the forgotten man

ROBERT CRAIS

An Orion paperback

First published in Great Britain in 2005
by Orion Books
This paperback edition published in 2006
by Orion Books,
an imprint of The Orion Publishing Group Ltd,
Orion House, 5 Upper St Martin's Lane,
London WC2H 9EA

An Hachette UK company

9 10

Reissued 2011

A CIP catalogue record for this book
is available from the British Library.

ISBN 978-1-4091-3561-6

Printed in Great Britain by Clays Ltd, St Ives plc

The Orion Publishing Group's policy is to use papers
that are natural, renewable and recyclable products and
made from wood grown in sustainable forests. The logging
and manufacturing processes are expected to conform to
the environmental regulations of the country of origin.

www.orionbooks.co.uk

*For Pat
with all my love*

ACKNOWLEDGEMENTS

On the personal side, Dr. Robert Beart and his elite team at the USC/Norris Cancer Center must be thanked for giving her back to me. In that effort, Dr. Randy Sherman, also of USC and the Keck School of Medicine, gave us emergency access we otherwise might not have had. The debt cannot be repaid.

On the research side, help, expertise, and advice came from many fronts: Detective-3 John Petievich, retired, consulted on matters relating to the LAPD. Craig Harvey, Chief Coroner Investigator of L.A. County's Department of Coroner, was generous with his time and patient with my questions. And, again, Dr. Randy Sherman was essential for the introductions and the science.

On the literary side, Jason Kaufman, my editor, contributed enormously to the evolution and development of this manuscript. Thank you.

The Empty House
Temecula, California

Late during one of those perfect twilights when the sky shimmered with copper like the last pulse of heat burning out of a body, Padilla and Bigelow turned off the highway onto a narrow residential street that brought them directly into the sun. They reached for their sun visors at the same time, both of them squinting, as Padilla thought, Christ, it was like driving head-on into hell.

Bigelow sat forward when he saw the women in the street.

'On the left. I'll call it in.'

Bigelow had three months in the car, compared to Padilla's nine years and change, so he was still excited by that stuff, the radio, the days when Padilla let him drive, and responding to a possible capital crime.

'Call, but try not to sound so excited. You sound like you got a chub over this. Let me tell you something, you get these calls, they're bullshit, they want attention, they're just confused, they're drunk, whatever, so try to sound like you know what's what.'

'Okay.'

I

'Sound bored, like you finally figured out being a cop is bullshit.'

'You think I'm going to embarrass you?'

'It crossed my mind.'

The women and children stood in the street between rows of cramped stucco houses, everyone in shorts and sandals, maybe seven or eight of them altogether. Ford pickups and an occasional boat were parked in their driveways. The neighborhood was similar to Padilla's, only Padilla was closer to town where the valley was green, not out here where the hills flattened into something like desert. Out here, landscaping was lava rock, blue gravel, and dead grass.

Padilla pulled over and got out as Bigelow made the call. He hated getting out of the car. Even at twilight, it was a hundred and five.

'Okay, what do we have? Who called?'

A heavyset woman with thin legs and wide feet stepped past two teenaged girls.

'That would be me, Katherine Torres. She's on the floor. I think it's her, but I couldn't tell.'

They had been dispatched to a 911, the Torres woman screaming her neighbor was dead with blood everywhere. Dispatch put out the call and now here they were, Padilla and Bigelow, uniformed patrol officers with the Temecula Police Department. Katherine Torres' hand waved as if a nervous life possessed it.

'All I saw were feet, but I think it's Maria. I called through the screen 'cause I knew they were home, so I looked in. The feet are all wet – and the legs – and I don't know, it looks like blood.'

Bigelow joined them as Padilla eyed the house. The sun was almost behind the mountains and most of the houses were showing lights. The house in question was dark. Katherine Torres could have seen anything – a towel someone dropped on the way from the shower, a spilled Dr Pepper, or feet wet with blood.

Padilla said, 'They got a dog?'

'No, no dog.'

'How many people live here?'

One of the teenaged girls said, 'Four, the parents and two children. They're really nice. I sit for the little girl.'

Bigelow, so anxious to get to the house that he shifted from foot to foot like a kid having to pee, said, 'Anyone hear any shouting, fighting, anything like that?'

No one had heard anything like that or anything else.

Padilla told the women to wait in the street, then he and Bigelow approached the house. The ground crunched under their boots. Large black ants crossed the earth in an irregular line, come out in the deepening twilight. The copper sky had purpled in the west as the darkness chased the sun. The house was quiet. The air was still in the way it can only be still when it floats in the emptiness of the desert.

Padilla reached the front door and knocked hard three times.

'Police officer. Frank Padilla with the police. Anyone home?'

Padilla leaned close to the screen, trying to peer inside, but it was too dark to see anything.

'Police. I'm going to open the door.'

Padilla drew his flashlight, trying to recall how many times he had tapped on doors and windows all hours of the night, usually checking on old people

3

someone feared had passed away, and twice they had, but only twice.

'Officers here! Coming inside, knock knock.'

Padilla pulled open the screen. He and Bigelow snapped on their flashlights at the same time, just as Bigelow said, 'I smell something.'

Their lights fell to the woman's body, early to mid-thirties, facedown on the living room floor, most of her hidden behind an ottoman that had been pushed to the center of the floor.

Bigelow said, 'Oh, man.'

'Watch where you step.'

'Man, this is nasty.'

Outside, the woman called from the street.

'What do you see? Is it a body?'

Padilla drew his gun. His heart was suddenly so loud he had difficulty hearing. He felt sick to his stomach and scared that Bigelow was going to shoot him. He was more afraid of Bigelow than the murderer.

'Don't shoot me, goddamnit. You watch what you shoot.'

Bigelow said, 'Jesus, look at the walls.'

'Watch the goddamned doors and where you point that gun. The walls can't kill you.'

The woman was wearing frayed cutoff jean shorts and a Frank Zappa T-shirt torn at the neck. Her shirt and legs were streaked with crusted blood. The back of her head was crushed, leaving her hair spiked with red gel. Another body lay between the living room and the dining room, this one a man. His head, like the woman's, was misshapen, and his blood had pooled in an irregular pattern reminding Padilla of a birthmark on his youngest daughter's foot. The floor was smudged

4

as if they had tried to escape their attacker and splatter patterns ribboned the walls and ceiling. The weapon used to kill these people rose and fell many times, the blood it picked up splashing the walls. The smell of voided bowels was strong.

Padilla waved his pistol toward the hall leading to the bedrooms, then toward the kitchen.

'I'll clear the kitchen. You wait here watching the hall, then we'll do the rooms back there together.'

'I ain't moving.'

Padilla said it all louder than necessary, hoping if someone heard him they'd jump out the window and run. He moved past the man's body, then into the kitchen. The body of a twelve-year-old boy was on the kitchen floor, partially beneath a small dinette table as if he had been trying to escape. Padilla forced himself to look away. All he thought about now was securing the damned house so they could call in the dicks.

Bigelow called from the living room, 'Hey, Frank –'

Padilla stepped back through the door. The rooms were bright now because Bigelow had turned on the lights.

'Frank, look at this.'

Bigelow pointed to the floor.

In the light, Padilla saw little hourglass smears pressed into the carpet; tiny shapes that Padilla studied until he realized they were footprints. These footprints circled the bodies, tracking from the woman to the man, then into the kitchen and out again, around and around each body. The prints led into the hall toward the bedrooms.

Padilla stepped past Bigelow along the hall. The footprints faded, grew dim, and then vanished at the final door. Padilla stepped into the dark room, his mouth dry, and flashed the room with his flashlight before turning on the lights.

'My name is Frank Padilla. I'm a policeman. I'm here to help.'

The little girl sat on the floor at the foot of her bed with her back to the wall. She held a soiled pillowcase to her nose as she sucked her index finger. Padilla would always remember that – she sucked the index finger, not the thumb. She stared straight ahead, her mouth working as she sucked. Dried blood crusted her feet. She could not have been more than four years old.

'Honey?'

Bigelow came up behind him, stepping past to see the girl.

'Jesus, you want me to call?'

'We need an ambulance and Social Services and the detectives. Tell them we have a multiple homicide, and a little girl.'

'Is she okay?'

'Call. Don't let the people outside near the house, and don't let them hear you. Don't answer their questions. Close the front door on your way out so they can't see.'

Bigelow hurried away.

Frank Padilla holstered his weapon and stepped into the room. He smiled at the little girl, but she didn't look at him. She was a very small girl with knobby knees and wide black eyes and blood smudges on her face. Padilla wanted to go to her and hold her the way he would hold his own daughter, but he didn't want to scare her, so he did not approach. She was calm. Better for her to remain calm.

'It's okay, honey. It's going to be okay. You're safe now.'

He didn't know if she heard him or not.

Frank Padilla stood looking at the tiny child in the bloody house with the miniature footprints she made as she walked from her mother to her father to her brother, unable to wake them, going from one to the other, circling through red shallows like a child lost at the shores of a lake until she finally returned to her room to hide in plain sight against the wall. He wondered what had happened to the little girl and what she had seen. Now, she stared at nothing, nursing her finger like a pacifier. He wondered if she still wore a diaper and if the diaper needed changing. Four was old for a diaper. He wondered what she was thinking. She was only four. Maybe she didn't know.

When the first team of detectives arrived, Padilla agreed to stay with the little girl in her room. Everyone thought staying in her own room would be better than having her wait for the social workers in a radio car. They closed the door. More detectives arrived, along with several patrol cars, two Coroner Investigators, and a team of criminalists from the Sheriffs. Padilla heard car doors slam and men moving in and around the house and voices. A helicopter circled overhead, then was gone. Padilla hoped the perp would be found hiding in a garbage can or under a car so he could get in a couple of hard shots before they hauled the sonofabitch away. That would be sweet, two jawbreakers right in the teeth, pow pow, feel the gums come apart, but Padilla was here with the little girl and that would never happen.

Once while they waited, Max Alvarez, who was the

senior homicide investigator and Padilla's wife's uncle, eased open the door. Alvarez had thirty-two years on the job, twenty-four on South Bureau Homicide in Los Angeles plus another eight in Temecula.

Alvarez spoke softly. He had seven children, all of them now grown and most with families of their own.

'She okay?'

Padilla nodded, fearful that speaking might disturb her.

'How about you?'

Padilla only nodded again.

'Okay, you need a break, let us know. The social workers are on their way. Ten minutes, tops.'

Padilla was relieved when Alvarez left. Part of him wanted to do the cop work of finding the perps, but more of him had assumed the role of protecting the little girl. She was calm, so protecting her meant preserving her calm, though he worried about what might be happening in that little head. Maybe her being so calm was bad. Maybe a child like this shouldn't be calm after what happened.

Two hours and twelve minutes after Padilla and Bigelow entered the house, field workers from the Department of Social Services Juvenile Division arrived, two women in business suits who spoke softly and had nice smiles. The little girl went with them as easily as if she was going to school, letting one of the women carry her with the woman's jacket covering her head so she wouldn't see the carnage again. Padilla followed them out, and found Alvarez in the front yard. Alvarez's face was greasy from the heat and his sleeves were rolled. Padilla stood with him to watch the social workers buckle the little girl into their car.

'How's it look?'

'Robbery that got outta hand, most likely. We got the murder weapon, a baseball bat they dropped behind the garage, and a couple of shoe prints, but we're not drowning in evidence. And the interviews so far, nothing, no one saw anything.'

Padilla studied Katherine Torres and the civilians who still lined the street. Padilla wasn't a detective but he had seen enough crime scenes to understand this was bad. The first few hours after a homicide were critical; witnesses who knew something tended to step forward.

'That's bullshit. Workday like this, all these women and kids at home, they had to hear something.'

'You think wits always got something to say, you've been watching too much television. I worked a case in L.A., some asshole stabbed his wife twenty-six times at eight P.M. on a Thursday night, them living on the second floor of a three-story building. This woman, her blood trail started in the bedroom and went all the way to the hall outside their front door, the woman dragging herself all that way, screaming her head off, and not one other tenant heard. I interviewed those people. They weren't lying. Forty-one people at home that night, having dinner, watching TV, doing what people do, and no one heard. That's just the way it is. These people who were killed in here, maybe all three of them were screaming their asses off, but no one heard because a jet was passing or some mutt was barking or the fuckin' *Price Is Right* was on television, or maybe it just happened too damned fast. That's my call. It happened so fast nobody knew what to do and it never even occurred to them to scream. What the fuck. You can't say why people do anything.'

Alvarez seemed both pissed off and spent after that, so Padilla let it ride. The social workers got themselves buckled in, and started their car.

'Why you think they didn't kill the little girl?'

'I don't know. Maybe they figured she couldn't finger them, her being so little, but my guess right now is they didn't see her. The way her footprints lead back to her room, she was probably in there sleeping or playing when it happened and they left before she came out. We'll let the psychologists talk to her about that. You never know. We get lucky, maybe she saw everything and can tell us exactly what happened and who did the deed. If she can't, then maybe we'll never know. That's the way it is with murder. Sometimes you never know. I gotta get back to work.'

Alvarez joined another detective and the two of them walked around the side of the house. Padilla didn't want to go back to work; he wanted to go home, take a shower, then drink a cold beer in his backyard with his wife while his children watched television inside, but, instead, he stood and watched.

The social workers were slowly working their car around the civilians and cops crowding the street. Padilla couldn't see the little girl. She was too small to see, as if the car had swallowed her. Padilla had been a cop long enough to know that the murders that had occurred tonight would haunt everyone involved for the rest of their lives. The neighbors who lined the tape would worry that the killers might return. Some would feel survivor's guilt, and others would grow fearful. Insecurities would flare, marriages would fail, and more than one family would sell their house to get out of Dodge before it happened to them. That's the way it was with murder. It would haunt the people who lived here and the cops who investigated the case and the friends and relatives of the victims and the little girl most of all. The murder would change her. She would become someone other than who she would have been. She would grow into someone else.

Padilla watched the car turn onto the highway, then crossed himself.

Padilla whispered, 'I'll pray for you.'

He turned and went back into the house.

Part One
NEXT OF KIN

CHAPTER 1

They called me to view the body on a wet spring morning when darkness webbed my house. Some nights are like that; more now than before. Picture the World's Greatest Detective, reluctant subject of sidebar articles in the *Los Angeles Times* and *Los Angeles* magazine, stretched on his couch in a redwood A-frame overlooking the city, not really sleeping at 3:58 A.M. when the phone rang. I thought it was a reporter, but answered anyway.

'Hello.'

'This is Detective Kelly Diaz with LAPD. I apologize about the time, but I'm trying to reach Elvis Cole.'

Her voice was coarse, reflecting the early hour. I pushed into a sitting position and cleared my throat. Police who call before sunrise have nothing to offer but bad news.

'How'd you get my number?'

I had changed my home number when the news stories broke, but reporters and cranks still called.

'One of the criminalists had it or got it, I'm not sure.

Either way, I'm sorry for calling like this, but we have a homicide. We have reason to believe you know the deceased.'

Something sharp stabbed behind my eyes, and I swung my feet to the floor.

'Who is it?'

'We'd like you to come down here, see for yourself. We're downtown near Twelfth and Hill Street. I can send a radio car if that would help.'

The house was dark. Sliding glass doors opened to a deck that jutted like a diving platform over the canyon behind my house. The lights on the opposite ridge were murky with the low clouds and mist. I cleared my throat again.

'Is it Joe Pike?'

'Pike's your partner, right? The ex-cop with the sunglasses?'

'Yes. He has arrows tattooed on the outside of his delts. They're red.'

She covered the phone, but I heard muffled voices. She was asking. My chest filled with a growing pressure, and I didn't like that she had to ask because asking meant maybe it was.

'Is it Pike?'

'No, this isn't Pike. This man has tattoos, but not like that. I'm sorry if I scared you that way. Listen, we can send a car.'

I closed my eyes, letting the pressure fade.

'I don't know anything about it. What makes you think I know?'

'The victim said some things before he died. Come down and take a look. I'll send a car.'

'Am I a suspect?'

'Nothing like that. We just want to see if you can help with the ID.'

'What was your name?'

'Diaz –'

'Okay, Diaz – it's four in the morning, I haven't slept in two months, and I'm not in the mood. If you think I know this guy, then you think I'm a suspect. Everyone who knows a homicide victim is a suspect until they're cleared, so just tell me who you got and ask whatever it is you want to ask.'

'What it is, we have a deceased Anglo male we believe to be the victim of a robbery. They got his wallet, so I can't give you a name. We're hoping you can help with that part. Here, listen –'

'Why do you think I know him?'

She plowed on with the description as if I hadn't spoken.

'Anglo male, dyed black hair thin on top, brown eyes, approximately seventy years but he could be older, I guess, and he has crucifix tattoos on both palms.'

'Why do you think I know him?'

'He has more tats of a religious nature on his arms – Jesus, the Virgin, things like that. None of this sounds familiar?'

'I don't have any idea who you're talking about.'

'What we have is a deceased male as I've described, one gunshot to the chest. By his appearance and location, he appears indigent, but we're working on that. I'm the officer who found him. He was still conscious at that time and said things that suggested you would recognize his description.'

'I don't.'

'Look, Cole, I'm not trying to be difficult. It would be better if –'

'What did he say?'

Diaz didn't answer right away.

'He told me he was your father.'

I sat without moving in my dark house. I had started that night in bed, but ended on the couch, hoping the steady patter of rain would quiet my heart, but sleep had not come.

'Just like that, he told you he was my father.'

'I tried to get a statement, but all he said was something about you being his son, and then he passed. You're the same Elvis Cole they wrote the stories about, aren't you? In the *Times*?'

'Yes.'

'He had the clippings. I figured you would recognize the tats if you knew him, me thinking he was your father, but it sounds like you don't.'

My voice came out hoarse, and the catch embarrassed me.

'I never met my father. I don't know anything about him, and as far as I know he doesn't know me.'

'We want you to come take a look, Mr. Cole. We have a few questions.'

'I thought I wasn't a suspect.'

'At this time, you aren't, but we still have the questions. We sent a radio car. It should be pulling up just about now.'

Approaching headlights brightened my kitchen as she said it. I heard the car roll to a slow stop outside my house, and more light filled my front entry. They had radioed their status, and someone with Diaz had signaled their arrival.

'Okay, Diaz, tell them to shut their lights. No point in waking the neighbors.'

'The car is a courtesy, Mr. Cole. In case you were unable to drive after you saw him.'

'Sure. That's why you kept offering the car like it was my choice even though it was already coming.'

'It's still your choice. If you want to take your own car you can follow them. We just have a few questions.'

The glow outside vanished, and once more my home was in darkness.

'Okay, Diaz, I'm coming. Tell them to take it easy out there. I have to get dressed.'

'Not a problem. We'll see you in a few minutes.'

I put down the phone but still did not move. I had not moved in hours. Outside, a light rain fell as quietly as a whisper. I must have been waiting for Diaz to call. Why else would I have been awake that night and all the other nights except to wait like a lost child in the woods, a forgotten child waiting to be found?

After a while I dressed, then followed the radio car to see the dead.

CHAPTER 2

The police were set up at both ends of an alley across from a flower shop that had opened to receive its morning deliveries. Yellow tape was stretched across the alley to keep people out even though the streets were deserted; the only people I saw were four workers from the flower mart and the cops. I followed the radio car past an SID van, more radio cars, and a couple of Crown Victorias to park across the street. No rain was falling there in the heart of the city, but the clouds hung low, and threatened.

The uniforms climbed out of their radio car and told me to wait at the tape. The senior officer went into the alley for the detectives, but his younger partner stayed with me. We hadn't spoken at my house, but now he studied me with his thumbs hooked onto his gun belt.

'You the one was on TV?'

'No, he was the other one.'

'I wasn't trying to be rude. I remember seeing you on the news.'

I didn't say anything. He watched me a moment longer, then turned to the alley.

'Guess you've seen a homicide scene before.'

'More than one.'

The body was crumpled beside a Dumpster midway down the alley, but my view was blocked by a woman in a T-shirt and shorts, and two men in dark sport coats. The woman's T-shirt was fresh and white, and made her stand out in the dingy alley as if she were on fire. The older suit was a thick man with shabby hair, and the younger detective was a tall, spike-straight guy with a pinched face. When the uniform reached them, they traded a few words, then the woman came back with him. She smelled of medicinal alcohol.

'I'm Diaz. Thanks for coming out.'

Kelly Diaz had short black hair, blunt fingers, and the chunky build of an aging athlete. A delicate silver heart swayed on a chain around her neck. It didn't go with the rest of her.

I said, 'I'm not going to know this man.'

'I'd still like you to take a look and answer a few questions. You okay with that?'

'I wouldn't be here if I wasn't.'

'I'm just making sure you understand you don't have to talk to us. You have any doubts about it you should call a lawyer.'

'I'm good, Diaz. If I wasn't good, I would have shot it out with these guys up in the hills.'

The younger cop laughed, but his partner didn't. Diaz lifted the tape, and I stooped under and walked with her to the Dumpster. When we reached the others, Diaz introduced us. The senior detective was a Central Station homicide supervisor named Terry O'Loughlin; the other guy was a D-1 named Jeff Pardy. O'Loughlin shook my hand and thanked me for coming, but Pardy didn't offer to shake. He stood between me and the body like I was an invading army and he was determined not to give ground.

O'Loughlin said, 'Okay, let him see.'

The cops parted like a dividing sea so I could view the body. The alley was bright with lights they had set up to work the scene. The dead man was on his right side with his right arm stretched from his chest and his left down along his side; his shirt was wet with blood and had been scissored open. His head was shaped like an upside-down pyramid with a broad forehead and pointy chin. His hair showed the stark black of a bad dye job and a thin widow's peak. He didn't look particularly old, just weathered and sad. The crucifix inked into his left palm made it look like he was holding the cross, and more tattoos showed on his stomach under the blood. A single gunshot wound was visible two inches to the left of his sternum.

Diaz said, 'You know him?'

I cocked my head to see him as if we were looking at each other. His eyes were open and would remain that way until a mortician closed them. They were brown, like mine, but dulled by the loss of their tears. That's the first thing you learn when you work with the dead: We're gone when we no longer cry.

'What do you think? You know this guy?'

'Uh-uh.'

'Ever seen him before?'

'No, I can't help you.'

When I looked up, all three of them were watching me.

O'Loughlin flicked his hand at Pardy.

'Show him the stories.'

Pardy took a manila envelope from his coat. The envelope contained three articles about me and a little boy who had been kidnapped earlier in the fall. The articles hadn't been clipped from the original newspaper; they had been copied, and the articles clipped from the copies. All three articles made me out to be more than I was or ever had been; Elvis Cole, the World's Greatest Detective, hero of the week. I had seen them before, and seeing them again depressed me. I handed them back without reading them.

'Okay, he had some news clips about me. Looks like he copied them at the library.'

Diaz continued staring at me.

'He told me he was trying to find you.'

'When this stuff hit the news I got calls from total strangers saying I owed them money and asking for loans. I got death threats, fan letters, and time-share offers, also from total strangers. After the first fifty letters I threw away my mail without opening it and turned off my answering machine. I don't know what else to tell you. I've never seen him before.'

O'Loughlin said, 'Maybe he hung around outside your office. You could have seen him there.'

'I stopped going to my office.'

'You have any idea why he would think he's your father?'

'Why would total strangers think I'd loan them money?'

Pardy said, 'Were you down here or anywhere near here tonight?'

There it was. The coroner's office was responsible for identifying John Doe victims and notifying their next of kin. Whenever the police took action to identify a victim, they were acting to further their investigation. Diaz had phoned me at four A.M. to see if I was home; she had sent a car to confirm I was home, and asked me down so they could gauge my reaction. They might even have a witness squirreled nearby, giving me the eye.

I said, 'I was home all night, me and my cat.'

Pardy edged closer.

'Can the cat confirm it?'

'Ask him.'

Diaz said, 'Take it soft, Pardy. Jesus.'

O'Loughlin warned off Pardy with a look.

'I don't want this to become adversarial. Cole knows we have to cover the base. He's going out of his way.'

I said, 'I was home all night. I spoke to a friend about nine-thirty. I can give you his name and number, but that's the only time I can cover.'

Pardy glanced at O'Loughlin, but didn't seem particularly impressed.

'That's great, Cole; we'll check it out. Would you be willing to give us a GSR? In the interest of helping us. Not to be adversarial.'

O'Loughlin frowned at him, but didn't object. A gunshot residue test would show them whether or not I had recently fired a gun – if I hadn't washed my hands or worn gloves.

'Sure, Pardy, take the swabs. I haven't killed anyone this week.'

O'Loughlin checked his watch as if he suspected this was going to be a waste of time, but here we were and there was the dead man. Diaz called over a criminalist, and had me sign a waiver stating I knew my rights and was cooperating without coercion. The criminalist rubbed two cloth swabs over my left and right hands, then dropped each into its own glass tube. While the criminalist worked, I gave Pardy Joe Pike's name and number to confirm the call, then asked O'Loughlin if they made the murder for a botched robbery. He checked his watch again as if answering me was just another waste of time.

'We don't make it for anything right now. We're six blocks from Skid Row, Cole. We have more murders down here than any other part of the city. These people will kill each other over six cents or a blow job, and every goddamned murder clears the same. He sure as hell wasn't carrying government secrets.'

No, he was carrying news stories about me.

'Sounds like you've got it figured out.'

'If you'd seen as many killings down here as me, you'd have it figured, too.'

O'Loughlin suddenly realized he was talking too much and seemed embarrassed.

'If we think of anything else to ask you, we'll follow up. Thanks for your cooperation.'

'Sure.'

He glanced at Diaz.

'Kelly, you good with letting Jeff have the lead on this? It'll be a good learning experience.'

'Fine by me.'

'You good with that, Jeff?'

'You bet. I'm on it.'

Pardy turned away to call over the coroner's people, and O'Loughlin went with him. Two morgue techs broke out a gurney and began setting it up. I studied the body again. His clothes were worn but clean, and his face wasn't burned dark like the people who live on the streets. When I glanced up at Diaz, she was staring at him, too.

'He doesn't look homeless.'

'He's probably fresh out of detention. That's good news for us; his prints will be in the system.'

The alley was a long block between commercial storefronts and an abandoned hotel. The letters from the old neon HOTEL sign loomed over the dark street. I could read the hotel's faded name painted on the bricks – Hotel Farnham. But without the police lights, it would have been impossible to read. The darkness bothered me. The body was a good sixty feet from the near street, so he either took a shortcut he knew well or came with someone else. It would have been scary to come this way alone.

'It was you who found him?'

'I was over on Grand when I heard the shot – one cap. I ran past at first, but I heard him flopping around in here and there he was. I tried to get a handle on the bleeding, but it was too much. It was awful, man . . . Jesus.'

She raised her hands like she was trying to get them out of the blood, and I saw they were shaking. The clothes she wore were probably spares from another cop's trunk. She had probably changed out of her bloody clothes in the ambulance and washed with the alcohol. She probably wanted to throw away her blood-soaked clothes, but she was a cop with a cop's pay so she would wash them herself when she got home, then have them dry-cleaned and hope the blood came out. Diaz turned away. The coroner techs had their gurney up, and were pulling on latex gloves.

I said, 'No wallet?'

'No, they got it. All he had were the clippings, a nickel, and two pennies.'

'No keys?'

She suddenly sighed, and seemed anxious and tired.

'Nothing. Look, you can take off, Cole. I want to finish up and get home to bed. It's been a long night.'

I didn't move.

'He mentioned me by name?'

'That's right.'

'What did he say?'

'I don't remember exactly, something about trying to find you, but I was asking what happened – I was asking about the shooter. He said he had to find his son. He said he had come all this way to find his boy, and he never met you, but he wanted to make up the lost years. I asked him who, and he told me your name. Maybe that isn't exactly what he said, but it was something like that.'

She glanced at me again, then looked back at his body.

'Listen, Cole, I've arrested people who thought they were from Mars. I've busted people who thought they were *on* Mars. You heard O'Loughlin – we got bums, junkies, drunks, crackheads, schizophrenics, you name it, down here. You don't know what kind of mental illness this guy had.'

'But you still have to clear me.'

'If you were home all night, don't worry about it. He'll be in the system. I'll let you know when the CI pulls a name.'

I turned away from the body and saw Pardy staring at me. His pinched face looked intent.

'It's not necessary, Diaz. Don't bother.'

'You sure? I don't mind.'

'I'm sure.'

'Okay, well, whatever; your call.'

I started back to my car, but she stopped me.

'Hey, Cole?'

'What?'

'I read the articles. That was some hairy stuff, man, what you did saving that boy. Congratulations.'

I walked away without answering, but stopped again when I reached the yellow tape. Diaz had joined O'Loughlin and Pardy as the coroner's people bagged the body.

'Diaz.'

She and Pardy both turned. Rigor had frozen the corpse. The techs leaned hard on the arms to fold them into the bag. A hand reached out from the dark blue plastic like it was pointing at me. They pushed it inside and pulled the zipper.

'When you get the ID, let me know.'

I left them to finish their job.

CHAPTER 3

Early in the fall, three men stole my girlfriend's only son, Ben Chenier. An ex-LAPD officer named Joe Pike and I saved the boy, but many people died, including the three kidnappers. Bad enough, but those three men had been hired by Ben's own father and were not your garden-variety criminals – they were professional mercenaries wanted under the International War Crimes Act. What with all the bodies, Joe and I faced felony charges, but the governments of Sierra Leone and Colombia interceded along with – get this – the United Nations. The lurid nature of a father contracting the abduction of his own child fed a wildfire of sensationalist journalism, but even before the worst of it, Lucy Chenier concluded that life with yours truly was not worth the risk, so she took her son and went home. She was right to leave. Being with me wasn't worth a four A.M. phone call saying a murdered stranger claimed to be the father I never knew.

I drove back to my house through a light rain, pretending my life was normal. When I reached home, I made scrambled-egg burritos, then turned on the early news. The lead story reported that the Red Light Assassin had struck again. The RLA had been killing traffic cameras for several weeks, and the camera death toll was now up to twelve, each camera snipered dead-center through the lens with a .22-caliber pellet gun. Web sites devoted to the Red Light Assassin had been set up; T-shirts bearing slogans like FREE THE RED LIGHT ASSASSIN sold on every freeway off-ramp; and all of it had come about because the city had installed traffic cameras to ticket rush-hour motorists who slid through the red. Which, in L.A.'s killer traffic, meant everyone. The news anchor tried to keep a straight face, but her coanchor and the weather guy goofed on the rising 'body count,' and had themselves in spasms. No mention was made of the nameless man found murdered in a downtown alley. Murdered people were common; murdered cameras were news.

I turned off the television, then went out onto my deck, feeling listless and unfocused. The rain had shriv-eled to a heavy mist and the sky was beginning to lighten. Later, homicide detectives would be asking my neighbors if they had seen me entering or leaving my house last night. Pardy would probably flash a picture of the dead man, and ask if anyone had seen him in the area, and my neighbors would be left wondering what I had done. I thought I should call to warn them, but calling would look bad so I let it go. Mostly, I wanted to call Lucy, but I had wanted to call her every day since she left, so that wasn't new. I let that one go, too, and watched as the canyon slowly filled with light.

People who lived on the hillsides would soon emerge from their homes to inspect the slopes, searching for cracks and bulges. The world grew unstable when rain fell in Los Angeles. Soil held firm only moments before it could flow without warning like lava, sweeping away cars and houses like toys. The earth lost its certainty, and anchors failed.

A black cat hopped onto the deck by the corner of my house. He froze when he saw someone on the deck, all angry yellow eyes, but his fury passed when he recognized me.

I said, 'Yes, I am standing in the rain.'

He said, 'Omp.'

He walked along the side of the house keeping as far from the mist as he could, slipped into the dry warmth of the house, then licked his penis. Cats will do that. He probably thought I was stupid.

When my mother was twenty-two years old she disappeared for three weeks. She disappeared often, walking away without telling anyone where she was going, but always came back, and that time she came back pregnant with me. My mother never described my father in any meaningful way, and may not have known his name. I did not reveal these things to the reporters who mobbed me for interviews after the events with Ben Chenier, but somehow the information found its way into their stories. I regretted not having read the clippings Diaz found in the alley. One might have mentioned the situation with my father, which could have inspired the old man to fabricate his fantasy. That was probably it and I should probably forget it, but I wondered if he had tried to contact me. When I stopped going to my office, I turned off my answering machine and tossed the mail, but that was weeks ago. If the dead man had written to me since then, his letter might be waiting in my office.

I went inside, put out fresh food for the cat, then drove down through the canyon to the little office I keep on Santa Monica Boulevard.

Mail was scattered inside the door where the postman drops it through the slot. I gathered it together, put on a pot of coffee, then turned on my message machine. The Elvis Cole Detective Agency was officially back in business. Of course, since I had ignored everything offered to me for the past six weeks I didn't exactly have something to do.

I went through the mail. A lot of it was bills and junk, but seven pieces were what I thought of as fan mail: a handwritten marriage proposal from someone named Didi, four letters congratulating me for bringing three mass murderers to justice, an anonymous nude photo of a young man holding his penis, and a letter from someone named Loyal Anselmo who described Pike and me as 'dangerous vigilantes no better than the monsters you murdered.' Some people are never happy.

I kept four of the letters with the intention of sending thank-you notes and dumped the others. After thinking about it, I pulled Anselmo's letter from the trash and put it into a file I kept for death threats and lunatics. If someone murdered me in my sleep I wanted the cops to have clues.

I poured a cup of coffee and felt disappointed that nothing had led back to the dead man. It was possible he had written me and I had tossed his letter, but I could never know that. He could have called when my machine was turned off, but I would never know that, either.

I was trying to figure out a new avenue of detection when the phone rang.

'Elvis Cole Detective Agency. Back on your case, and just in time.'

'It's me, Diaz. You at your office, or is this call being forwarded? I already tried your house.'

'I'm at the office. Did you get an ID?'

'I'm sorry, we didn't. I thought for sure this dude would be in the system, but he's not. The coroner investigator ran him through the Live Scan as soon as they got to the morgue, but nothing came up.'

The Live Scan was an inkless fingerprinting process that digitized fingerprints, and instantly compared them with files at the California Department of Justice in Sacramento. If nothing came up, then he had never served time or been arrested in California.

'Okay. What happens next?'

'Sacramento will roll the prints through NLETS. We still have a shot with the Feds, but it could take a few days. You said you got a lot of mail and calls you didn't answer –'

'I came in to check, Diaz. There's nothing. He could have sent something earlier, but I don't have anything now. I just went through the mail.'

'I hate to ask this but I'm going to ask anyway. I'm going over to the morgue. Would you meet me there?'

'I thought Pardy had the case.'

'Pardy does, and he's back from the medical examiner. He says the deceased is totally covered with these insane tattoos. I know you didn't recognize him, but maybe something in the ink will ring a bell.'

I felt a little dig of anger, but maybe it was shame.

'He's not my father. There's no way.'

'Just come look, Cole. One of his tats might give you a name or a place. What can it hurt?'

I didn't say anything, and Diaz pushed on.

'You know where the coroner is, down by the USC Medical Center?'

'I know.'

'They have a parking lot in front. I'll meet you there in half an hour.'

I put down the phone, then went into the bathroom and looked at myself in the mirror. The dead man had a head like a praying mantis and I had a head like a rutabaga. I didn't look anything like him. Nothing like him. Nothing.

I went down to my car and made my way to the morgue.

CHAPTER 4

Invisible Men

Frederick Conrad, which was the name he now used, hustled through the trailer park toward his truck when Juanita Morse lurched from her double-wide like a brown recluse spider springing a trap.

'Frederick!'

She hooked his arm with a dried-out crone's hand, trapping him even though he was frantic to leave.

'Frederick, you were so nice last week when I was down with my legs, bringing my groceries like you did. Here, this is for you, a little something.'

Frederick fell into character without missing a beat, hiding his fury with the lopsided Frederick Conrad grin everyone knew so well. He pressed the dollar back into her hands.

'Please, Juanita. You know better than that.'

'Now you go on, Frederick, you were so nice to see after me like that.'

So Frederick took the dollar, feigning appreciation, his furious rage arcing like downed power cables while his eyes remained calm. *He wanted Payne to come home. He needed to find out what happened. He was terrified that Payne had confessed.*

That traitorous prick, Payne. (Payne Keller being the name he now used.)

'You really don't have to, Miz Morse, but thank you. Is your leg better?'

'It still burns, but at least I'm not down. I put the heating pad on this morning and took the Tylenol.'

Frederick patted her hand as if he gave a shit about every burning pulse in her withered body.

'Well, if you need anything else, you let me know.'

Pat-pat. Smile. You hideous hag.

Finally rid of her, Frederick hurried to his truck, wanting to crush her nasty throat just to grind the bones. He fired up the Dodge, then slowly drove the two-point-six miles to Keller's gas station, Payne's Gas & Car Care. Frederick was well known as the slowest driver in town.

He parked behind the service bays, hung the slow-witted grin on his face again like an Open For Business sign, and sauntered into the office.

'Hey, Elroy, I called three or four times this morning, but you didn't answer. You hear from Payne?'

Elroy Lewis was Payne's other full-time employee. He was a skinny man in his late forties with a roll of flab melting over his belt and yellow fingers from chaining Newport cigarettes. Lewis's dog, Coon, was sleeping in the middle of the floor. Coon, a lazy dog with bad hips, wagged his tail when he saw Frederick, but Frederick ignored him. Lewis put his elbows on the counter, and sulked.

'No, he didn't, and I gotta talk to you 'bout that. We got stuff to talk about.'

Frederick stepped over the dog and made his way to Payne's office, doing a pretty good job of pretending everything was okay.

'Well, he called me last night, and said he was gonna give you a call. I guess he got busy with his sister.'

'Goddamn, how long is it gonna take that bitch to die?'

'You should be ashamed of yourself, Elroy, sayin' something like that. She's his sister.'

Payne Keller had disappeared eleven days ago without a word or note to anyone. When Payne turned up missing, Frederick fed Elroy a bullshit story about Payne's sister being T-boned by a drunk driver, but, truth was, Frederick had no idea. Payne's sudden disappearance terrified him. Payne could be anywhere and might say anything; Payne and his buddy, Jesus, confessing their sins.

I hope you're dead, you bastard. I hope your heart split open like a rotten grapefruit. I hope you put a gun to your head. I hope you're dead, and I hope to hell you didn't take me with you.

Frederick had decided to cover their tracks, and prepare for the worst. Elroy followed him into Payne's office.

'Well, I'm sorry about his sister, but it's goddamned rude, you ask me, him leaving without a word. The wife and I are going to her parents' next week. Payne knew I had that time off and said I could go.'

Frederick rounded Payne's desk, took the keys from the top drawer, and flashed the big easy grin.

'Then go, Elroy. That's why Payne called last night, to ask if I'd cover for you. I said sure.'

Elroy looked doubtful.

'You will?'

Frederick came back around the desk as a white Maxima pulled up to the self-service pumps. A teenage girl got out, looking confused by the pump. Frederick noted how Elroy stared at the girl.

'Heck, Elroy, I don't mind. You'd do it for me and we'd both do it for Payne. No problem.'

Now Elroy looked guilty for being pissed off.

'Listen, when you talk to Payne again, tell him I wish the best for his sister.'

'I'll tell him. You bet.'

'I never knew Payne had a sister.'

'You better see if that girl outside needs help. I gotta swing up by Payne's to feed his cats.'

Elroy glanced at the girl again, and Frederick knew what he was thinking; the tight low-cut jeans, the cropped shirt showing a fine flat belly, the dangly thing in her navel.

Sure enough, Elroy said, 'Yeah. I'd better get out there. C'mon, Coon.'

Elroy nudged Coon to his feet as Frederick went back through the service bay to the storage shed in back of the station. He used Payne's keys to unlock the three padlocks and the steel security bar that kept the shed safe. He found the shovel and a two-gallon can Payne used to bring gas to stranded motorists, then searched behind the boxes of air filters, brake fluid, and Valvoline for the old Tri-Call vending machine Payne used to have out front for peanuts and Snickers. Payne and Frederick had better hiding places for their secret things, but Payne kept the shed to stash their goods.

Frederick checked to see that Elroy was busy with the girl. As if on command, Coon planted his face square into the girl's kibble. Elroy made a big deal of scolding the dog as the girl laughed, then grabbed Coon's face so he could sneak a cheap rub on the girl's privates. Frederick had seen Elroy run that trick a hundred times. Elroy trained his mutt to head straight for the cush bush, and Coon never let him down.

Frederick unlocked the vending machine, and fished out a leather case about three feet long. It was heavy, but the weight was comforting. He tucked the case under his arm, relocked the shed, then brought everything to his truck. Elroy was still pretending that he was trying to keep Coon off the girl's goodies, and here was the girl, red-faced and laughing, but not getting into her car. Frederick pumped two gallons of premium into the can (figuring the premium would burn hotter), loaded two cans of propane into his truck, then tooled away. Elroy never even glanced over to see.

A couple of miles along the road, Frederick pulled over and opened the case. A cut-down Remington 12-gauge pump gun was inside, already stoked with six rounds of number-four buck. Jammed in with the shotgun was a plain white envelope holding a thousand dollars in twenties and matching Illinois driver's licenses – both now out of date – but showing Frederick Conrad and Payne Keller with different names. Frederick jacked a shell into the chamber, tucked the shotgun under the front seat, then pulled back onto the road.

It crossed Frederick's mind to stomp on the accelerator and rip out of town, but that would be like waving a red neon flag. If Payne hadn't ratted him out, running would be a major mistake – their mutual disappearances would be obvious to even the dumbest cops. Frederick had to find out what happened to Payne, and he had to get rid of the evidence.

Payne's place was only another mile ahead, all by itself and hidden by trees so no one could see what they did.

CHAPTER 5

The Department of Coroner was split between two modern cement buildings at the edge of the County-USC Medical Center, across the river from the main jail. The north building housed administrative offices for thirty-five or so coroner investigators, and the south building housed the labs. The medical examiners parked their vehicles at the front of the buildings, but the bodies were delivered at the rear. Probably so the patients at the Women's and Children's Hospital wouldn't see the stiffs.

I parked across the street and met Diaz outside the main entrance. She had changed into jeans and a blazer, and was holding what looked like a gas mask with two purple cylinders jutting from its face.

I said, 'What's that?'

'It's a particle filter. We have to wear them when we go down to the service floor with the bodies.'

'Why do we have to wear something like that?'

'TB, SARS, Ebola – you wouldn't believe what these stiffs are carrying. This one's mine. We'll get something for you downstairs.'

'Ebola?'

Ebola was the African virus that dissolved your cells so you melted into a puddle of goo.

Diaz shrugged as she turned away.

'They say wear it, I wear it. Let's get this done so I can get some sleep.'

The receptionist gave us visitor passes, then we took the elevator down to the service floor. The smells of disinfectant and cavity blood hit me when the doors opened, and we stepped out into a lavender hall. An ultraviolet light burned high on one wall, and a bug zapper hissed as it cooked a fly. Germ control.

Diaz led me around the corner into another long hall where two steel gurneys were parked, each bearing a body wrapped in heavy translucent plastic. Red liquid pooled within the plastic.

'I thought we needed masks when we were with the bodies.'

'You're not going to catch anything. Don't be a sissy.'

I tried not to breathe.

The coroner investigator was a tall man with framed glasses and bushy hair named Dino Beckett. I had seen him at the crime scene, but didn't meet him until he emerged at the end of the hall and Diaz introduced us. He was wearing a cloth mask like doctors wear in an operating room, and handed a similar mask to me.

'Here, pull the elastic band over your ears and squeeze the metal strip across your nose.'

I did like he said while Diaz pulled on her larger mask.

'How come her mask is bigger?'

'Her mask filters one hundred percent of the air,

which is what you're required to wear if you go in the autopsy room like the homicide detectives. The mask we're wearing only filters ninety-five percent of the air.'

'What about the other five percent?'

Diaz said, 'Jesus Christ, Cole, don't think about it. Where is he, Dino?'

We followed him into a long narrow room where the air was cold. A rash of goose bumps sprouted over me, but not from the chill. Racks on the walls were stacked from the floor to the ceiling like bunks in a submarine, with each rack holding two bodies. The bodies were wrapped with murky plastic, but not so murky that you couldn't see nude bodies within. Feet poked through gaps in the plastic, some with tags wired to the big toe. I tried not to look, but bodies filled the wall.

Beckett said, 'This is nothing. We have three rooms like this.'

'Are all these people waiting to be autopsied?'

'Oh, no. Most of the bodies you see here are waiting to be claimed by their next of kin, or identified.'

'You get many you can't identify?'

'We bag around three hundred John Does a year, but we put a name to most of them. Doesn't matter where they come from, either. We've had illegals from Mexico, Central America, even China, and we've run'm down. We'll name your guy, too.'

Several pairs of feet were so translucent I could see a dim smudge of bones within the flesh. Beckett explained that some of the bodies had been on the racks so long the fluids had drained from the tissue; they had been waiting for years.

Beckett brought us past the racks to a gurney at the far end of the room.

'Okay, here we go. You'll need gloves if you want to touch something.'

We gloved up, then Beckett peeled open the plastic. John Doe #05-1642 was naked, with a brown paper bag between his knees and a case file clipped to the gurney. The bag contained his bloodied clothes, which would be placed in a drying room before they were examined. Beckett removed the bag, then stood back.

Diaz said, 'Jesus, Pardy was right. This guy thought he was the Illustrated Man.'

Beckett grunted at the body like it was a lab specimen.

'Weird, huh? I've never seen one like this, the way he did it. All the tats are upside down.'

Crucifixes of differing sizes and designs dotted his forearms and thighs and belly, all of them upside down. The tattoos were upside down because they were self-inflicted. They would have been right-side up as he looked at them when he pushed ink into his skin. Some of the crosses were brittle thin lines, but others were blocky structures with shading and shadows. Weeping Jesuses and upside-down words were spread between the crosses: PAIN, MERCY, GOD, FORGIVE ME. They looked like they had been drawn by a child. I felt queasy. These marks were not religious; he had desecrated himself.

When I glanced at Diaz, she was watching me again. I felt a bubble of irritation.

'What is it? You think I look like him?'

'You don't look anything like him. Do the tattoos ring a bell?'

'Of course not. It's nothing but crosses.'

Diaz glanced at Beckett.

'Does he have more on his back?'

'Uh-uh. It's all in front where he could reach. None of his ink is identifying – like the name of a ship, or a gang sign, or something like that – it's just what you see.'

Diaz frowned at the body, then shook her head.

'Okay, I want you to check him for sex. If you get a smear, log it for DNA.'

'Pardy already told me.'

'Fine. Dope, too. He was in that alley for something.'

Beckett shifted the bag to make a note, and the bag gave me an idea.

'Did you see if his name was in his clothes?'

Beckett grinned.

'Always, and inside his shoes, too. I got burned like that on my first case – here's this dude, flattened with no ID and no prints in the file, turns out his mama wrote his name inside his belt, and that's how we made the ID.'

I nodded, and looked back at Diaz.

'And you didn't find any rings, watches, a wallet –'

'He was stripped, Cole. Just the clippings and seven cents.'

I studied the body again, feeling remote and detached. His chest was smooth and thin beneath the tattoos, with a farmer's tan showing pale flesh against dark arms. Other than a thin scrape at the base of his neck, no other marks were apparent. The lower half of his body showed a mottled lividity where his blood settled; the bloodless tissue above had taken on a waxy sheen that seemed to highlight the tattoos. The pucker of the entry hole was purple and blue with a pepper of gunpowder

45

particulate surrounding it. He had been shot close, the muzzle not more than two feet away. His fingers showed no evidence of rings, but his left wrist carried the pale outline of a missing watch. A faint dimple crossed the outside of his hip below his left pelvis, so slight it might have been a fold or a crease.

I said, 'What's that?'

Beckett reached under the gurney for the case file, and tipped out a large X-ray.

'A surgical scar. There's another on his opposite leg just like it. Here, we already got the plates.'

He held the X-ray up to the overhead light. The shadows and smudges of the pelvic ball joint were off-set by perfect white bars that ran along the outside of each femur. Beckett pointed them out.

'It looks corrective, so he probably had the surgery when he was a kid. These white bands are some kind of appliance. Appliances like this will sometimes have a manufacturer and serial number. If these do, we should be able to trace the manufacturer to the hospital, and pick up his ID.'

Diaz said, 'When will he hit the table?'

Beckett checked his clipboard.

'Tomorrow afternoon, looks like. Might wash over to the day after, but I think we'll cut him tomorrow.'

I stared at the body again. Its face had hardened with rigor into a distorted mask. One eye was closed, but the other drooped open. The skin was stretched tight over bony cheeks and the hollows of his eyes were pronounced. His mouth hung open as if he were sleeping and might wake. I wanted to close it.

Something touched me. I lurched. Diaz was watching me.

'Cole? You okay?'

'Sure. What happens next?'

Diaz stared at me another moment, then glanced at Beckett.

'Okay, Dino, we're done. I need close-ups of the body tats and his face. Something that doesn't make him look like *Night of the Living Dead*, okay?'

'No prob. I'll meet you at the elevator.'

Beckett pushed the body away as Diaz and I peeled off our gloves, and I followed her back to the hall. When we were away from the bodies, she considered me again.

'Here is what happens: I'm going to drop the pictures back with Pardy so he can make copies, then I'm going to bed. Pardy will hand out the pictures to the patrol commander so we can try to find someone who knew this guy.'

'Has Pardy ever worked a case before?'

'This is a big chance for him, Cole. Pardy came up from Metro. He's hungry, and he wants to make a name for himself. He'll be fine.'

I looked back at the swinging door with the walls of bodies behind it, some that had been there for years.

'You mind if I work it?'

'Meaning what? Pardy isn't good enough, so the World's Greatest has to pitch in?'

'I want to know why he thought he was my father. Wouldn't you want to know why someone said that about you?'

'We haven't even cleared you yet.'

'You'll clear me. C'mon, Diaz, think about it. I might even find the shooter.'

Her eyes hardened with something I could not read

deep in their dark pools. She smiled at me, but her smile held no humor, and was also unreadable. She shook her head.

'I hope you're being straight with me.'

'About what?'

'I hope you're not keeping something from me, Cole.'

'Like what?'

'You don't recognize him?'

'All I know is a man who told you he was my father is lying on ice.'

She stared with the hard eyes, then she turned away down the hall.

'Sure, Cole. You want to look, look. You're the World's Greatest Detective. It says so in the papers.'

Beckett met us at the elevator a few minutes later, and gave Diaz the pictures. She pulled off her mask, considered the picture of the dead man's face, then gave me one of the prints.

'Here. You might need this.'

'Thanks.'

'You can take off the mask.'

I left it on. I didn't take off the mask until the elevator opened and we stepped into cool fresh air. We walked out together, then parted to go to our cars. When I reached my car I looked back at her. She was standing beside a dark blue Passat, studying his picture. She glanced up to look at me, and saw I was watching. She tried to pretend she wasn't comparing us, but I sensed that she was. She got into her car, and drove quickly away.

CHAPTER 6

Hidden

Payne Keller owned sixteen acres of elm thicket, brush, and pine trees, bought for squat in a probate because the cabin was falling apart. He had dug a new septic tank, a new well, replumbed the place, put in new gas lines, had a natural-gas tank set, put on a new roof, and paid to run new phone and power lines from the main road. Frederick had encouraged Payne to get a trailer like him, but Payne wanted his privacy. Frederick had to admit that Payne's privacy had come in handy, time to time.

Frederick bumped along the long private drive over potholes and erosion cuts until he reached Payne's cabin. The dusty white house was still. Frederick slipped the shotgun from under the seat, then climbed out of his truck. Payne used to have a real nice place, but now the eaves were heavy with cobwebs, and the house was streaked with dirt like mascara when a woman cried.

'Payne! Hey, buddy, you home?'

Frederick stood absolutely still, listening. He sensed the house was deserted, but stepped up onto the covered porch, keeping an eye on the windows. He unlocked the dead bolt, and pushed open the door. Inside, twelve Christs stared down at him from twelve crucifixes nailed to the walls. More Christs stood on the TV. Christ bore witness from the entertainment center, the bookcase, and the end tables. Frederick knew that even more Christs waited in the bathroom and kitchen and bedroom.

'PAYNE⁈'

Calling, just for show. If Payne had betrayed him, a policeman or reporter might be anywhere.

Frederick felt the Jesuses watching him, and closed his eyes. A buzzing started in his head, and if he didn't make it go away the buzzing would grow into voices.

'Make them stop, Payne. Make them go away.'

The buzzing gradually faded, and Frederick pulled himself together. He hurried into the kitchen to check the message machine, and found two new messages, but one was from Elroy and he had left the other. Frederick had checked the house twice a day every day since Payne disappeared, hoping to find a message that would give some clue about Payne's fate, but all he ever found were the messages he left expressing concern for Payne's well-being (also for show), and the messages from Elroy.

Frederick deleted the messages, then scrounged a box of trash bags from the cupboard, relocked the house, and returned to his truck for the shovel. He hurried around the side of the house into the woods, then followed a dry creek bed until he was at the base of a large rock. Frederick considered the trees both ways along the gulley, but wasn't sure if he was in the right spot or not. He felt confused and fuzzy, but also excited.

Frederick moved with increasing strength.

He climbed uphill behind the rock, then suddenly recognized his surroundings with a precision that made every leaf as familiar as old friends. He felt a rush of confidence.

'Yes, it is,' he said, smiling. 'Yes, it is.'

He put his weight into the shovel, and levered up the earth. Frederick Conrad, which was the name he now used, worked with great purpose. The shovel struck something hard. He clawed away the dirt, and uncovered the first skull.

CHAPTER 7

Six hours earlier, the streets had been empty, but now pedestrians churned the sidewalks, bike messengers whipped between cars like tweaked-out humming-birds, and the shops along Grand and Hill had become an open bazaar. The police were gone. The yellow tape, area lamps, criminalists, and patrol cars had vanished, erasing all evidence that a murder had occurred. To the untrained eye, it was another flawless day in the City of Angels.

I drove back to the crime scene, pulled to the curb outside the flower mart, and studied the mouth of the alley. I couldn't do any more than the police, and wasn't sure why I wanted to try. I never once – not then at the beginning – believed that John Doe #05-1642 was or could be the father I had never known. He was more like a client who had hired me, and the person I had been hired to find. Maybe I was bored after so many weeks not working; maybe I didn't want to go back to a house that felt pointless without Lucy and Ben. It was easier to lose myself in murder; it was merciful to focus my anger at someone else.

The Big Empty was a moldering area east of the convention center and south of the business district, unclaimed by the homeless, who tended to gather several blocks north at the parks and missions of Skid Row. The streets were lined with wholesale outlets, cut-rate office space, garment resellers, and businesses that closed at dusk; the bars, hotels, apartments, and missions were ten blocks or more to the north, and not an easy walk from the alley. John Doe #05-1642 either lived in the area or had been seeking a destination, though there wasn't much in the area to seek. I studied my Thomas Brothers map. I wanted to talk to the people who worked at the flower mart, then search the area for businesses that might have been open.

I turned across traffic into the alley, and parked. When I got out of my car, a thin man in a form-fit pink shirt came out a service door. His arms were filled with cardboard boxes that had been flattened, and his face pinched into a pruned knot when he saw me.

'You can't park there. They'll tow it.'

'Police business. A murder occurred here at two forty-five this morning. The police will be around to talk to you.'

'Someone was already here. A tall man. He was brusque and rude, and that doesn't look like a police car.'

I drive a 1966 Sting Ray convertible, which would probably look more like a police car if I washed it. It's yellow.

'It's not, and I'm not, but I'm looking into the case. Were you here at your shop around three this morning?'

He looked irritated at having been asked. I guess the rudeness had put him off.

'I've already talked to the police. Of course I wasn't here. I don't sleep here. I wasn't here when it happened, and I don't know anything about it.'

I gave him what I hoped was a friendly smile, trying to ease his irritation.

'All right. Maybe you can help me out with something. I'm trying to figure out why the victim was in this area at that hour. I was going to look around for businesses that might have been open at that hour. You know of anything?'

His faced tightened and he seemed even more irritated.

'No, I don't, and you can't leave your car. Delivery trucks can't get through with your car.'

Thirty feet away, a man had bled to death from a bullet to the chest, but here was this guy, pissy. I studied the space between my car and the far side of the alley. There was plenty of room.

'There's no place else to park, and I won't be long.'

'See the sign on the wall, "No Parking"? If you don't move your car, I'll call the police.'

I stopped trying to be friendly, and told him to call. People like him give me hives.

I took longer than I needed just to spite him. I spent two hours walking the surrounding twelve square blocks, but counted only six restaurants and two Starbucks, none of which would have been open at two forty-five in the morning. There was no reason for the John Doe to have been in the area unless he was on his way to somewhere else.

After a while I went back to the alley. My car had not been towed, but a mountain of garbage bags was piled behind it. I guess the man in the pink shirt figured if he couldn't have me towed, he would block me in. Pissy.

I went to the Dumpster. The alley had been washed clean after the police released the scene. The blood was gone, and disinfectant had been sprayed. No chalk marked the body's outline and no evidence buttons marked a telltale trail of forensics, but veins in the tarmac remained damp with the disinfectant.

I looked up and down the alley, trying to imagine it at two forty-five that morning. It would not have been an inviting place to walk, but fear is relative. The cross streets were well lit, but John Doe #05-1642 chose darkness. Maybe the darkness meant safe harbor, or maybe he had been chased. The shooter might have already been in the alley when the victim entered, resulting in a crime of opportunity, but most homicides are committed by family, friends, or acquaintances; the odds promised that the victim and the shooter knew each other. If they entered together, the alley would not have seemed so foreboding. The victim and his killer might have sought out the darkness together, but to what end? I thought over what Diaz described: She heard the shot, found him no more than three minutes later, and asked what had happened. Instead of telling her who shot him or how it happened, he told her he was trying to find me. Identifying me as his son, and saying he wanted to make up for the lost years were his dying words. I didn't like knowing that. Had he entered this particular alley to find me? Did he believe he was going to someplace where I would be? Had the shooter claimed to know me and promised an introduction?

I stared down at the place where his body had been

and imagined them facing each other against the Dumpsters. The gun came out, the victim resisted –

– *bang* –

I closed my eyes and saw it, the withered dead man suddenly alive and on his feet, facing an assailant hidden by shadows –

– *bang* –

– one shot pounded home low to the right of his sternum, missing his heart but ripping his arteries and lungs. The kinetic energy dumped into his body staggered him. A hydrostatic shock wave pulsed through his tissues along the wound channel, rupturing the cells nearest the wound and surfing the blood in his arteries straight to his brain. The spike of pressure blew out capillaries and shorted his senses; he went blind, deaf, and unconscious in a heartbeat, and he dropped in his tracks like a boxer stepping into a powerhouse hook. A larger gun – a .45 or .44 – would have killed him instantly by rupturing the vessels in his brain with a hundred simultaneous strokes, but with the smaller gun, his consciousness slowly returned as Diaz found the alley. Pain and fear would have boiled up with his returning senses, and he had screamed and thrashed as she described. His vision and hearing returned. He was able to think again, and speak, even though he was dying. Someone had shot him, and then he was dying, but he hadn't told her who, or why – the most important thing in the world to him was to tell her he was my father and that he was trying to find me. To make up the lost years.

I bent to touch the ground.

Why me?

I searched the ground around the Dumpsters. The

cops had been over it, but I looked again, searching a few feet in one direction, then the other, then along the far wall, trying to remember if the police had recovered a shell casing. I searched the sills of the delivery doors opposite the Dumpsters, found nothing, then worked my way back across the alley, looking into the cracks and pocks in the tarmac. The detectives and the criminalist had searched these same areas, but I looked anyway. Chipped tarmac, jagged brown glass that had once been a beer bottle, and weathered paper were spread evenly where the criminalist had left them. I let myself down into a push-up position to look under the first Dumpster, and saw a bright rectangle partially wedged between the Dumpster's left rear wheel and the wall. It seemed too obvious a thing for the police to have missed, but maybe the cleaning crews had dislodged it from a less obvious place when they sprayed down the area.

I pushed the Dumpster aside, then picked up the card at its edges. It was a plain blue plastic card with a white triangle pointing off one end beneath the words INSERT HERE. A magnetic strip ran the length of the card on the opposite side. I was pretty sure it was a key card like they use in hotels. The name of the hotel and the room number weren't printed on the card because you don't want a stranger knowing which room the key opens, but I thought the information might be readable on the magnetic strip. There might even be fingerprints.

I could have brought the card to Central Station and left it for Pardy and Diaz, but I didn't want to wait three days for results. I phoned an LAPD criminalist named John Chen. John and I had worked together in the past, but when I reached his office at the Scientific Investigations Division, they told me he had the day off. Perfect. I hung up, then phoned a detective I knew on the Hollywood Station Juvenile Section named Carol Starkey. Starkey had been a bomb technician with LAPD's Bomb Squad until some bad breaks made her change jobs, so she knew almost as much technical stuff as Chen.

When Starkey answered, she said, 'You finally calling to ask me out?'

'No, I'm calling to see if you can recover information off a key card for me.'

I explained about the card, the body, and what I was doing.

She said, 'No shit? You think this guy is your father?'

'No, I don't think he's my father. I just want to find out what's on the card.'

'Call Chen. Chen knows how to do that.'

'Chen has the day off.'

'Hang on.'

She put me on hold. While I waited, I stacked the garbage bags the man in the pink shirt had piled around my car into a huge mound against his door. Pissy.

Starkey came back on the line.

'Chen will meet us at SID in an hour.'

'I thought he had the day off.'

'Not anymore.'

I hung up, then checked my watch. It had been almost nine hours since John Doe #05-1642 had been murdered. The key card was about to open a door to his identity, and to far more than I wanted to know.

Part Two
FATHER KNOWS BEST

CHAPTER 8

APD's Scientific Investigation Division shared its location with the Bomb Squad, where Carol Starkey had spent three years strapping into an armored suit to de-arm or destroy improvised explosive devices while everyone else hid under a tree. You've seen bomb techs in the news. They're the men and women dressed in what looks like a space suit, bent over a box or a backpack that's loaded with TNT, trying to render it safe before it explodes. Starkey was good at it, and loved it, until it finally went bad. Starkey and her supervisor were killed on the job, blown apart in a trailer park by a keg of black powder and nails. The medics brought her back and the surgeons stitched her together, but they wouldn't let her go back to the Squad. She worked in Criminal Conspiracy for a while, and now she worked on the Juvenile desk, but she still missed the bombs. Some woman, huh?

Starkey was leaning against a dark blue Bomb Squad Suburban when I pulled into the parking lot. She was in her early thirties, with a long face, limp hair, and a dark gray pin-striped suit that went with her attitude.

She was smoking.

I said, 'Those things will kill you.'

'Been there, done that. Chen's inside, sulking 'cause I made him come in.'

'Thanks for setting this up, but you didn't have to make the drive. I know you're busy.'

'What, and miss the chance to flirt with you? How else am I gonna get you in the sack?'

Starkey is like that. She turned toward the building, and I followed, the two of us threading our way between parked cars.

She said, 'So what's the deal on the vic? You don't think he's related?'

'No, I don't think he's related. He was just obsessed or confused. You know how people get, like stalkers when they fix on a movie star. That's all it is.'

'Lemme see that picture.'

I had told her about the morgue shots, but I was irritated she wanted to see. She looked at the pictures, then me, then back at the pictures. It left me feeling vulnerable in a way I didn't like. She finally shook her head and handed them back.

'You don't look anything like this guy.'

'I told you.'

'He looks like a praying mantis and you look like a rutabaga.'

'This is what you call flirting?'

Starkey squeezed between a couple of cars that were parked too close together, then waited as I walked around. She seemed thoughtful as we continued on, and maybe embarrassed.

She said, 'Listen, maybe I shouldn't've joked about it. I didn't know about you not knowing your father. I can see how this would be weird for you.'

'It's not weird. I'm not doing this because I think he's my father.'

'Whatever.'

'Don't make more out of it than there is.'

'Tell you what, let's change the subject while we're still speaking to each other. Have you heard from Ben? How's he doing down there?'

Starkey had helped in the search for Ben Chenier. We met on the night he disappeared.

'He's doing well. We don't talk as often as we used to.'

'And the lawyer?'

The lawyer was Lucy Chenier.

'We don't talk as often as we used to.'

'I guess I shouldn't have brought that up, either.'

'No. I guess not.'

Starkey badged our way past the receptionist, then led me along a hall toward a sign that read TECHNICAL LABORATORY. SID was divided into three parts: the Technical Laboratory, the Criminalistics Laboratory, and the Administrative Unit. Chen, like the other field criminalists, worked freely between the Tech Lab and the Criminalistics Lab, though he could and did refer to specialists when needed.

Chen scowled when he saw us. He was tall and thin, with ill-fitting glasses and the hunched posture of someone sporting chronic low self-esteem. Some of the criminalists wore lab smocks, but most of them wore street clothes. Only John Chen wore a pencil caddy. He glanced around, making sure no one else was nearby. Furtive.

'Today is my day off. I spent all morning waxing my car. I was gonna cruise Westwood for pussy.'

Chen is like that. His sole motivation in all things is publicity, promotion, and sex. Not necessarily in that order.

Starkey said, 'That's more than we needed to know, John. Just work the card.'

'I'm just saying, that's all. You guys owe me.'

He held out his hand, making a little hand-it-over gesture.

'Let me see it.'

I was carrying the key card in my handkerchief. I laid it on the bench, then folded back the handkerchief. Chen lifted his glasses, and leaned close to see.

'Did this belong to the vic or the shooter?'

'I don't know. It was in the alley, so I have to follow it. It might not belong to either one of them.'

Chen peered closer, looking dubious, then glanced up at me.

'This guy really your father?'

I was getting a headache. I wanted whatever I could get from the key card and I wanted to get out of there.

'He was a deluded old man who *thought* he was my father. That's all.'

'Starkey said he was your father.'

Starkey said, 'I got it wrong, goddamnit. Cole doesn't look anything like him. I saw the pictures.'

I said, 'Are you going to look at the card or not?'

I was sorry I called them.

Chen brought the card to a workstation that looked like a Napster geek's dream: A desktop computer was wired to what appeared to be VHS, VHS-C, BETA, 3/4', 8mm, and digital tape decks, along with DVD/CD players, mini-CD players, and several different swipe-card readers that might have come from your local supermarket. A sign on the wall read NO MAGNETS, NO INFO, NO JOB. Lab rat humor.

Chen went to work on the computer, bringing up different windows on the screen.

'Most of the work we do here is with counterfeit credit and ATM cards, but we can analyze commercial key cards, too. Most hotels in the U.S. buy their systems from one of three magnetic-lock companies, and they all use the same coding. We'll try the commercial codes first. Who's the detective in charge?'

'Kelly Diaz. She's Divisional Homicide at Central.'

Chen typed in her name.

'I'll have to call her for the case number. Does she put out?'

Starkey punched him in the back, told us she had to get back to work, then stalked out of the lab.

I said, 'Jesus, John, show a little class.'

Chen seemed disappointed with my answer, but not embarrassed that he had asked. He glanced after Starkey and lowered his voice still more.

'You owe me for this, man. Tell your girlfriend she owes me, too.'

'Starkey isn't my girlfriend.'

Chen rolled his eyes.

'Yeah, sure.'

Chen finished filling in the boxes, then picked up the key card with a pair of plastic forceps and swiped it through a card reader. The information embedded in its magnetic strip instantly appeared on the computer.

00087662///116/carversystems//
0009227//homeawaysuiteso47//
0012001208//00991//

Chen tapped at the screen.

'Here it is, dude. It's from the Home Away Suites chain. The oh-forty-seven is probably the location. The one-sixteen is probably the room number. All this junk on the left side is just coding sequences. You don't have to worry about that.'

I copied the information into my notebook. Room 116 at Location 47.

'What's Carver Systems?'

'The company that made the lock. Remember I said only three or four companies make this stuff? That's them. Does Diaz know you have the card?'

'Not yet. I was going to give it to her later.'

Chen looked worried.

'I can't do this off the books. This is a homicide.'

'I'm not asking you to do it off the books. Diaz knows I'm working the case. She's good with it.'

'Then I'd better keep the card. I can have the CI send over the vic's prints to see if we get a match.'

'Can you make a duplicate for me?'

'You mean make you another key card?'

'Yeah. Now that you have the codes, can you put them on another card?'

'Make you a key for room one-sixteen?'

'Yeah.'

Chen looked uneasy again, cocking his head like a nervous parrot.

'This isn't some kind of grudge thing, is it, you thinking someone murdered your old man? If you kill somebody, it'll be my ass.'

'He isn't my father.'

'I'm going to tell Diaz I made a dupe for you. I'll tell Starkey, too.'

'Tell them. That's fine.'

Chen dug around in a cabinet until he found a box of blank cards. He typed on the computer some more, swiped a new card through the reader, then handed it to me. He didn't look happy about it.

'Room one-sixteen.'

'Thanks, John. I owe you.'

'You better not kill anyone.'

I pocketed the card and started back through the lab.

'Hey, Elvis.'

I stopped. John Chen was staring at me with the wary parrot eyes, only now the eyes seemed sad.

'I don't look like my father, either.'

I went out to my car, but Starkey had already gone.

CHAPTER 9

Home Away Suites was a chain of cheap no-frills motels geared to drive-by salesmen and people on their way to somewhere else. They were big in the Midwest, but had only six locations in Southern California, with two in the L.A. area, one being in Jefferson Park just south of mid-city, the other in Toluca Lake. Jefferson Park was closer to downtown, so I got their number from information, and called from the SID parking lot. A chipper young woman answered.

'Home Away Suites, your home away from home, may I help you?'

'Is this location number forty-seven?'

'Pardon me?'

'You have several locations, and each location has a number. I'm trying to find number forty-seven.'

'I don't know anything about that.'

She didn't ask me to hold on, she didn't offer to find out, she simply stopped talking. Home Away probably didn't hire for initiative.

'Could you ask someone, please?'

'Okay. Hold on.'

Okay.

A few minutes later she came back on the line.

'Sir?'

'I'm here.'

'We're number forty-two. You want the Toluca Lake location.'

'Could you give me their address?'

'I'll have to look it up.'

'Never mind. I'll call information.'

Welcome to the exciting world of Private Detection.

I got the address from the information operator, then headed around the north side of Griffith Park, across Burbank, and into Toluca Lake.

Toluca Lake is a small treesy community wedged between Universal Studios and Burbank where the Ventura and Hollywood freeways merge. Most residents have never seen the lake as it is surrounded by expensive homes, but the larger community is a comfortable mix of middle-class homes, well-kept apartment buildings, and sidewalk businesses.

I followed Riverside Drive across the back of Toluca Lake to Lankershim Boulevard, then slipped under a freeway overpass and into North Hollywood. The Home Away people had cheated the location, but I guess they figured close was good enough. So much for truth in advertising.

Home Away Suites #47 was a gray stucco box; no restaurant, no room service, no frills. Just the kind of place for a traveling salesman or a family on a limited budget. I parked on the street, and entered a lobby as plain and simple as the outside. A bored young man in a gray blazer sat behind the registration desk, reading. An older couple was standing at a rack of tourist brochures, probably trying to decide between standing in line for the Leno show or driving to Anaheim for Knott's Berry Farm. Beyond the registration desk was a set of stairs, and a long straight hall leading to the first-floor rooms.

I wanted to talk to the clerk, but I also intended to search the room even though the clerk probably wouldn't go for it. I knew I would enter the room when I had Chen make the duplicate key, and I knew I wasn't going to wait for the police to get it done. I crossed the lobby like any other registered guest, and went down the hall. Room one-sixteen was in plain view of the couple at the brochure rack, but not the desk clerk. I rapped lightly on the door, listened, then slipped the card into the lock. I pushed open the door, and went in.

The room was empty.

Like the motel, it was spare and plain, with an alcove for a closet and a small bath beyond the alcove. The lights were off, the drapes were pulled, and the air smelled of cigarettes. Everything was neat and tidy because the housekeeper had already made her rounds. Two pairs of men's slacks and two shirts hung in the alcove above a battered gray suitcase. I checked the suitcase for a name tag, but the suitcase was tagless. No telltale clues stood out on the bed or dresser to tie the room to the man in the alley, and the nightstand drawers were empty.

The bathroom was empty, too, except for a small black toiletries case. I was hoping for a prescription bottle showing a name, but it held only the usual anonymous travel articles available at any Rite Aid. I went back to the alcove, and checked the pants hanging on the rail. The pockets were empty. The suitcase was unlocked, so I opened it. A naked woman smiled up at me. She was on the cover of one of those freebie sex newspapers filled with ads for strippers, outcall services, and massage parlors. This one was the *Hard-X Times*. I lifted it aside, and stared down at myself.

In a way I didn't understand, my chest hurt, as if a pressure had built within me until some part of me cracked and the pressure escaped. The picture was part of an article about me published in a local magazine. The reproduction was poor and murky, like it might have been copied off a library microfiche; my eyes were dark smudges, my mouth was a black line, and my face was mottled, but I knew it was me. I found two more articles under the first, one I remembered from the *Daily News* and another from the *L.A. Weekly*.

This was his room.

John Doe #05-1642.

I put the articles aside and searched the rest of his suitcase. I felt through his underwear and three rumpled shirts, then felt along the inside lining of the suitcase for some kind of identification, but instead I found something hard and round inside a roll of socks. I unrolled the socks and counted out $6,240 in twenties, fifties, and hundreds.

I counted the money twice, put it back in the socks, then finished searching the room. Nothing identified the occupant, almost as if he was purposefully trying to hide himself.

I put everything back as I had found it, let myself out, and went back to the lobby. The older couple was gone. A name tag on the clerk's blazer read *James Kramer*.

I gave him my best cop tone.

'My name is Cole. I'm investigating a homicide, and we believe a person or persons involved might be a guest at your motel. Do you recognize this man?'

I held out the morgue shot, and watched Kramer's mouth tighten.

'Is he dead?'

'Yes, sir, he is. Do you recognize him?'

'He looks kinda different, like that.'

They always look different when they're dead. I put away the picture, and took out my notepad.

'We're trying to identify him. We believe he was staying in room one-sixteen. Can you tell me his name?'

Kramer moved to his computer and punched in the room number to bring up the invoice.

'That's Mr. Faustina – Herbert Faustina.'

He spelled it for me.

'Could you give me his home address and phone?'

He read off an address on College Ridge Lane in Scottsdale, Arizona, then followed it with a phone number.

'Okay. How about his credit card number?'

'He paid cash. We do that if you put down a three-hundred-dollar cash deposit.'

I tapped my pad, trying to figure out what to ask next while he stared at me. You should never give them a chance to think.

He said, 'What did you say your name was?'

'Cole.'

'Could I see your badge?'

'If he made calls from his room, those calls would show up on his bill, right?'

He was beginning to look nervous.

'Are you a policeman?'

'No, I'm a private investigator. It's okay, Mr. Kramer. We're all on the same side here.'

Kramer stepped back from the desk to put more distance between us. He didn't look scared; he was worried he would get in trouble for answering my questions.

'I don't think I should say any more. I'm going to call the manager.'

He turned to pick up his phone.

'You need to do something before you call. Someone else might have been involved, and they might be in his room. That person might be injured and need help.'

He held the phone to his face, but he didn't dial. His eyebrows quivered, as if he was sorry he had ever taken a crappy job like this.

'What do you mean?'

'Check his room. Just peek inside to see if someone needs help, then you can call your manager. You don't want someone dying in that room.'

He glanced back toward the hall.

'What do you mean, dying?'

'Faustina was murdered. I knocked on his door before I came to you, but no one answered. I don't know that anyone is inside, but I'm asking you to check. Make sure no one is bleeding to death, then call.'

Kramer glanced toward the hall again, then opened the desk drawer for his passkey and came around the desk.

'You wait here.'

'I'll wait.'

When he disappeared down the hall, I went behind the desk. Herbert Faustina's account still showed on the computer. I found the button labeled CHECKOUT INVOICE, and pressed it. A speedy little laser printer pushed out Herbert Faustina's final room charges on three pages. I took them, and left before Kramer came back. I did not wait. The World's Greatest Detective had struck again.

CHAPTER 10

Ten hours start to finish, and I had Faustina's name and address, and a list of every call made from his motel. I was thinking about calling Diaz and Pardy when I realized I was hungry, so I picked up a couple of soft tacos from Henry's Tacos in North Hollywood and ate them on the benches out front. I wolfed down the tacos like a starving dog, then bought two more, slathering them with Henry's amazing sauce. I would probably have Faustina's life story by dinner, and his killer by bedtime. LAPD would probably beg me to clear their other unsolved cases, and I thought I might go along. Largesse is everything.

When I finished eating, I worked my way up Laurel Canyon to the top of the mountain, then along Woodrow Wilson Drive toward my house. I was feeling pretty good until I saw the unmarked sedan parked in front of my house, and my front door wide open.

I parked off the road beyond my house, then walked back to check out the car. It was an LAPD detective ride with a radio in the open glove box and a man's sport coat tossed casually on the back seat. My friend

Lou Poitras was a homicide lieutenant at Hollywood Station, but this wasn't his car. Also, Lou wouldn't leave my front door hanging open like an invitation to bugs and looters.

I went inside. Pardy was on my couch with his arms spread along its back and his feet up on the coffee table. He didn't get up or smile when he saw me. A black Sig hung free under his arm.

'You have a nice little place here, Cole. I guess it pays off, getting your name in the papers.'

'What are you doing?'

'I was up here asking your neighbors about you. They say your car was here all night, so I guess you're in the clear unless something else comes up.'

'I meant what are you doing here in my house.'

'I saw your door open, but got no answer. I thought you might be dead or injured, you being a party to a homicide investigation, so I came in to render assistance.'

I went back to my front door and examined the jamb. Neither it nor the lock showed signs of having been jimmied. I left the door open and went back to the living room. Two cabinets beneath my television were ajar and the stack of phone books on the pass-through between my dining room and the kitchen wasn't in its usual place. Pardy had searched my house.

'I can't believe you came into my house like this.'

'I can't believe you went back to my crime scene this morning. I find it suspicious.'

'Diaz knows I'm working the case. She gave me her blessing.'

'Did she?'

'Ask her.'

'O'Loughlin gave me the lead, and I don't need any help. Consider this a courtesy call.'

Pardy suddenly stood. He was taller than me, with angular shoulders and large bony hands, and he stood close to intimidate me.

'Don't come around my case anymore. I don't want you talking to my witnesses, I don't want you at my crime scene, and I don't want you contaminating my evidence.'

'I'll bet you don't want me finding evidence you missed, either.'

He was here because of the key card. When I arrived at the alley that morning, Pardy had been shining a flashlight under the Dumpsters. It had been his evidence to find, only he hadn't found it. When Chen notified Central Homicide about the card, O'Loughlin must have asked about it, and now Pardy felt shown up.

'I'm sorry you got burned, but what was I supposed to do, pretend I didn't find it?'

'Funny how you found a card that wasn't there. I'm thinking maybe you planted it, looking to show us up.'

'You don't know what you're talking about.'

'I know you're a publicity slut, Cole. You might have murdered that bum just for the ink – the dumb cops can't close the deal, so the superstar asshole rides to the rescue, page one above the fold?'

I was pissed off and tired, and the wonderful spicy soft tacos had grown sour and old.

I said, 'Have you been to the Home Away Suites yet?'

Pardy's face tightened and his red skin looked like parchment pulled over a skull. I shook my head because I knew he hadn't.

'No, Pardy, you haven't. While you were dicking around up here, I went to the motel. The vic was listed on their register as Herbert Faustina. When the reporters interview you, you can tell them the superstar asshole had to give you his name because you were up here going through my house without a search warrant while I was working the case. They'll probably make me out to be Sherlock Holmes after that.'

Pardy's face pinched even tighter.

'What did you do at the motel?'

'I talked to a clerk named Kramer. He's probably gone off duty by now, but you can catch him tomorrow. Tell O'Loughlin I covered that one for you, too.'

I didn't tell him I had entered the room, and I wasn't going to give him Faustina's bill. I decided I would still call Diaz, but Pardy could swing it himself.

He said, 'You think you know, but you don't, Cole. You don't have any idea. Stay out of my case. You're nowhere around this or I'll have your ass.'

I should have let it go. I should have just nodded, and he would have walked out, but I didn't like that he had come into my house, and I liked it still less that he thought he knew me when he didn't know me at all.

'Wrong, Pardy, which is something you'd know if you had paid attention at the Academy. I can pursue any matter I choose so long as I don't interfere with or obstruct you in doing your job. You might not like it, but if you arrest me on those grounds, you'll have to make a case not only to the district attorney but also to Internal Affairs. You'll get to tell them how you entered my home without paper, and how you missed the key card and showed up late at the motel. You'll even get to tell them how you tried to front me off even though everything I've done today has been done with the full knowledge and permission of LAPD. You'll look sweet with all that, Pardy. O'Loughlin might even help you pack.'

Pardy watched me with the hard eyes as if his body had gone rigid, and he didn't know what to do because nothing was playing out like he imagined. Then he made it worse.

'I don't think you understand, Cole. Where's your gun? Let me see the gun you killed all those people with.'

Pardy raised his right hand and rested it on the Sig's grip. A film of sweat made his forehead shine.

'I want to make sure you understand.'

The hammer cocking on the Colt .357 Python at my front door sounded like cracking knuckles. Pardy turned to the sound, and shouted his warning like when he was in uniform.

'LAPD!'

Joe Pike said, 'So?'

Pike stood framed in the shadows of the open front door with his .357 down along his right thigh. Pike was six feet one, with short brown hair and ropy muscles that left him looking slender even though he weighed two hundred pounds. He was wearing a sleeveless gray sweatshirt, jeans, and the Marine Corps sunglasses he pretty much wore 24/7, inside and out, daytime or night. Light from the setting sun caught the glasses, and made his eyes glow.

Pardy kept shouting, but had the sense not to pull out his gun.

I said, 'This is my partner, Joe Pike. You read about him in the newspaper, too.'

'I'm a police officer, goddamnit. Police officer! Put down that weapon! Tell him to put down the goddamn gun.'

I looked at Pike.

'He wants you to put down your gun.'

'No.'

'What do you want to do, Pardy? You want to have a shoot-out? You were finished. If you want to arrest me, I'll go with you and we can sort this out with O'Loughlin down at the station. Did you want to place me under arrest?'

Pardy glanced back at me, and the moment was done. He could press it, but his shit was weak and he knew it. He was so tight his voice squeaked like a bad hinge.

'Sit this one out.'

Pardy lurched around like a sailing ship tacking into the wind. Pike stepped down out of the entry to let him pass. When Pardy reached the door, he looked back at me. He didn't seem scared; he seemed certain.

'Sit this one out.'

'Good night, Pardy.'

Pardy left, and after a minute his car pulled away. When it was gone, Pike holstered his .357.

'Was this about your father?'

Just like that.

'He isn't my father, for Christ's sake. How do you know about this?'

'Starkey.'

'Are you two phone buddies now?'

'She was concerned.'

Pike knew much of it from Starkey, but I filled in the rest. Joe Pike had been my closest friend and only partner for almost twenty years, but we had never much shared the facts of our childhoods to any great degree. I'm not sure why, only that it had never seemed necessary and maybe even felt beside the point. Maybe it was enough that we were who we were, and were good with that; or maybe we each felt our baggage was lighter without the weight of someone else's concern. When I reached the part about the Home Away Suites, I showed Pike the bill with Faustina's name and address. Pike glanced at it.

'This isn't the right area code for Scottsdale. His address and phone number don't go together.'

The motel record showed 416 as the area code for Faustina's home number.

'What's Scottsdale?'

'Four-eighty.'

I brought the invoice to the phone, and punched in the number. A computer chimed immediately to inform me that no such listing existed. Next, I booted up my iMac, signed on to Yahoo's map program, and entered Faustina's address. No such street existed in Scottsdale. I leaned back in my chair and glanced up at Pike; everything I thought I knew about Herbert Faustina was wrong.

'His phone number and address don't exist. He made them up.'

Pike studied the invoice again, then handed it back.

'My guess is he made up more than that. Maria Faustina was the first saint of this millennium. She was canonized for her trust in God's Divine Mercy. Five gets you ten he was using an alias.'

Pike knows the most surprising things.

I unfolded the morgue photos and showed him the picture of Herbert Faustina's tattoos.

'I guess he sought mercy.'

'Maybe,' Pike said. 'But mercy for what?'

CHAPTER 11

Yard Work

Frederick made three trips down to Payne's house that day, not that so much was left after all these years, but the bags were awkward. Each time he came down, he was terrified the police would be waiting. He crept through the trees, gut-sick with fear until he saw that the coast was clear.

Once everything was down, Frederick fired up Payne's gas grill. He used four full cans of propane, then mixed the ashes with gasoline and burned them in a fifty-five-gallon drum Payne used for burning trash. After the second burn, he bagged the residue, then scrubbed the drum with Clorox. He drove the ashes out along Highway 126 to Lake Piru, washed out the bags with lake water, then stopped at two nurseries in Canyon Country before heading back. Late that afternoon when the sun was beginning to weaken, he dusted Payne's property with a generous mix of warfarin, ant poison, cayenne pepper, and arsenic. The police might eventually bring dogs to search the property, but when their mutts hoovered up Frederick's little surprise, they wouldn't last long. Frederick felt satisfied with a job well done.

With the evidence gone and the grounds laced with poison, Frederick let himself back into Payne's house to think. Payne had always told him they would be punished. Frederick thought he meant they would burn in Everlasting Hell – especially after Payne began tattooing himself and talking to Jesus – but maybe it wasn't that at all. Frederick woke every morning knowing that someone somewhere was hunting them; entire armies were probably trying to find them.

Maybe now they had.

Thoughts swirled through Frederick's head like whispering voices, and he felt himself beginning to panic.

'Stop.'

Frederick sat motionless at the table except for his right leg. His foot bounced with a will of its own, separate and apart from him, faster as the buzzing grew louder.

'Make it stop.'

Frederick knew he was in trouble. They were trying to get him, and they might have already found Payne – mercenaries, masked assassins, maybe even criminals; hired killers paid to find and punish them. Maybe they had snatched Payne and his car, too; made their move so quickly that Payne simply vanished.

Frederick realized if they found Payne, then they might be watching him right now. He felt the weight of their eyes. He heard their covered whispers.

Frederick's foot bounced until the table shook; a ceramic Jesus danced to the edge of the table and fell. When it shattered, Frederick clutched his leg, and pounded his thigh –

'Stop it! STOPITSTOPITSTOPIT!'

He lurched to his feet, stumbled into the kitchen, and saw a fresh message waiting on Payne's machine. Someone had called that day while Frederick worked in the yard.

Frederick played the message, and a voice he had heard only once – the time he let Payne talk him into going to the Catholic church that Sunday – came from the machine.

'Payne, this is Father Wills. I hope you're well, but I'm concerned I haven't heard from you. Please call or come by. It's important we continue our discussion.'

Frederick's stomach clenched, and he tasted sardines.

What discussion?

Father Wills was a priest, and priests took confession.

What had Payne told him?

What was the knowing suspicious tone in Father Wills's voice?

Payne had probably confessed his ass off to every priest and minister and rabbi in town. Frederick started shaking, and the buzzing returned –

Frederick deleted the message.

He breathed hard, drawing in ragged and hideous breaths until it occurred to him that Payne might have told his confessor where he was going and what he was going to do. Father Wills might know.

Frederick decided to ask.

CHAPTER 12

During the nine days Herbert Faustina resided in the Home Away Suites, he made forty-six phone calls, but none were to any number I recognized. He had not phoned my office. The bill listed each number dialed and the duration of the call because the motel charged by the minute. Of the forty-six numbers dialed, Faustina had called 411 an even dozen times. Pike and I divided the remaining thirty-four numbers between us, then began dialing to see who answered, me on the house line and Pike on his cell.

The first two calls Faustina made were to the information operator. A woman with a steady voice answered on the third.

'Los Angeles Police, West L.A. Station. May I help you?'

I was surprised, and wasn't sure what to say.

'This is the police. May I help you?'

'Is there an Officer Faustina?'

'I don't see that name on the roll.'

'Do you recognize that name, Faustina?'

'Who is this?'

I apologized and hung up. Faustina had spoken to the West L.A. Station for six minutes, which was long enough to be transferred through every unit in the building. He might have asked to speak with me, and, when I wasn't there, asked for J. Edgar Hoover. Anyone loopy enough to believe he was my father would want Hoover on the case.

I glanced over at Joe.

'He called West L.A. Station. How about that?'

Pike said, 'Uh.'

A man with a gruff voice answered the next number. 'Police, Southeast.'

When I hung up, Pike was waiting.

'Another station?'

'Yeah. He called Southeast.'

'He also called Newton.'

Herbert Faustina had spoken with Southeast for eleven minutes, and Newton for eight. The next three numbers brought me to Pacific, the 77th, and Hollenbeck.

When I leaned back, Pike had still more.

'Devonshire, Foothill, and North Hollywood.'

Three more of LAPD's eighteen patrol areas.

'Okay, this is strange. Why would he call all these police stations?'

'The newspapers described you as a detective. Maybe he thought you were a police detective, and called the stations trying to find you.'

'Possible.'

Pike shrugged and returned to his phone.

'Or not.'

The next number connected me to a Rite Aid pharmacy, and the ninth with the Auto Club. The tenth number brought me to LAPD's Hollywood Station, but the eleventh was different. A man with the hushed voice of a late-night disk jockey answered on the first ring.

'Golden Escorts, discreet and professional.'

Faustina had spent twenty-three minutes on the phone with Golden Escorts. I remembered the little throwaway newspaper in his suitcase, the one showing the naked woman with metallic blue hair – the *Hard-X Times*. I hung up.

'He had more on his mind than finding me. He called an escort service.'

'Golden Escorts?'

'You got them, too?'

'Twice. He called them last Wednesday, then again on Friday. Maybe he thought call girls would know how to find you.'

'Humor doesn't suit you.'

Pike's face was flat and expressionless. Maybe he meant it.

We checked the call dates and saw that during Faustina's nine days at Home Away Suites, he had phoned Golden Escorts three times. He called them on his second night at the motel, then again on his fifth and ninth nights. The ninth night was yesterday – the night he was murdered. I felt a little pop of adrenaline when I tied the escort service to the date of his death. It felt like a clue.

I said, 'Keep dialing, and let's see what else we get.'

The remaining calls included two more police stations. All together, he had phoned twelve patrol areas out of the eighteen into which LAPD divides Los Angeles. The remaining calls also included three take-out restaurants, a Pep Boys auto parts, two churches in North Hollywood, and the Crystal Cathedral. No one at any of these places recognized his name or remembered his call. Excepting the information number, Golden Escorts was the only number he phoned more than once, and the only escort service.

When we finished identifying every number Faustina called, I phoned Golden Escorts again. The same man answered in exactly the same way.

'Golden Escorts, discreet and professional.'

'I saw your ad in the *Hard-X Times*.'

'Groovy. You need a date for tonight?'

'Can I get someone to come to my motel?'

'No problem. We take cash, Visa, and MasterCard, no AmEx, and we offer both male and female escorts for nonsexual outcall companionship. Prostitution is illegal and that's not what we sell. Anything that happens between you and the escort, well, that's between you and the escort. You understand?'

He gave me the boilerplate in case I was Vice.

'I understand.'

'Groovy. Tell me where you are, how much you want to spend, and what kind of companion you're looking for.'

'I'm at the Home Away Suites. You know where it is.'

'Like the back of my teeth.'

'Groovy. I'd like the same girl I had last time.'

'You've used us before?'

'Oh, sure. Three times.'

'Who is this?'

'Herbert Faustina.'

The line went dead. After three conversations, he knew Faustina's voice well enough to know I wasn't him.

I called a friend of mine at the phone company and gave her the number. If it turned out to be a cell, we would have to backtrace through the billing address, and all of that could take a long time. If we got lucky, it would be a hard line. We were lucky. Ninety seconds later she gave me their address.

Groovy.

CHAPTER 13

Golden Escorts occupied a tiny clapboard house in Venice north of the canals, six blocks from the ocean. The neighborhood was typical of Venice, where microscopic houses were set on lots so narrow they shouldered together like cards in a deck. To the untrained eye, many streets in Venice looked like tenements, sporting broken sidewalks, beach-bum decor, and rent-a-wreck parking, but the cheapest house on the block would go for six hundred thousand dollars. Location was everything.

The house itself was a Craftsman knockoff sporting a tiny front porch, yellow paint, and a weather vane shaped like a whale. The windows were lit, but women with heavy makeup weren't lingering on the sidewalk and a red light didn't burn over the door. Escort services weren't brothels with prostitutes lying around in negligees; they functioned more like dispatchers for independent contractors – they ran ads, fielded calls, and doled out assignments by phone. Sometimes they provided a driver for the girl, but most times not, and the smaller services were almost always located in a private home or apartment.

Pike and I parked on the cross street, then walked back to the house like two citizens out for a stroll. Pardy and Diaz would have to hope for cooperation, but Pike and I weren't Pardy and Diaz.

Pike said, 'Give me a minute.'

He waited for a car to pass, then slipped down along the east side of the house and vanished into the shadows. I continued on to the next corner. It was a nice night in Venice. The ocean smelled fresh. Six minutes later, Pike reappeared. I walked back and joined him in front of the house.

'One man, one woman. Kitchen's in the rear, living room in front, bed and a bath to the right of the kitchen. She's making dinner and he's in the living room with a headset and computer. Looks like they live here.'

'Don't you hate it when people drop by at dinner-time?'

'They're going to hate it more.'

We waited for two more cars to pass, then went to the front door. Pike stood to the side so he wouldn't be visible when the door opened. You see Joe Pike, you know you have trouble. I put on my best nonthreatening smile, and knocked.

After I knocked the second time, the door opened, and a man in his early thirties peered out. He had dark hair combed back, a wide face, and a cordless telephone headset. The earpiece was pushed to the side because he had come to the door.

He said, 'What's up?'

I smiled wider, then pushed him hard in the chest, catching him off guard and shoving him backward. Pike came in behind me. Not particularly discreet, but very professional.

'Hey, what is this? What are you doing?'

'You don't have a problem. We just want to talk to you.'

The man backpedaled, pushing out both hands like he was trying to quell a riot.

'You're the guy who called.'

Pike stepped past him into the living room. The guy with the headset tried to back up so he could see both of us at the same time, but he was already against the wall.

'Where are you going? Hey, I live here. This is my home. Get out of here.'

'What's your name?'

'Fuck you. Get out of my house.'

A wallet was in a bowl on a table inside the front door. I found his driver's license and compared him to the picture. Yep, it was him. Stephen Golden, the proud proprietor of Golden Escorts. Criminals amaze me. I dropped his wallet back into the bowl as a woman came out of the kitchen. She had a narrow face with a gap between her front teeth and soft eyes, but she didn't scream or make a scene, either. You don't make a scene when you're afraid of the police. I gave her the encouraging smile.

'It's okay. The police will be here in a little bit.'

The man said, 'That's bullshit. They have some kind of beef with a client.'

'We don't have a beef. One of your clients is dead.'

The woman said, 'Oh, that's terrible.'

He snapped at her, his voice harsher toward her than me even though I had invaded his home.

'Don't say anything. We don't know anything about that. They can't just come in here.'

I gave more of my smile to the woman, like he wasn't in the room with us, just me and her.

'What's your name?'

'Marsha.'

He said, 'Don't say a goddamned thing.'

Marsha's face had the translucence of murky water: pale skin, faded freckles, and lashless eyes that gave her an innocence she probably did not possess. She wore a Tenacious D T-shirt over shorts, with butterflies tattooed above her ankles. The shirt was cropped and the shorts were low, letting a tattoo peek out across her lower belly.

'It's going to be fine, Marsha. Do you know what Stephen does for a living?'

'Yeah, it's our business. We don't hurt anyone.'

'You his wife, girlfriend, what?'

'Don't talk to him! It's none of his business!'

It was just me and Marsha.

'We live together.'

'Okay, cool. You don't have to be afraid.'

'I'm not.'

A laptop computer was set up on a dinner tray by a club chair in the corner of his living room so Golden could watch TV while he worked. I went over and looked at it.

'Get away from there! Leave my stuff alone.'

Pike said, 'Shh.'

A six-line phone base with an auto-forwarding repeater was on the floor next to the chair, slaved to the computer. A phone directory was set up on the laptop, showing what was probably the names and numbers of his prostitutes. A Telecredit window was open to run Visa and MasterCard charges, so the computer probably held his billing ledgers and records of who earned what. I went back to him.

'Okay, Stephen, here's what we want. A man named Herbert Faustina was staying at the Home Away Suites up in Toluca Lake –'

'I don't know anything about that.'

'Three times during the past nine days, Mr. Faustina phoned you –'

'That's not true.'

'We know because the phone records show he called your number.'

'I run a legitimate business. What happens between –'

'Faustina called you last night for the third and final time. This morning, at approximately two forty-five, he was shot to death. You see where I'm going with this?'

Golden crossed his arms and chewed the inside of his lower lip. He shook his head.

'I'm going to call my lawyer.'

'No. We're not the police, so we're not going to waste time with your lawyer. The police will probably roll by tomorrow. You can call your lawyer when you talk to them, but right now you're on your own. We're going to go see whoever you sent to Faustina.'

'I don't file a W-2 for these people. I got pager numbers, and maybe a cell. I don't even know their real names, most of them, let alone where they live.'

'So page them. Stephen, look, you're going to cooperate because you are now a link in a homicide investigation and so are the three people you sent to Faustina. If you don't cooperate with the police, they will stretch you. If you don't cooperate with me, I'm going to take

95

your computer and all of that stuff over there to West L.A. Sex Crimes.'

His computer probably showed the prostitutes he employed, a history of his credit card transactions that would include the identities of his johns, and possibly even banking and account information that would reveal how he hid his money from the IRS.

He looked incredulous.

'You can't steal my stuff.'

'Stephen, please. How are you going to stop us?'

Golden glanced at Pike again, but now he seemed more thoughtful than afraid.

'What if I cooperate?'

'If you don't, I can give your records to the police. If you do, we can make them disappear. You see what I'm offering?'

I was offering him a way out of a major pimping and pandering bust.

Marsha said, 'Dinner's ready, Stephen. Would you please tell them so they'll leave?'

Golden glared at her as if he suddenly hated her as deeply as he hated anything, but then he pushed away from the wall and went to his computer.

He said, 'Come over here. I want you to see.'

He dropped into the club chair and used a mouse to open what appeared to be a calendar on his computer. He went to each of the three dates and copied the names of the women he had sent to the Home Away Suites, then opened an address book to show me their entries: Janice L., Dana M., and Victoria.

'You see? I have the pagers and the phones, but I don't have their addresses. I can page them, but I can't say when they'll get back to me. We're not talking about

96

the most stable people. Sometimes these girls disappear and I never hear back.'

'Aren't they on call?'

Marsha said, 'People have lives, you know? Stephen isn't the only person they work with.'

With. Not for.

Now Golden looked impatient.

'Look, you want me to page them right now, I'll page them.'

He stalked back to the phone and punched in a number. When he heard the pager's squeal, he held out the phone as if I could hear it from across the room.

'See? A tone. I'm paging.'

He tapped in his phone number, then hung up and tossed his headset onto the club chair.

'She's paged. You guys wanna have dinner? We can page the other girls, then sit here all night waiting for them to call back while they're out sucking dick.'

I looked at Pike, but Pike was immobile. Pike would sit with Golden for weeks if we had to; maybe even forever. Pike would also put a gun to Golden's head and pull the trigger if Golden didn't come through.

I didn't like not knowing where to find them, and I liked it less because any one of them might have been involved in Faustina's murder. If one of them was linked with the homicide, they weren't likely to call back, and certainly wouldn't cooperate, but Golden seemed like my only way to reach them.

'What about their last names?'

'If they gave me a last name, it would be bullshit. You think I file W-2s for these people?'

He spread his hands again, the universal sign of the man caught in the middle.

'Look, I'm trying to cooperate here, but all I can do is what I can do. When they call, I'll tell them to talk to you. If you want to page them yourself, go ahead, but all you're going to do is scare them.'

Golden was right. I felt half-assed and caught short. I had blundered into his house exactly like the cowboy Pardy accused me of being, and now I didn't have anything to show for it. I tried to think of something smart to ask, and felt even more half-assed because thinking was hard.

'Did Faustina pay with a credit card?'

'No, he paid cash.'

'Which girl saw him last night?'

'I wrote the names in the order they saw him. That was Victoria. She saw him last.'

'Did Victoria or the other girls tell you about him, like something he said or did?'

'They don't tell me anything and I never ask. I don't want to know. You probably won't want to know, either.'

'But you spoke with Faustina when he called?'

'Yeah.'

'What did he say?'

'You wanna know what he wanted, like did he want a blow job or anal?'

Pike shoved Golden in the back of the head.

Marsha said, 'Don't be smart, Stephen. You make it worse when you're smart.'

'Did he say where he was from or what he was doing in L.A.?'

Golden was still rubbing his head.

'I don't make conversation with these people. I tried to feel him out about what he wanted from the girl – some things cost more than others, and some girls won't

98

do certain things. All he said was she had to be a nice person. Understanding, he said. He just wanted someone he could talk to. That's all he said.'

'Did the girls tell you what he talked about?'

'I don't give a shit. We agree on a price, and I get my cut. One hour for two hundred bucks. I don't care what they do.'

I thought about Faustina wanting only to talk, and wondered if it was true. Six hundred dollars for three hours of talking was a lot of talking.

'The man called you three times in less than two weeks. I can see the first call being all business, but you must have developed a familiarity with him, maybe joked about what a good customer he was, something like that.'

'Yeah, I joked around with him a little, but we didn't talk. He didn't have the gift of gab, you know? Me, I like to talk. Him, he just seemed kinda awkward and sad.'

'Did he mention his family?'

Golden laughed.

'Some dude calling for a whore doesn't bring up his family. Look, I don't want to be best buddies with these people. I don't give a shit who they are or where they're from. I tie up my phone with one guy, no one else can get through – I'm losing money. Like now.'

I tried to think of something else to ask, but it was clear Golden didn't have anything more to offer. I folded the list of names and put it away.

I said, 'Okay, Stephen. Page them and set it up for tomorrow, then give me a call –'

I took out a business card and put it in the little bowl with his wallet.

'You can reach me at this number, and I know that you will.'

Golden's face brightened, surprised that Joe and I were going for it and anxious to get us out of his house. You could almost see the wheels turning behind his bushy eyebrows. As soon as the girls called back, he would warn them, tell them to split town, and then be on the horn to his attorney. He might even leave town himself.

I said, 'You know how I know, Stephen?'

'Hey, I said I would, didn't I? You're giving me a big break here.'

'That's right. And I'm also taking your computer.'

I closed his laptop, then jerked out the cables. Golden's eyes widened and he lurched forward, but Pike touched his arm.

Pike said, 'Stay.'

Golden froze in place between us. Marsha went back to the kitchen and called from the door.

'For Christ's sake, Stephen. Dinner's going to suck.'

I tucked his computer under my arm and moved to the door.

He said, 'That's fucking stealing! You can't just come into someone's house and steal their stuff!'

'I'm not stealing it – I'm holding it hostage. If your girls come across, you'll get it back. If they don't, it goes to the police.'

Pike opened the door, then glanced back at Golden. Pike shook his head, and went out.

Golden said, 'This is bullshit!'

'Call me tomorrow morning or it goes to the cops.'

'Fuck you, you asshole! Fuck Faustina, too!'

I stopped, and turned back to him when he said it.

His face paled, and his rage became something soft.

I said, 'What?'

He shook his head.

I let myself out, pulled the door shut, and stood on the porch. Pike was in the street, his sunglasses reflecting red like nighttime cat eyes. Inside, Marsha called Stephen Golden to dinner.

CHAPTER 14

A gentle onshore breeze carried the smell and the taste from the sea, six blocks away. A thin maritime fog swirled overhead, bright with reflected light. The fog dampened neighborhood sounds, and left the world feeling empty. Pike watched me approach. When I reached him, we were in the street, two guys just waiting. We had no reason to wait, but something felt unfinished. I stared at Golden's house, wondering if I had forgotten an obvious question or an even more obvious conclusion. When I looked at Pike again, he was still watching me.

'I saw how you looked at him. A couple of times in there when he said things.'

'What do you mean?'

'Are you all right with this?'

I glanced back at the house, but its face hadn't changed. It was a house. I didn't know if I was all right or not. I tried to explain.

'I work a case for other people. It's always about someone else. This time, too; Faustina is a stranger – but it ended up feeling like I was here about me. I wasn't sure what to ask. None of it seemed as clear.'

I thought about it.

'I guess.'

We stood in the street. Out on Main, a horn blew. A dog barked as if fighting for its life, and then the barking abruptly stopped. I smelled garlic.

After a while, Pike said, 'You did fine.'

We walked back up the street to his Jeep, then made the long drive back to my house, bumping along in traffic like a million other Angelenos, but the sense that my night's work was unfinished remained. We left the 405 at Mulholland and drove east along the spine of the mountains, neither of us speaking. The fields of light on either side of us that marked the city and the valley did not glitter that night. They were hidden behind lowering clouds. The stalled spring rain had thinned throughout the day, but now was returning.

When we reached my house, Pike let me out at the mouth of my carport. He spoke for the first time since we had left Venice.

He said, 'It was the word, sad. Sad has an ugly weight.'

I knew right away what he was saying, and knew he was right.

'Yes. It was when Golden said Faustina seemed sad. He wasn't just a stiff on a slab anymore. He was real, and what he felt was real. You're right about that word.'

'You want to go grab a beer or something?'

'No, I'm good,' I said.

'We could go back to Golden's. Put two in his head for using that word.'

'Let's quit while we're ahead.'

I got out, closed his door, but didn't watch Pike drive away.

My house was quiet, and empty. For the first time that day, I thought about Lucy. I wanted to hear her voice. I wanted to say something funny, and be rewarded with her laugh. I wanted to tell her about Herbert Faustina, and let her help me carry the weight of that word – sad. I wanted everything to be as it had been between us because if only I had her then maybe this business about Faustina wouldn't feel so important.

But Lucy and Ben weren't inside and they weren't down the hill in their apartment. They were two thousand miles away, building a new life.

I checked the phone, but no one had left a message. I washed my hands, took a Falstaff from the fridge, then put out fresh food for the cat. I called him.

'Hey, buddy. You here?'

I opened the French doors to the deck and called him again, but he did not appear.

I leaned against the kitchen counter. The phone was three feet away. I went into the living room and turned on the tube. Maybe the Red Light Assassin had racked up another score. I went back to the phone, dialed most of Lucy's number, then stopped, not because I was scared but because I didn't want her to hurt and that was the way she wanted it. It should have been easy; just stop pretending that she wanted to hear my voice as much as I wanted to hear hers.

After a while, I opened another Falstaff, then decided to take care of the unfinished business.

Carol Starkey

It was almost ten that night when Starkey idled past Elvis Cole's house, trying to work up the nerve to stop. His car was in its usual place, his house was lit, and her palms were as damp as the first time she faced down a bomb when she was a rookie tech with LAPD's Bomb Squad.

Starkey, pissed at herself, said, 'Jesus Christ, moron, just *stop* for Christ's sake. He's *home*. You drove all the way *up* here.'

The entire drive up from Mar Vista, Starkey had badgered herself as to what she would do and how she would do it: She would knock on his door, bring him over to the couch, and sit his ass down. She was gonna say, *Hey, listen to me, I'm being serious – I like you and I think you think I'm cool, too, so let's stop pretending we're only friends and act like adults, okay?* – and then she would kiss him and hope to hell he didn't toss her out on her ass.

Starkey said, 'All you gotta do is *stop*, go to the door, and *do it!*'

Starkey didn't stop. She crept past his house on the crappy little road, turned around in a gravel drive, then eased back with her lights off like some kind of lunatic stalker pervert, talking to herself the entire time because – her shrink said – hearing another human voice was better than hearing no voice at all, even if it was your own.

Touchy-feely bullshit.

Starkey parked up the street from Cole's house so she could keep an eye on things while she got herself together. If he came out he probably wouldn't recognize her car. Jesus, if Cole caught her sitting out here she would drive right off the cliff, no shit, just flat out punch the gas and pull a hard left straight down to the center of the earth and never come back.

'Cole,' she said. 'You must be the densest man in Los Angeles and I am certainly the most pathetic female, so why can't we just get on with this?'

Starkey felt around for her cigarettes and was disgusted to find she had only eight or nine left. They wouldn't last long. She lit one, sucked down half with one ferociously hot pull, then exhaled through her nose, feeling grumpy and frustrated. Here she was, a tough-ass bomb cop who had de-armed, defused, and defeated more than enough bombs to blow Cole's house right off the mountain, who had, herself, been blown apart in a goddamned trailer park, come back to tell about it, then gone on to beat and bury the most notorious serial bomber in U.S. history (that asshole, Mr. Red, who had blown up *her* house in the process, that prick!), and she couldn't work up the nut to bang on Cole's door. And then bang *him*.

It wasn't for lack of trying. Starkey had asked Cole out, flirted with him shamelessly, and pretty much done everything short of putting a gun to his head. But Cole, that idiot, had it bad for his *lawyer*, the Southern Belle.

Starkey scowled as if she had bitten a turd.

'Looo-ceee.'

Every time she thought about Lucy Chenier, she pictured Lucille Ball, all that wild red hair, bulging eyes, and loony bullshit with Ethel Mertz. She could hear Ricky's voice.

'*Looo-ceee, I hooaaannn!*'

How could Cole say her name without laughing?

Starkey finished the cigarette, tossed it, then lit another. Starkey wasn't short on nerve, but her stupid shrink had suggested she wasn't so much afraid of Cole's rejection as she was of eventually losing him. Starkey hadn't had the best of luck when it came to men. Not so many years ago she was head over heels in solid with her sergeant-supervisor on the Bomb Squad, Sugar Boudreaux, who *still* left her shaking when she thought about him, but Sugar had been killed with her in the trailer park. Then there was Jack Pell, the ATF agent she met on the hunt for Mr. Red. Starkey had been hitting the booze pretty good back then, and she was coming off Sugar and the effed-up ripped-apart surgical nightmare that was her patched-together body. One third of her right breast – missing in action; one fourth of her stomach – gone; three feet of intestine – adios; her spleen – *what* spleen?; and the Big Casino – her uterus . . . and everything that went with it. Pell had been tender, and his passionate mercies had gone a long way toward helping her kick the booze, but after a while they both realized it wasn't The Love, Pell with his own uncertainties and Starkey with hers, both of them with so far yet to go.

'Love'm and lose'm.'

And maybe that was her fear – if she had Cole then she would lose him, just as she lost Sugar and Pell – so it was safer to simply want him.

Psychobabble bullshit.

Starkey lit another cigarette, then slouched down in the seat, watching his house. She had liked Elvis Cole since they met on the night the little boy went missing. She liked his dopey sense of humor and the fierce way he tried to be normal even though he wasn't; she liked how he had given every part of himself to find that boy, and the loyalty she saw in his friends –

Starkey grinned.

– and it didn't hurt he had a hot ass, either.

Starkey's laughter faded, and the hole it left filled with sadness. Truth be told, she had a crush on him, she was fascinated by him, she *dwelled* on him, and she wanted him to want her as much as she wanted him.

Maybe he didn't like her.

Maybe she wasn't his type.

He was still in love with Lucy Chenier.

Starkey let smoke drift from her mouth, up and over her face like a cloud, hiding her. She hadn't taken a drink in ten months. She wouldn't start now.

All she had to do was go to his door and knock.

'Do it!'

Starkey pushed herself upright, flicked the cigarette away, then started her car as –

Thirty yards away in his carport, brake lights came on and the grungy yellow Corvette backed out.

Starkey said, *'Shit!'*

She ducked, praying to Christ he didn't see her as the Corvette's tail swung around. She wedged herself all the way down on the seat, damn near under the wheel, and when she finally looked up he was gone.

CHAPTER 15

The Missing

'Father? Father, are you here?'

'I'm coming, dear.'

Father Clarence Wills – called Father Willie by the patrons of Our Lady of Righteous Forgiveness Church – hoisted his creaky bones up from the floor of his closet and stepped into his office. Mrs. Hansen, who assisted him in his clerical duties, was waiting in the door with her purse and jacket.

He said, 'I was just trying to get those papers away. Why is it all the empty file space is at the bottom of these old cabinets?'

'You're limping.'

'I'm always limping. It comes with age and too much port wine.'

Father Willie loved telling her things like that. Every time, she would cluck at him just as she did now, and, every time, he would smile, letting her know it was all just a naughty tease. Mrs. Hansen was short, overweight, and probably the only person in town shorter, fatter, and older than Father Willie.

'It's dark out, Father. I'd like to be getting home.'

'That's fine, dear. We're finished for the day.'

'I don't like leaving after dark. It's not safe out in the night.'

'You could have gone two hours ago.'

'You were still working.'

'And I'll work after you leave. Just a few more things. Here, I'll see you out to your car.'

She clucked again as he pulled on his jacket. The thin air was growing nippy.

'You big men think I'm silly, but something happened to all those people and it always happened at night. Javier is the same way, making fun of me like it's all in my head.'

Javier Hansen was her husband. Between them, Mr. and Mrs. Hansen had five children, sixteen grandchildren, and two great-grandchildren, every one of them 'corn-fed and farm-raised' as her husband liked to say, and all of them currently living somewhere else.

'I'm not making fun, dear, but that was years ago and there was never any fact to go with the rumors. People get carried away with these things, and then start believing in werewolves.'

'Six people don't just up and vanish.'

'Six people spread over twenty years. Wives leave their husbands, husbands leave wives, children run away, people move on.'

'People *say* something when they move, good-bye or good riddance. They pay their bills and close their accounts – they don't just disappear like they were snatched off the face of the earth. Those children didn't just leave.'

110

Mrs. Hansen had worked herself up into a snit, though Father Willie had to agree about the children. Three of the six missing were minor children, the two little Ames girls and that Brentworth boy, gone missing in the span of eight months almost ten years ago. They hadn't just moved on like the adults might have, not those little girls and the boy. That was a clear-cut crime, no doubt about it, though the police had never been able to prove it or even name a suspect.

Father Willie felt glum at the memory, and suddenly got it in his head to tease Mrs. Hansen out of her snit.

'Well, I'm not going to let anything happen to you, dear, you can be sure of that!'

He pulled out a shiny black Kimber .45-caliber semi-automatic, and waved it overhead.

'Silver bullets! In case it's a werewolf!'

Mrs. Hansen, who well knew about the Father's gun, rolled her eyes and turned away, smiling in spite of herself.

'You put that thing away before you hurt yourself!'

'The Lord will keep me safe; it's the werewolves who better watch out.'

Father Willie was no stranger to firearms, as Mrs. Hansen and everyone else who worked at the church knew. Father Willie was an avid sports marksman, and the gun had been a Christmas gift from his youngest brother. Having gotten Mrs. Hansen to smile, Father Willie slipped the pistol into his jacket, caught up to her in the hall, and saw her out to her car.

Set back from the main road and surrounded by pines, the small parking lot seemed deserted with only two cars remaining, one being his Le Baron, the other her four-wheel-drive Subaru. Father Willie had always thought the middle darkness of early spring lent his church a cloak of isolation, though now the parking lot seemed unusually dark.

She said, 'Don't you work too late. You're not a young man. And don't get into that port wine until you're home. I don't want the police finding you on the side of the road.'

'Drive safely, Mrs. H. I'll see you tomorrow.'

Father Willie held the door for her, then watched her drive up the narrow road into blackness. He snuggled his hands into his pockets, his right hand just naturally finding the pistol's grip. As Mrs. Hansen's headlights disappeared, he saw his breath in the moonlight and suddenly realized why it was so dark – the two enormous security lamps that automatically came on when it got dark, hadn't. The lamps were perched on their poles like two dead owls.

Father Willie made a mental note to tell the custodian in the morning, then started back to his office.

'Father?'

The voice startled him, but then Father Willie saw the man's embarrassed smile. The smile put him at ease.

'Gosh, Father, I didn't mean to scare you. I thought you saw me.'

The man was large and fleshy, with a receding hairline and soulful eyes. His hooded sweatshirt made him appear even larger, standing in the shadows like he was, with his smile floating in darkness. Father Willie smiled awkwardly, too, because he was so startled that he was sure he squirted a whiz. Age brought a weak bladder.

'I know we've met, but I don't recall your name. Sorry.'

'Frederick – Frederick Conrad, not Freddie or Fred –
I work for Payne Keller, myself and Elroy Lewis.'

'That's right. Payne.'

Father Willie remembered. Frederick had once come
to Mass with Payne, and when they were introduced,
Frederick had pointed out that his name was not Freddie
or Fred, but Frederick. Now Frederick shuffled closer,
and Father Willie thought his eyes seemed lonely and
cold.

'I know Payne's been seeing you, Father, and I'm
hoping you know what's going on.'

'What do you mean, son?'

'Payne's missing. He hasn't been home and he didn't
tell me or Elroy he was going, and we're left with his
station to run. Tell you the truth, I'm worried. It's not
like Payne to just up and go like this. I'm scared.'

Father Willie stood thinking. He had no wish nor
right to share the matters of counsel with a parish-
ioner, but Payne had spoken often of Frederick Conrad,
and Father Willie himself had grown concerned about
Payne's absence. Payne was a troubled man, so deeply
troubled that Father Willie often probed him for the
possibility of suicide.

Father Willie saw the concern on Frederick's face,
and weighed what he could offer.

'Payne didn't tell you he was going away?'

'No, sir, and I'm getting scared. I'm thinking I
should call the police.'

Father Willie thought calling the police might not
be such a bad idea. His conversation with Mrs. Hansen
about folks gone missing had put the spook into him,
though he also knew that Payne had made plans.

'Frederick, I don't think you need to call the police

just yet. If you're truly worried, you should follow your heart, but Payne was planning a trip to Los Angeles. That much I can say. I didn't know he would go so soon or be gone so long, but he did tell me he was going.'

Something like a ripple worked across Frederick's face, and his eyes grew smaller.

'Why Los Angeles?'

'I can't really get into it, Frederick. Suffice it to say that Payne felt the need to make peace with himself. You ask him when he gets back.'

Frederick wet his lips.

'Can you tell me how to reach him?'

'I'm sorry.'

'Well, he just left us, Father. We have this station to run.'

Father Willie wanted to go home, but Frederick didn't move. The priest already regretted the conversation, reminding himself this was why you could never tell people anything – they always wanted to know more, and seemed to feel it was their right.

'I really don't know what else to tell you. Maybe tomorrow you should call the police like you said.'

Father Willie tried to turn, but Frederick caught his arm, and the force of it almost pulled Father Willie off his feet.

'He was planning this trip? It was Los Angeles, you said?'

'I think you'd better calm down.'

'Why was he going to Los Angeles?'

Father Willie stared into Frederick's eyes, and felt a fear he had not known since his days volunteering on death row at the penitentiary. He found the pistol in his pocket, and gripped it, then came to his senses. He let go of the gun. He drew his hand from his pocket and patted Frederick's hand, the same hand that held tight to his arm.

'Let go, son.'

The eerie wrongness faded from Frederick's eyes, and he made an embarrassed smile.

'Jesus, I can't believe I did that, Father. I'm sorry. I'm just so worried about Payne, is all. Can you forgive me?'

'Of course I can. Let's talk about this tomorrow.'

'I'm just worried, you know.'

'I can see that.'

'Listen, will you let me confess to you? I'm not a Catholic, but would that be okay?'

'We can talk, son. You can tell me anything you need to say. Let's talk about it tomorrow.'

'I want to confess, is all. Just like Payne. I got a lot to get off my chest. Like Payne.'

Father Willie wanted to comfort this man, but could not divulge that Payne's anguish had remained private. Payne had never confessed, not the things that most tortured him. Payne wanted to confess, knew he desperately needed to confess, but he had not yet found the strength. Father Willie had been seeing Payne as a counselor to help him find that strength, but – so far – had failed.

Frederick stepped away and slipped his hands into his pockets.

'Let's go inside, Father. I won't keep you. I know you want to go.'

'We can talk tomorrow. Whatever it is, it will keep. You can come back tomorrow.'

'Tomorrow.'

'That's right.'

'You're sure it was Los Angeles, where he went? You won't tell me why, but you know it was Los Angeles?'

'Payne's reasons are between himself and God.'

'I'll have to go find him. I got no other choice.'

'We can talk about it tomorrow.'

'Okay, tomorrow. I can find him tomorrow.'

Father Willie turned away, but didn't have the chance to slip his own hands back into his pockets. Something powerful lifted him off his feet and carried him struggling to the side of the church. He glimpsed a truck hidden in the darkness.

He did not see the blade, but felt it.

CHAPTER 16

When I first came to Los Angeles, I made the drive on Route 66, mostly because of an old television series I enjoyed as a child, two cool guys played by Martin Milner (the rich mama's boy trying to come into his own) and George Maharis (the rootless loner from the wrong side of town), off in search of themselves and adventure along America's pre-interstate coast-to-coast highway (Route 66). Route 66 began in Philadelphia and tracked its way through the center of the country to L.A. where it merged with Sunset Boulevard, then Santa Monica Boulevard, rolling inevitably west until it reached the amazing amusement park that bloomed along the length of the Santa Monica pier. I had followed the highway to its end, not running from but going to, like Milner and Maharis, searching until I reached the sea. It wasn't the first time I had sought out an amusement park, and now I sought one again.

I left my home that night amid the deepening sense that some important business I started a long time ago had remained unfinished. I drove back to the ocean and parked on a bluff overlooking the Santa Monica pier, not so far from Stephen Golden's home in Venice. I got out of my car, climbed over a low fence, and stood at the edge of the bluff. Below me, the lights of the Ferris wheel and the roller coaster spun across the black sea. The bluff was fragile from erosion and uncertain in its nature. Signs warned the unwary not to cross the fence because more than once the precipice had calved like ice from an iceberg, but the earth felt firm to me. Maybe I didn't recognize the danger.

I watched the swirling lights, and wondered if Herbert Faustina had also come to this pier.

Once upon a time I ran away to join the circus. I ran away because my mother told me my father was a human cannonball. Do you think that's silly? My mother never told me my father's name, or showed me a picture, or even described him. Maybe she didn't know these things. Neither my grandfather nor my aunt knew any more than me. After a while, it didn't matter whether he was a human cannonball or not; her description was my truth. If she said my father was a human cannonball, then he was a human cannonball.

I searched, but I did not find him. In my boyhood fantasies, he sometimes came to find me.

Learning a Trade

WILSON

The private detective was a short oval man named Ken Wilson. He wore a dark gray business suit and tan Hush Puppy loafers that didn't go with the suit. Creases cut his jacket and pants because of the long drive, but he smelled of Old Spice and he checked his hair before he got out of his car. Appearance was important in his line of work; people were suspicious of someone ill-kept.

Wilson was one hundred sixty-two miles from home, having made the long drive to collect a fourteen-year-old runaway named Elvis Cole. This was the third time Wilson had tracked down the kid, and at least one other dick had worked for the family before him. Wilson had to hand it to the kid, he had perseverance. He kept trying to find his father.

The carnival was set up at the edge of a small town in a field used mostly for crop dusters. Wilson left his car in the parking area and walked through an arched gateway beneath a shabby banner that proclaimed: Ralph Todd's 21st Century Shows & Diversions!!! Twin rows of tents swallowed anyone who walked through the gate, but not before running them past roach-coach food stands and game arcades that Wilson suspected were magnets for pedophiles. Everything looked patched together and poorly maintained. Wilson thought that if this was the twenty-first century they could keep it.

The manager's trailer was at the opposite end of the midway behind the tents that housed the featured attractions: Whores billed as 'exotic dancers,' a freak show featuring a three-eyed cow, and, behind a final banner, the midway's star attraction, the Human Fireball . . . See him flash thru the sky like a blazing meteor!!! Wilson cynically noted that every banner ended with three exclamation points. The future was hyperbole.

A dwarf who smelled of vegetable soup pointed Wilson between the tents to a silver Airstream trailer.

It was dull and spotted with grime. A small sign on the door read MANAGER. The manager would be a Mr. Jacob Lenz, with whom Wilson had spoken. Mr. Lenz would be expecting him.

Wilson rapped at the door and let himself in without waiting to be asked. Time was money.

'Mr. Lenz? Ken Wilson. I appreciate your cooperation.' Wilson offered his hand.

Lenz was a broad, heavy man with lined skin and small eyes. He stood to take Wilson's hand, but he didn't look happy about it.

'I just wanna get this straight, you know? I don't want any trouble with the family.'

'There's no trouble. He's done this before.'

'I can't keep track of all the people around here. Kids come, they go, I don't know who belongs to who. I just wanna do the right thing.'

'I understand.'

Wilson took out a picture and held it up. It was a black-and-white school photograph taken two years earlier.

'Now let's be sure we're talking about the same boy. Is this Elvis Cole?'

'Yeah, that's him, but he tells everyone his name is Jimmie.'

'His name was Philip James Cole until his mother changed it. He used to go by Jimmie.'

'She changed his name to Elvis?'

Wilson ignored the question because the answer left a sour ache in his stomach. Wilson felt bad for the kid. Here was this little boy, one day out of the blue, his mother changed his name to Elvis; not Don or Joey – Elvis. Here's this poor kid with no idea who his father is because the crazy bitch won't tell anyone, and bammo – she feeds him a bullshit story that his father was a human cannonball. Wilson believed that parents should be licensed.

'Does the boy know I've come for him?'

'You didn't want me to say, so I didn't say. You want me to get him?'

'It's best if you take me to him. That way he won't run.'

'Whatever you want. I jus' don't want no trouble with the family.'

'There's no trouble.'

'I'm glad to get rid of him, all the trouble he made. He was a pain in the ass.'

Wilson followed the manager out past a giant tarpaulin showing a stripper crooking her finger. The paint was faded and her hairstyle was ten years out of date. A voice balloon over her head read: C'mere, big boy!!!

Wilson clucked to himself.

Three exclamation points.

These people were something.

ELVIS COLE

Elvis Cole, fourteen years old, heard about Ralph Todd's 21st Century Shows & Diversions from a kid named Brucie Chenski who lived in the trailer park where Elvis and his mother stayed when his Aunt Lynn threw them out. Brucie was sixteen years old, the only other teenage boy in the park, and a sociopathic liar.

First day they met, Brucie told Elvis his older brother was a dealer and the two of them were going to San

Francisco to get Free Love. Everything Brucie said was like that: large dramatic adventures involving his brother, dope, and Female Conquest. Elvis never believed him. Then one day Brucie said, hey, bro, my brother and I fucked these whores at the carnival. The part about the carnival nailed Elvis's attention like an iron spike through his feet.

What carnival?

The carnival out past the water tower, Brucie says, Jesus, they got this one girl was in Playboy, I saw her picture right out of the magazine, tits out to here, they got rides, a retarded midget that eats worms, these strippers who are total slut whores, my brother sold this girl some acid and she sucked our dicks while –

Elvis interrupted.

They got a human cannonball?

Yeah . . .

Elvis walked away, just like that, not even caring when Brucie called out the carnival was already gone.

Elvis hitched a ride to the water tower, which sat on a great wide pasture at the edge of town. As Brucie warned, the carnival was gone and the pasture was empty. Elvis kicked through litter for almost two hours until he found a poster that showed the dates and locations for the carnival's next four stops. That was enough.

Elvis hitchhiked to the highway, where, twenty minutes later, two college girls gave him a ride. He caught up with Ralph Todd's midway two days later, one hundred forty-six miles from home.

He had gone to find his father.

*

That first night, when Elvis finally reached the carnival, he saw a huge banner spread across the gates to the midway that showed a blazing man flying through the air –

See Him EXPLODE from a Cannon!!!
See Him BURST into Flames!!!
See Him DEFY Death!!!
The AMAZING Human FIREBALL!!!
every night at 9pm!!!

It was five minutes before nine when Elvis went through the gates.

A crowd was gathered at the end of the midway. Elvis could see the cannon over the heads of the people in front of him: a long red, white, and blue tube as big around as a manhole, lying atop a flatbed trailer. The strip show was on one side (SEE exotic GO-GO DANCERS from the FAR EAST!!!) and the freak show on the other (SEE the LSD BABY!!! DEFORMED by MOD science!!!).

Elvis shoved his way to the front of the crowd only to find the crowd had gathered for the freak show. A sign hanging from the cannon read: NO SHOW TONIGHT.

Elvis felt a frantic despair, like he had lost his last good chance of finding his father, then pushed back through the mob. He found a ticket kiosk where he asked when the Fireball was going to perform.

A woman with two missing front teeth said, 'Might not be for three or four days. Eddie hadda fly to Chicago.'

'He's coming back?'

'Sure, kid, but he won't catch up to us until the next town. You're gonna miss his show.'

Three or four days. That wasn't so bad. Elvis decided he would wait for three or four weeks, if that's what it took. All he had to do was wait. All he had to do was be around when Eddie got back.

Eddie.

Elvis.

Same first letter.

Maybe that's why his mother had changed his name.

Elvis drifted along the midway until the carnival closed. He was hungry and cold, but he hid in the tall grass behind the tents until the grounds were empty and the thrill rides were dark, and then he slipped back into the midway. He slept beneath the cannon. Saying the name out loud.

Eddie.

The next morning, Elvis watched as the roustabouts and carnies emerged from trucks and trailers to begin their day. They streamed across the midway into a large kitchen tent set up behind the trucks. Elvis fell in with the crowd. He joined a line and was given a tray filled with eggs and French toast, pretending to be just another teenager in the crowd.

That afternoon he met Tina Sanchez.

He was walking along the midway past a ball-toss concession when a woman cursed angrily in Spanish. She stood on a bucket, straining on her tiptoes to reach a row of stuffed cats on a very high shelf.

Elvis said, 'Can I get that for you?'

She twisted around to see him, then stepped down from the bucket. She was short and sturdy, and almost as old as his grandfather.

'Unless I grow another six inches, I guess you'll have to. Climb over the counter there, young mister.'

Elvis hoisted himself over the low counter into the booth. Wire baskets filled with worn softballs were lined beneath the counter, and the side walls of the booth hung with rainbow-colored animals. Rows of fluffy silhouette cats lined shelves at the far end of the booth. You got three balls for a quarter; if you knocked down three cats, you got a prize.

She said, 'I gotta take down the top row. Just drop'm into this bucket here, okay?'

'How did you put them up there?'

'I had a young fella working for me, but he left last night. They do that, you know. Probably after a woman. Now I gotta find a ladder.'

Elvis pulled down the top row of targets, putting them into the bucket like she asked. Each cat was eight inches tall, and wedged into a little groove built into the shelves. Fluffy hair stuck out around the cats so they looked bigger than they were. Elvis figured that with all the hair and the tight bases, it would be almost impossible to knock off a cat unless you hit it dead center.

'That's a big help, young mister. You want a prize or a dollar?'

'I guess the dollar, but I'll take that guy's job instead. I'm looking for work.'

She frowned at him.

'How old are you?'

'Sixteen.'

She frowned harder.

'I'd say more like thirteen or fourteen, you ask me. You a runaway?'

'I'm trying to find my father.'

She pulled a dollar from her pocket and pushed it toward him. She added a second dollar.

'Take this and go back to your mama. She's gonna be worried sick. You're too young to be off by yourself like this. You could be murdered.'

Elvis's mother had been leaving him alone since he was a baby, but he didn't tell her that. His mother vanished three or four times every year for as long as he could remember. He woke on those mornings to find her gone – no word, no note, just gone. He never knew when or if she would return, and when she did, she never told him (or his grandfather or his aunt) where she had been or what she had done. She was like that. But every time she left, he – secretly in his secret heart – prayed that she was going to find his father, and this time – this time – would bring him home. Which is why he loved her still; for the hope that one day she would bring his father home.

Elvis glanced at the cats filling the bucket.

'How are you going to get them back on the shelf?'

'I'll get a ladder.'

'Tell me where it is and I'll get it for you.'

She looked up at the shelf that was beyond her reach, and a little smile played at her lips.

'What's your name?'

'Jimmie.'

The woman abruptly put out her hand, and Elvis knew he was in. She had one of the strongest grips he had ever felt.

'You can stay long enough to help me fix up these cats and put them back, but after that you gotta go home.'

An hour later she offered him the job, and that night she let him sleep on the floor in her tiny Airstream trailer.

Elvis Cole ran for coffee when Tina needed a refill, wiped each of the one hundred eighteen softballs (he counted) with an oiled cloth, and touched up the shelves where the nightly onslaught chipped, splintered, and bruised the paint; he retrieved thrown balls, replaced targets that had been knocked down, helped work the counter, and in between he tried to find out more about Eddie Pulaski.

Three days later, the midway was struck, packed, and trucked seventy-four miles where they set up in a new town. The following day, Elvis was eating lunch when several roughnecks took seats around him, their trays laden with food. They were young guys, with weathered skin and callused, banged-up hands.

A man with an anchor tattooed on his left forearm lit a Marlboro, then abruptly looked at Elvis.

'Seen you around. Who you with?'

'Tina Sanchez.'

The man blew a cloud of Marlboro and sucked food from his teeth.

'Nice lady, that Tina. She's been with this midway a long time.'

The man beside Elvis belched. He was the oldest.

'Hell, she's been here longer than me. They used to be with the Big Top, y'know, that whole family. You ever seen her bend a nail? She can bend a twelve-penny with her thumb, just push it right over, a little woman like that. They were tumblers.'

Elvis said, 'Do you guys know when the Human Fireball is coming back?'

'He's the big ticket, kid; the boss ain't gonna let that cannon sit. We're pullin' out the cannon for tonight's show.'

Elvis's heart pounded so hard he thought he would jump out of the chair. He made excuses all afternoon to leave Tina's booth, each time running to watch the roustabouts position the cannon and string a tall skinny net to catch Eddie Pulaski at the end of his flight.

By eight-thirty that night, the business at Tina's booth was furious. A crowd of high-school baseball players crowded the counter, firing balls in a competition to see who could peg the most cats. Five minutes before nine, an announcer's voice cut through the din of the crowd; the Human Fireball was only moments away from exploding into the air, Come one, come all, SEE if he survives!!!

Tina rolled her eyes, and waved him away.

'Oh, go on, go! You wanna see him so bad you gonna pee yourself.'

Elvis sprinted down the midway and pushed through the crowd. More than a thousand people had already gathered and the show had begun. The Human Fireball stood atop the upraised cannon with a microphone in his hand.

Eddie Pulaski looked nine feet tall in a white leather jumpsuit festooned with red and blue stars. He had shadowed eyes, flowing black hair combed back over his skull, and shoulders at least three feet wide! He gestured broadly to the crowd with wide sweeps of his arm, explaining that the cannon was charged with high explosives, enough to bring down a small skyscraper, enough to hurl him high over the midway into the far net.

The crowd oo-ed and ah-ed.

And if that wasn't enough, Eddie exclaimed, he would be doused with gasoline and burst into flame, hurling through the sky like a blazing fireball!

The crowd oo-ed and ah-ed again, but then Eddie raised his hands for silence. Only questions remained:

Would he land safely in the net, or would a stray breeze blow him off course?

Would the explosive charge be too much or too little?

Would he fly fast enough to snuff the blazing flames or would he burn alive in the far net?

There was only one way to find out!!!

Elvis pushed forward to get closer, shoving past men who cursed and boys who hit him.

Eddie tossed the microphone to an assistant, another assistant splashed him with a bucket of liquid, and Eddie hoisted himself into the cannon without another word.

The crowd fell silent.

Elvis Cole's heart pounded.

The assistant counted down through the microphone: ten! . . . nine! . . . eight! . . .

The crowd counted with him, their voices a thundering chant.

The second assistant lit a ring of flames around the mouth of the cannon.

. . . three! . . . two! . . . one! . . .

The Human Fireball thundered from the cannon in a whoosh of white smoke. He burst into flames as he passed through the ring of fire and arced into the night. Long flames trailed behind him, blowing out as he reached the peak of his flight, and then he landed safely in the net. Eddie Pulaski bounced to his feet as the crowd cheered. He raised his hands to the applause as if he were the King of the Universe, asked the crowd to tell their friends – Last show tomorrow night, friends! – then he gripped the edge of the net, swung down, and was gone.

His father was gone.

Elvis shouldered between milling bodies and slipped between the canvas banners into the darkness behind the midway, desperate to catch the man. His heart thundered and his ears hummed. He ran as hard as he could to catch up, and rounded a truck just as Eddie Pulaski climbed into a long blue trailer. The trailer door shut. Elvis told himself to keep moving, to pound on that door, to show Eddie Pulaski the picture of his mother, you remember her don't you, fourteen years ago? He had come so far and wanted it so much, but his feet did not move. Elvis ached deep in his center, an ache so sharp and terrible that he knew he could not stand to ache more.

Elvis stared at the closed door of the trailer, then turned and walked away.

Now that Elvis knew where Pulaski lived, he soaked up bits of the man's life: the white Ford pickup parked near the trailer; a small charcoal grill standing cold outside the trailer door; two empty beer cans standing upright in the grass. Elvis slipped past the truck to peek inside, seeing the ashtray overflowing with butts, a roll of duct tape on the bench seat, and a shrunken head dangling from the mirror. Elvis drank the details *as if each was a missing piece to the puzzle of his life. He took out his mother's picture and held it up, showing her face to the truck and trailer and grill.*

'This is where he lives. This is him.'

Elvis paced the midway most of the night, anxious and sick. He returned to Eddie's trailer again and again, circling it like a dog afraid to go home. When he finally tried to sleep, he couldn't, and he let himself out of Tina's mobile home while she slept.

The midway was quiet that morning except for the kitchen crew and the carny who walked the three-eyed cow. Elvis returned to Pulaski's mobile home, but it was still quiet. He slipped between the tents and went to the cannon. It had been lowered and pushed beneath the banners. Elvis climbed onto the flatbed and ran his hand along the barrel. He peered into the muzzle.

'Get the hell down from there!'

The Human Fireball was glaring up at him, a cup of steaming coffee in one hand and a cigarette dangling from his lip. He was wearing a thin cloth robe over shorts, an undershirt, and unlaced shoes.

'C'mon, kid, get down or I'll have Security on your ass.'

Elvis jumped to the ground.

Eddie Pulaski was shorter than he seemed last night. His hair was thin and pockmarks cut his jaw.

'I was just looking. I work for Tina Sanchez. Wiping the balls, you know? And stacking the targets.'

The Fireball squinted, then nodded.

'I guess I seen you.'

Elvis shivered, but not with the morning cold. He was certain that Eddie Pulaski recognized him, maybe not clearly, and maybe not well, but with some deep part of himself that remembered one of his own.

The Fireball sucked off his cigarette, then hacked up phlegm and swallowed it.

'Either way, you bein' new, lemme set you straight about somethin'. Don't mess with my stuff. Everyone on the 'way knows not to mess with my stuff. My ass depends on this gear, so I can't have anyone fuckin' around with it.'

'I'm sorry. I didn't touch anything.'

'Forget it, just so you mind. You see the show last night?'

'You were amazing.'

The Fireball placed his coffee on the flatbed, then hoisted himself up. He didn't look happy.

'I just fixed the fucker, but I didn't like the way it sounded last night, made this funny poppin' noise when it let go. You don't wanna hear shit pop when you do what I do for a livin'. C'mon up, you want. I'm gonna open her.'

Elvis pushed himself onto the flatbed as if he were weightless. He felt electric with energy as he followed after Pulaski. He wanted to hear every word the man spoke; he wanted to drink in everything he was willing to teach, just as a son learns from his father.

Pulaski twisted a row of catches along the cannon's housing and let down its side. Elvis was surprised by what he saw: The cannon barrel didn't fill the housing; a heavy steel spring with coils as thick as his wrists ran on steel rails where the barrel should be. Chains stretched along the springs down into gears and pulleys and what looked like heavy electric motors.

Elvis said, 'I thought it was a cannon.'

Eddie took a deep drag on his cigarette, flicked the butt away, then went to work tinkering in the motor.

'Use your fuckin' head. A man can't shoot himself out a real cannon; the g-force would bust your spine, and the barrel pressure would scramble your brain. It's a catapult. The smoke and other stuff is shit for the marks.'

Elvis felt disappointed, but somehow thrilled, too, and the mix left him confused. He didn't like it that Eddie Pulaski was a liar, but Eddie was also sharing secrets exactly the way a father would share with his son. Elvis suddenly pulled out the photograph of his mother, and held it up.

'You're my father.'

The Fireball twisted around. His eyes went to the picture.

'This is my mother.'

'Did you say what I think you did?'

'My father was a human cannonball. My name used to be Jimmie, but she changed it to Elvis so it would be like your name, just like your name but not, you see how they both begin with an E? You see how they have five letters?'

The Fireball stepped back from the cannon and shook his head once.

The words spilled out. They had been building for fourteen years.

Elvis said, 'I look just like you, don't I? She didn't name me Eddie because she still keeps the secret. She never told anyone about you, and she never will. Look at the picture. You see my mom?'

Pulaski's eyes softened in a way more frightening than if they had blazed with hatred.

'I've been looking for you all of my life. I had to find you. I found you.'

Pulaski stared across the midway, then glanced back. Elvis was desperate to hear how Pulaski and his mother met and how much they meant to each other and that Pulaski missed her and had always wanted a son, but Pulaski didn't say those things. His voice was gentle.

'Kid, listen, I never met your mother. Look at me. We don't look anything alike. I'm not the guy you've been looking for. I'm not your father.'

The Fireball's face filled with pity, which hurt more than a slap.

'My father is a human cannonball.'

Pulaski shook his head.

'I worked shrimp boats out of Corpus Christi fifteen years ago. I've only done this eight years.'

'You're him.'

'I'm not.'

Elvis felt as if he was floating in soft gray fuzz. He looked at the cannon that wasn't a cannon. He looked at Pulaski, with his thin upper body and thick legs, his thin wiry hair and stubby fingers. They looked nothing alike. Nothing.

'You're a fake. Everything about you is fake.'

Elvis felt the tears run down his face. He wanted to run, but his feet didn't move. He shouted as loudly as he could, shouted because he wanted everyone on the midway to hear.

'FAKE! THAT'S NOT A CANNON! IT'S A SPRING!'

Pulaski didn't grow angry. He only looked sad.

'C'mon, kid.'

'HE'S A LIAR! NOTHING HERE IS REAL!'

134

Pulaski hugged him close, wrapping his arms around him tight, but never once raising his voice.

'Stop it, boy. I'm not your old man. I'm nobody's old man.'

'YOU'RE NOTHING BUT A LIE!'

Pulaski held tight, and Elvis wanted to be held; he wanted to hold on forever, but then it all seemed wrong and he pushed Pulaski away, and ran without thinking. He jumped from the flatbed and ran as hard as he could, seeing nothing through the diamonds in his eyes, just colored light that shimmered and moved like the made-up fantasy of a rainbow; he ran past Tina Sanchez's trailer and the still-sleeping skeletons of the thrill rides; he ran until he fell to the ground, hating everything and everyone in the world, and himself most of all.

FATHER KNOWS BEST

Wilson followed Jacob Lenz to a small Airstream set up behind the midway. It was polished and bright, speaking well of the owner. The door was propped open for the air.

Lenz rapped at the door, then went inside. Wilson stepped up behind him, blocking the door with his body so the boy couldn't get out.

Lenz said, 'Tina? A man is here for the boy.'

The kid was sitting on a couch with a short, dark woman who had probably been good-looking in her day. The kid recognized Wilson right away, and didn't seem surprised.

'Hi, Mr. Wilson.'

'Hiya, bud. You're a lot taller now.'

Lenz seemed surprised.

'You know each other?'

Wilson said, 'Oh, yeah, we've done this a few times.'

Wilson thanked Mrs. Sanchez for giving the boy a roof, then assured Lenz for the tenth time that the family did not want trouble and would not call the police. The old lady hugged the boy, and wiped at her tears. She seemed like a nice old gal. When Wilson shook her hand she damned near crushed his bones.

The boy didn't try to run. He had bolted the first couple of times Wilson bagged him, but now he seemed resigned. In a way that Wilson didn't expect, this left him feeling sad. They walked back to Wilson's car without incident, then began the long drive home.

'You hungry?'

'Uh-uh.'

'It's a long drive, five hours maybe.'

'I'm good.'

They drove in silence for more than an hour, and Wilson was fine with that. The boy was exhausted. He sat slumped against the door, staring out the window with an empty expression.

Having collected the kid three times, Wilson had gotten to know him a little bit. Wilson felt sorry for him, sure, but he also found himself liking the boy. His absentee mother was nuts, his grandfather was a stiff who clearly didn't want the boy, and they rarely lived in one place more than a couple of months, yet here he was shagging ass all over creation, chasing after shadows. He just wouldn't quit, which was both terrible and admirable at the same time. Wilson – he finally admitted to himself – was getting attached.

'How many times is this, four, five?'

The boy didn't answer.

'This is the third time I snagged you, and before me was that other guy. How many times have you gone chasing after a carnival?'

'I don't know. Six. I guess this makes six. No, seven.'

'Seven different human cannonballs.'

The boy didn't answer.

'You have a knack for this, I gotta give you that. Here you are, a kid, and you track these bastards down like a professional. You'd make a helluva detective.'

The kid's eyes glazed and he returned to staring out the window. Wilson drove another few miles in silence, trying to figure out what to say. He didn't like interfering in people's lives beyond what he was hired for, but someone needed to straighten out this kid, and no one seemed willing to do it.

Finally Wilson dove in.

'I want to tell you something maybe I shouldn't tell you. I shouldn't interfere with what goes on in your house, but, Jesus, seven times. Somebody's gotta set you straight.'

The boy glanced at him, then turned back to the window. Now came the hard part, but Wilson had started it so he would finish it.

'Everything your mother told you about your father being a human cannonball is bullshit. She made it up.'

The boy's face turned dark and hard, but he didn't say anything. He was a sharp kid. Down deep, he probably knew it was bullshit.

'Do you know where your mom goes when she disappears?'

The hardness dropped from the boy's face like fog

hiding from the sun. He stared at Wilson with wide, expectant eyes.

'How do you know she goes away?'

Wilson let his voice soften.

'Here your grandfather hires me to find you, you think he never hired me to find your mother?'

Wilson felt a last reluctant pang, but this boy needed to know; the kid needed to know what was real and what wasn't because no one else in his life did or cared.

'She's got what's called a delusional disorder. Whenever she feels, I don't know, "overwhelmed" is what they call it, she can't tell what's real and what isn't, so she runs away. Your father isn't a human cannonball. She might think he is, but she believes it because she imagined it, and she can't tell the difference. She's not lying to you. She just doesn't know what's real.'

Wilson glanced over. The boy was facing forward, staring at the coming highway, as stiff as a fence post in the wind. Wilson felt bad, but he was just trying to help.

'Look, this isn't my business. I just thought someone should tell you, is all.'

'I don't care. I'm going to find him.'

'Kid, I don't have any doubt you'll find him, but be careful what you wish for. Whoever he is, he won't be anything like you imagine.'

'I don't care.'

'I know you think that now, but once you find him, you can't unfind him. He'll be part of you forever.'

The boy's jaw worked, but his eyes never left the highway ahead.

'That's what I want.'

Wilson glanced over again.

Elvis Cole sat quiet as a clam, but now a great sloppy tear spilled down his face. Wilson felt like a heel and was sorry he brought it up. He gripped the wheel and went back to driving. Time was money. He wanted to get rid of the kid and get on with his life.

Part Three
BLOOD LINES

CHAPTER 17

Golden called at five minutes after eight the next morning. He probably hadn't been awake that early in years, but he also probably hadn't slept.

'All right, you bastard, I set it up with the girls. They'll talk to you, but they're scared, like anyone needs this kind of shit in their lives.'

'It's a high-risk profession.'

He told me when and where to see them, and how to contact them if I needed to change the plan. I copied their addresses and phone numbers. I hadn't expected that all three would agree to see me; I guess Stephen had some sway.

'Okay, Stephen. As soon as I talk to them I'll return the computer.'

'I think you're gonna fuck me up the ass is what I think. What kind of man walks into another man's house and steals his stuff? Like I should trust you?'

That's what you need at eight in the morning, a pimp assuming the moral high ground.

'You don't have a choice, Stephen, just like last night.'

'Yeah, well, I got friends, too, you bastard. I want my –'

I hung up. Beckett would probably hear back from the Feds today, and Pardy would run Faustina's name, but I didn't trust that Pardy would get back to me. If a missing-persons report had been filed on Herbert Faustina, it would show when his name was run and save me a lot of time. I called Starkey.

'Hey, you wanna do me a favor?'

'We have a spare desk over here. Why don't you bring your stuff and move in?'

'Would you run the name Herbert Faustina through the MPRs?'

I spelled it for her.

'Faustina your John Doe?'

'Yeah. I'm not sure that's his real name, but it'll save me a lot of time if you get a hit.'

'You want me to wax your car, too?'

Everyone is a comedian.

'Thanks, Carol. I appreciate it.'

An uneasy silence developed before she cleared her throat.

'Listen – why'd you call me with this? You could've called your pal, Poitras – he's sitting on his fat ass right down the hall here – but you called me. Why is that?'

Next to Joe Pike, Lou Poitras was my closest friend. He ran the homicide bureau at Hollywood Station, and I was godfather to one of his three children. I didn't understand what she was getting at, but she seemed irritated.

'I didn't think of him – I thought of you. Look, it's not a big deal if you're too busy or can't or whatever. I'll call Poitras. That's a good idea.'

'I'm not saying to call Poitras. Look, I'll run the god-damned name and call you later. Forget I said any-thing.'

'What's wrong?'

'Forget it.'

She hung up, and I thought maybe I should call her back, but I didn't. I locked the house and drove down the hill.

Victoria was the last.

Victoria had been the last of the three escorts to see Faustina, so I wanted to talk to her first. She was also the most reluctant to see me, Golden had said. She was married, and had children. She wouldn't agree to see me at her home, and didn't want me to call, but she agreed to meet me at Greenblatt's Delicatessen on Sunset after she dropped her kids at school. Great.

I eased into the morning chain of commuters creep-ing down Laurel to Sunset, then hooked a tight left, and parked behind Greenblatt's. Lucy and I had often gone there for bagels because it was close to my house, but when the memories of her came I pushed them away. I told myself it was important to stay focused, but the truth was I was tired of hurting.

The deli was crowded with people buying bagels and coffee to go. I strolled to the front of the store, then along the wine aisles, but no one looked like a poten-tial murderer or a soccer-mom escort with her eye out for a private detective.

I bought a cup of coffee, then carried it upstairs to a small dining area. It was crowded, too, but I knew Vic-toria as soon as I saw her. She didn't look away when our eyes met. She had black hair cut to frame her face, and pale skin, and was wearing an unzipped burgundy sweat jacket over a black tee and sweat pants. She watched with remote detachment as I approached.

I said, 'Victoria?'

'Let's do this in my car. We'll have more privacy.'

I followed her outside to a gleaming S-class Mercedes sedan. It was an eighty-thousand-dollar car. She pointed her key, and the Mercedes chirped. She hadn't bought the car by working as a prostitute; her money came from somewhere else. Probably her husband.

'Get in. We can talk in the car.'

Her Mercedes was parked facing out so we would be in open view of everyone entering and leaving the deli. She had probably planned it that way. When we closed the doors, the sounds of the city vanished with the heavy thump of sealing gaskets. Victoria folded her hands in her lap, and twisted a platinum wedding band on her left hand.

I identified myself, then asked to see her driver's license. She shook her head.

'I didn't bring it. Stephen said you aren't a police-man –'

I didn't see a purse, so she was probably telling the truth about her license. I slipped a digital camera from my pocket, and snapped her picture before she realized what I was doing. She covered her face after the flash, when it was too late.

'You bastard. You sonofabitch –'

'That one is for the night clerk at the motel. I'll also run the license plate on your car. You want to stop fooling around?'

She glared at me, but she didn't try to run, and she didn't make a scene. I took out the morgue shot of Faustina.

146

'Do you recognize this man?'

'Yes. Stephen said he's dead.'

'When and where did you last see him?'

'The night before last at the Home Away Suites. There wasn't any before or after – just the once. At about ten. Five minutes before ten.'

'Did you leave the motel with him?'

'It was an outcall date. I went to his room, I left – that's how it works.'

'So you didn't leave with him?'

'*No.* I don't know what he did after I left. I don't know anything about this. I don't want to be involved –'

She twisted the band harder, and shook her head, not as a negative, but to swing the hair from her eyes. Her calm expression and frantic fingers didn't go together, as if they belonged to different people.

'Victoria –'

'My name is Margaret Keyes.'

'Margaret. If you had to prove you weren't with him later that night, could you?'

She studied me for another moment with the same detachment she had shown earlier, then glanced past me at something she wanted me to see.

'See over there – the other Mercedes.'

A black Mercedes AMG sat at the far end of the parking lot. I couldn't see the driver clearly with the sun glaring off its windshield, but a man wearing sunglasses and a baseball cap sat behind the wheel.

She said, 'You see the AMG?'

'I see it.'

'That's my husband. When I left the motel, I got into his car and we found a quiet street. It was one of those little streets just above the freeway, I think by a school.

We had sex. After we finished, we went for dinner in Studio City. That would have been around eleven-thirty. We eat there all the time, so the maître d' will remember. We'll have the credit card receipt.'

I watched the AMG as she said it, then looked back at her, feeling uncomfortable that she had to open herself to me and a guy like Pardy.

She shrugged.

'I don't trick for the money. He likes it when other men pay for me. He likes waiting while –'

'Is he armed? If he gets out with anything in his hands, it's going to be a problem.'

'We didn't know what to expect. Stephen made threats. He said if I didn't talk to you, he would tell the police a lot more about me than the evening I spent with Faustina –'

She hesitated, to choose her words carefully.

'Stephen has pictures. We have children.'

'I'll talk to Stephen. I don't care what you did with Faustina sex-wise – I want to know what he said. Did he mention what he was doing here in L.A. or what he was going to do later that night? Did he mention any names? I don't need a description of the sex.'

The corner of her mouth curled again.

'Everything is sex.'

'Just answer my questions.'

'We prayed.'

She stopped, waiting for my reaction.

'You prayed?'

'He paid me two hundred dollars to pray. So tell me, was that sex or not? We knelt and he read from the Bible. That's what he wanted.'

'What did you pray about?'

'We asked God to forgive him, like, please forgive this man his sins, forgive this sinner, show him mercy, like that. I thought it would become sexual, but it didn't.'

'You prayed for an hour?'

'He paid for an hour, but he got a phone call and asked me to leave. I was probably with him about forty minutes. I got there at ten, so that was about ten-forty.'

The phone call could have been from the person he went to meet.

'Do you remember what he said to the phone?'

'No, I'm sorry. I wasn't paying attention, and then he let me out. I know he was still on the phone when I left.'

I made a mental note to recheck the calls Faustina made that night. One of his outgoing calls might have led to his getting the call she remembered. I glanced at her husband, but he was still tucked in his car. The lot attendant was busy directing traffic. Something in what she said bothered me.

'He walked you to the door, but he was still on the phone? Did you mean he was holding the phone when he brought you to the door?'

'That's right. You know how you cup it so people can't hear?'

'His phone was on the nightstand on the opposite side of the bed. It wouldn't have reached the door.'

'No, no, not that phone. His cell phone. It was one of those flip phones.'

A cell phone meant he could have made calls other than the calls that showed on his motel bill. A cell phone opened an untraceable world of possibilities unless I could learn his number. I made a note to ask Diaz if a cell phone had been found with his body.

Margaret Keyes said, 'Are we finished?'

'Yes. You've been a big help. I appreciate it.'

I glanced at her husband. She saw me looking, and smiled.

'Go introduce yourself. It would scare the shit out of him.'

I opened the door, then looked back at her.

'This thing you do, you do it for him?'

She laughed, and her eyes sparkled with cold fire.

'You can't even hope to understand.'

I didn't ask what she meant. I walked back to my car, then went to find the others.

CHAPTER 18

Hot Pursuit

After Frederick had taken care of Father Wills, he was scared to return to Payne's. He wanted to; he wanted to race back and search for anything that would tell him where Payne had gone and what he intended, but it was late when he finished with the priest. Even with Payne's house hidden the way it was, Frederick was frightened that filling his house with light in the middle of the night would draw unwanted attention.

Frederick went home and spent a fitful night, tossing and turning as he dreamed about killing Payne with the skewer from his Weber. The dream played out on the inside of his skull like one of those IMAX theaters, totally surrounding him as if it was real. In the fantasy, he saw himself drinking a Coors Light outside his mobile home while the Weber grew hot. The skewer glowed yellow over a huge mound of coals so hot the air rippled. Payne stepped out of the trailer, and said, 'I confessed. I went to Los Angeles, and told them our nasty little secrets, and now I feel better. They know all about us, and now the dead will carry you down into Hell, but it's okay because I feel better, and isn't that what confession is all about, me feeling better while you pay the price?' Frederick was swept by a tsunami of fear, betrayal, and indignation. In his fantasy, he snatched up the skewer and drove it through Payne's belly into his lungs, screaming, 'YOU TRAITOR!'

The next morning – before he opened the station – Frederick went back to Payne's when the sky was misty with light. He worried that Payne had written a confession or journal or diary, or had some sort of incriminating scrapbook hidden away. He searched every drawer, cabinet, box, closet, and hiding place he could think of, trying to find something that would explain why Payne had gone to Los Angeles, and whom he had gone to see.

Frederick searched high and low for the better part of three hours, growing more and more frantic at what Payne was saying, and where; finding nothing until he saw the Los Angeles Yellow Pages waiting on the kitchen counter. It was the San Fernando Valley East edition.

If Payne had gone to Los Angeles, he would need a place to stay.

Frederick opened the Yellow Pages to the section on hotels. Dozens of hotels were listed, but none of them stood out. Frederick flipped deeper into the book to find the listing for motels. A scrap of paper marked this page. A blue dot of ink indicated a motel in Toluca Lake.

Home Away Suites.

Frederick checked the time. Toluca Lake was less than thirty minutes away. If Payne was down there ratting him out, Frederick would make sure he paid.

CHAPTER 19

Where Margaret Keyes had met me in an anonymous location, Janice lived near Dodger Stadium and had no problem with me coming to her home. Janice shared an exclusive condominium with her boyfriend, a wealthy Israeli named Sig who wanted to make a name for himself directing gonzo porn ('Sig's family has so much money they shit green.'). Janice started talking the moment she opened her door, and talked so much I had to interrupt to keep her on point. Janice started tricking while a senior at an exclusive girls' prep school ('It was *nasty*, and I *LOVED* it!'), got implants on her eighteenth birthday ('They were a present from my mom.'), and started stripping while a freshman at USC ('It's like getting paid to be *me*!'). Janice talked so much it was like drowning in a verbal Niagara Falls. She told pretty much the same story as Margaret Keyes, except in her version Faustina had received no phone call – she had stayed for an hour, and was paid two hundred dollars in cash. To pray.

Dana Mendelsohn was the last escort on my list, but the first to have visited Herbert Faustina. I didn't expect Dana to tell me anything new. I stopped for an outstanding turkey burger at Madame Matisse in Silver Lake, then sat in my car, searching for Dana's address in the Thomas Brothers Guide. I had just found her street when my cell phone rang. It was Starkey.

She said, 'I left three friggin' messages. Didn't you get them?'

I looked at the little window on my cell phone. It showed no messages.

'I've had my phone with me all morning. It didn't ring and it doesn't show any messages.'

'I know I got the right number. It's your stupid voice on the message.'

My stupid voice.

I hated my cell phone. I was the last person in Los Angeles to enter the Jetsonian world of cellular communications, and I have regretted it ever since. Before I got the cell, everyone asked how I got by without one, and my clients complained. I weakened under the cultural weight of a city filled with satisfied cell users, ponied up, signed a service contract, and was doomed to crappy cell service. I rarely got a signal. When I got a signal, I couldn't keep the signal, or found myself in someone else's conversation. When someone called me, the phone rang sometimes, but not always. When someone left a message, the phone told me when it felt like it, or not at all. Everyone in my life was happy I got a cell phone except me. I wanted to throw it down a storm drain.

I said, 'Okay, let's pretend I got your messages, and now I've called you. Why am I calling?'

'I ran Faustina through the system. Nothing came up, which means he doesn't have a criminal record, and he didn't toddle off from a booby hatch.'

'Okay.'

'I also ran his name through the Social Security roll. The name Herbert Faustina doesn't show. Whoever he is, he doesn't have a Social Security number, which means Herbert Faustina probably doesn't exist. It's an alias.'

The Social Security system was off-limits to police without special court orders. Cops couldn't just ask for someone's Social Security information. Starkey had probably used a personal contact, and she would get burned if anyone found out.

'You didn't have to do that, Starkey. I wouldn't have asked you.'

'Don't worry about it, but since you're so slow on the uptake let me point out the obvious: I am definitely a woman you want on your side.'

'I guess you are.'

'I gotta get back to work. Try not to get killed.'

She hung up, but left me smiling.

Dana's address led me to a small red apartment building south of Melrose between La Brea and Fairfax on a street without character or charm. It was one of those older areas where single-family homes had been scraped away a house at a time, replaced by four- or six-unit apartment buildings built on the cheap by heirs, retirees, or doctors looking for a positive cash flow. Now the street was lined by small buildings that looked like they had been designed on paper napkins while everyone laughed about how much money they would make. Dana's building looked like a Big Mac carton.

I parked on the street, walked up along a short drive lined with garbage cans, and found her apartment under a set of floating stairs that led to the second floor. Two mountain bikes were chained to the stairs. I rang her bell, then knocked. Loud voices started up inside; a man and a woman arguing whether or not to open the door. Dana wasn't alone. I knocked again.

A tall good-looking man jerked open the door and gave me the dog eye. He was solidly built with a fine neck and thick shoulders, and he knew it; he stood tall in the open door, showing himself off. His hair was high and tight, and he was neatly dressed with two layers of Raiders apparel.

I said, 'Dana?'

'I'll Dana you up the ass, you talk trash to me.'

Behind him, Dana said, 'Please, Thomas, Stephen said I hadda talk to him.'

'Stephen don't live here.'

'Thomas. Let him in.'

A chunky young woman touched him out of the way. She was maybe five four, with peroxide-blond hair, a deep tan, and wide blue eyes that made her seem open and innocent. She was wearing a cropped T-shirt over shorts, with the T-shirt showing large breasts and a gold navel stud. She was about the same age as Janice, but she looked younger; she was a lifetime younger than Margaret.

She said, 'This is Thomas. He's not my boyfriend or anything. He's my roommate.'

I made him for her boyfriend, and probably her driver. Thomas didn't move far. His hands hung loose at his sides as he leaned toward me to let me know he was ready to unload.

'And what does Thomas do? He drive you to see Faustina?'

Thomas shook his finger at her before she could answer.

'It's not his damned business. You shouldn't talk to him or anyone else about this.'

'Stephen said we gotta.'

We.

'Fuck Stephen, gettin' us mixed up in this shit. They gonna put this on someone and it gonna be ME!'

Stephen told me he knew nothing about the drivers for his escorts, but apparently Thomas and Stephen knew each other. It made me wonder what else Stephen hadn't told me.

I moved past and looked at their apartment. It was simple and clean, with the living room breaking to the right, and a dining area and kitchen ahead. The dining table had been pushed into the far corner and set up as a desk with a desktop computer and a clutter of notes pushpinned to the wall. The chairs were hung with what looked like camera bags and backpacks. In the living room, a fluffy couch faced a cabinet that held a television, a CD player, and a row of color photographs of Dana spinning around a stripper's pole. She looked pretty good upside down.

I said, 'Nice pictures. Is that you?'

'What the fuck you care, is that her in the nice pictures? You think those pictures NICE? You want us to have a little coffee, pass time like we FRIENDS?'

I looked at him. The day had been a slow grind from morning to midafternoon with not much to show for it. He didn't like me looking at him, and glowered even harder.

He said, 'What?'

Dana came up beside me and pulled at my arm.

'He's scared of the three strikes. He has two convictions.'

'Don't tell him nothin' about me, not a goddamned thing.'

I understood his fear – if he caught another felony conviction he could go back to jail for the rest of his life.

I said, 'No one cares about you unless you know something about Faustina. Do you?'

'No!'

'Then that's all you have to say. The police are going to talk to Stephen. If he tells them you drove and you say you didn't, what's that going to look like?'

'I ain't sayin' nothin' to nobody! I canNOT be part of this!'

Dana's eyes worked up to full-scale tears.

'Stephen said we gotta.'

'Fuck Stephen! You leave me out of this and do NOT even mention my name! I don't want to hear my name, not ONE TIME!'

Thomas jabbed the air to show her what one time meant, then stalked around the corner into the dining room. Suddenly, after all the shouting, their apartment was silent. Dana wiped at her eyes and cleared her throat. She spoke softly so Thomas wouldn't hear.

'Stephen says it'll be all right. He said to cooperate.'

'This is a homicide investigation, Dana. The police won't be here to bust you – or Thomas. They just want to know about Faustina. You see?'

She glanced to make sure Thomas wasn't listening, then lowered her voice still more.

'Thomas took those pictures. He's a really, really good photographer. We're doing a pay site and he's taking the pictures of me. He's even building the web site for me. He knows all about that stuff.'

I nodded, and knew why she told me – all her dreams with Thomas were riding on the hope that Stephen had told her the truth – that everything would be all right.

'Dana, I want you to look at this.'

I showed her the morgue shot of Faustina and walked her through my questions exactly as I had with the others. Faustina paid Dana to pray for his forgiveness. He told her nothing about himself and his reasons for being in Los Angeles; they did not have sex; and, when they finished praying, he walked her to the door. During their hour together, he never mentioned where he was from, why he was in Los Angeles, how long he intended to stay, or any other person or place. The only difference with what I heard from the other escorts was that Dana had asked Faustina why he needed to be forgiven. I guess Dana wasn't yet so hardened that she no longer cared.

I said, 'Did he tell you?'

'He said for loving too much.'

'You asked him why he wanted God to forgive him, and he said for loving too much?'

'Isn't that sad?'

'What or who did he love too much?'

A woman he met once and never saw again? A son he never knew?

'I dunno. I said, how can you love too much? Loving someone is a good thing – you don't have to be forgiven for that. I wanted to make him feel better, you know, but he said love could be terrible, he said love could be the Fifth Horseman and could kill you as dead as the other four, and then he started crying and I felt so bad I started crying, and I put my arms around him because I wanted him to feel better, but he didn't want me touching him like that. He kinda unwrapped me and gave back my hands and said let's keep praying, okay?, asking me real nice, 'cause that's the only thing will make it better, so we kept praying, and I didn't even know what he meant until Thomas told me.'

Thomas's voice came quietly from the dining room.

'The Horsemen. She didn't know about the Four Horsemen, so I had to tell her what he meant by the fifth.'

He was watching us from the mouth of the dining room. The Four Horsemen of the Apocalypse were war, pestilence, disease, and famine – the four forces that could destroy the world. Herbert Faustina had added love to the list.

Thomas glanced at Dana, then me.

'We don't know nothin' about a murder. She didn't have sex with him or *solicit* anything, so this ain't prostitution. It ain't against the law to be paid for saying your prayers, am I right?'

'That's right. No harm, no foul.'

'So what can they pop me for if I drove her to pray?'

'Nothing.'

'All right, then –'

He nodded some more, still circling his commitment, then finally went for the meat.

'All right, he had a brown car.'

Dana looked horrified.

'Thomas –'

He stopped her with the finger.

'That asshole Stephen hadda bring me into this, now

161

I got to look out for me. All I did was drive you to pray, and now I'm gonna cooperate with the police and earn my love. You got to give to get, and I will NOT go to prison. This is me, being a good citizen. He had a brown Honda Accord. The left rear hubcap was missing and it had a big dent back there, right by the wheel.'

I stared at him, then looked at Dana, but Dana had an empty expression like she didn't have any idea what he was talking about.

'Were you in his car? Did you go for a ride with him?'

'She didn't go anywhere with the man. She finished with the praying like she said, and came out and got in the car – *my* car – and told me about what they did, the prayin', and that's when I set her straight about the Horsemen. Then we talked about what we want to do, get something to eat or go have some drinks or come home, and she says, hey, look, that's him.'

Dana suddenly nodded, as if she only now remembered and saw it clearly.

'That's right. He came outside.'

Thomas silenced her with the finger again and kept going. He had made the commitment, he had the floor, and nothing would stop him now.

'So now I'm lookin' 'cause I want to see this stupid john with all his prayin', and there he is. He got into a car and drove away, the brown Honda.'

'You see his license plate?'

'No, man, I was too busy lookin' at this goofy asshole, in there crying 'bout forgiveness.'

'Was it a California plate?'

'Never even looked. He come backin' out and there's this big-ass dent and the car all dirty. I tol' her, look at that piece of shit he drivin'. He got two hundred to spend on pussy, he oughta wash his car.'

I suddenly felt a pulse of my own hope. Brown Honda Accords were as common as sand fleas, but a brown Accord with a missing left rear hubcap and dented wheel well was a specific vehicle. The dent meant it wasn't a rental.

'Okay. Then what?'

'Nothing. What you think, what? He went off, and we went over to Stephen's, drop off his cut of the money. We shared a blunt, then came home. Stephen like to spark up, he get some money. He keep a lot of dope in that house.'

Thomas made a nasty smile when he mentioned the pot, like he was paying Stephen back for putting him in this position. He would mention it to the police, too.

I wanted to tell Diaz about the car. If Faustina's car was still near the scene, an alerted patrol officer might find it. Then we could trace his name and address through the vehicle registration. If the shooter was currently joyriding in Faustina's car, we might even catch the killer.

I thanked them for their time, then started out when I saw the pictures again. I looked back at them. Dana had come up beside Thomas, and slipped her hand into his.

I said, 'What Faustina said about love being the Fifth Horseman? He was wrong.'

I pulled the door, then hurried back to my car, and called Diaz. If I couldn't reach her, I planned to call Starkey, but Diaz answered on the third ring.

She said, 'Cole, is that you? I've been trying to get you the past hour.'

I hate my cell phone.

'I have a possible car description, Diaz. It's –'

'We have his name. Beckett got the ID from those things in his legs. We know Herbert Faustina's real name.'

John Doe #05-1642, also known as Herbert Faustina, had been identified through the appliances in his legs as George Llewelyn Reinnike, originally from Anson, California. I made her spell Reinnike. She told me to come to her office, and promised a full report. It was great news; so good that I did not feel the eyes, or notice that I was being followed.

CHAPTER 20

The Central Community Police Station was headquartered on Sixth Street, a few blocks south of the Harbor Freeway in downtown Los Angeles, and not far from the murder site. It was a five-story modern brick building dwarfed by surrounding skyscrapers, and constantly patrolled by bomb-sniffing dogs. LAPD's SWAT is headquartered at Central, as is the elite uniformed Metro Division. Like the other police stations in Los Angeles, it was known as a Division until someone decided that Division made the police sound like an occupying army. Now we had Community Police Stations, which sounded user-friendly.

I put my car in a civilian parking lot, entered through the main entrance on Sixth, and waited for Diaz to come get me. When the elevator finally opened, Pardy was the only one aboard. He was standing straight and stiff as if his suit was tight, and he did not look at me. His jaw worked as if he had bitten into a sour candy.

He said, 'Get on.'

I got on. Pardy hit the button to close the doors before

anyone could join us, then turned and squared his shoulders to face me.

'You could have filed a beef for what I did, but you didn't. For what it's worth, I appreciate that. I was out of line.'

He hesitated like he wanted to say something more, but finally turned back to the door. Sometimes these guys will surprise you.

'That was classy, Detective. Thank you.'

He nodded, still not looking at me, but now he seemed more relaxed.

'I spoke with Golden this morning. That was good work, you finding him so fast. I'm not going to ask why, but he's cooperating.'

'I inspire good citizenship.'

'Sure.'

'The girls who saw Reinnike will cooperate, too. They expect you to give them a pass.'

'They don't have anything to do with the shooting, they don't have to worry. All I'm about is the murder.'

'Make that clear to them, and you'll be okay.'

'After I saw Golden, I went by the Home Away Suites. I'm also not going to ask how you got Reinnike's bill, but don't do anything like that again. You understand what I'm saying?'

'I get you.'

'Diaz wants me to let it go, and I owe you one, so this is the one.'

'Did you go over the calls Reinnike made?'

Pardy took a moment to answer.

'He called damned near every police station in the city. I've been thinking about it.'

'Yeah, me, too.'

When the doors opened again, Pardy led me along a light beige hall that was lined with file cabinets, and into the Homicide Bureau. The homicide detectives were housed in a narrow room with too much furniture and not enough storage. Like the hall, the homicide room bristled with file cabinets.

Diaz was at the far end with two detectives who looked like middle-aged carpet salesmen. Pardy gestured toward her.

'Detective Diaz will show you where. I gotta get the file.'

Diaz met me in the center of the room, then led me to her desk. It was wedged against the wall, and faced another desk. A black female detective as small and brittle as a hummingbird was at the adjoining desk, quietly asking someone on the phone to tell her what happened next. She scribbled notes as she spoke, ignoring us.

'Siddown here, Cole. So does the name Reinnike or Anson, California, mean anything to you?'

Like she expected a lightbulb to flash over my head and me to shout, DADDY!

'No. Do you have anything on him?'

'Beckett ran the name through NCIC and DMV. No one by this name shows on their rolls, either; which means he resided out of state or held a license under another name.'

Like his alias, Herbert Faustina, George Llewelyn Reinnike was also a cipher.

Pardy returned with a black three-ring binder. It was his murder book. As the lead homicide detective, Pardy would file all the reports, witness statements, and relevant evidence he accumulated in this one binder.

Since this was his first case as the lead, it was probably the first time he had been responsible for the book. He draped a leg over the edge of Diaz's desk, and carefully snapped open the rings. There weren't many pages yet in the book, but more would be added as the case developed. He handed me a thin stack of reports.

'Okay, Cole, this is the medical examiner's prelim, and the records from the company that manufactured the appliances. You can read it here in front of us, and make notes, but you can't make copies. That's the way it is.'

I was anxious to read, but Diaz touched the reports before I could begin.

'Hang on. You said you had a vehicle description. Let's get started with that.'

Pardy made notes on a yellow pad as I repeated Thomas's description.

'They get the plate?'

Diaz cut off his question as if he was stupid.

'He would have told you if he had the plate. Keep going, Cole – did you get anything else?'

'They prayed.'

Diaz and Pardy waited the way I waited when Margaret Keyes first told me.

'Reinnike didn't have sex with them. He paid them to pray for him.'

Pardy laughed.

'That's bullshit. Are you making that up?'

'All three women told me the same thing. They prayed for his forgiveness.'

Diaz's dark eyes colored like smoke on the horizon.

'Why did he need forgiveness?'

'He didn't tell them.'

Pardy frowned at Diaz.

'I'm telling you, this sounds like bullshit. Golden probably tells all these whores to say that to beat the sex bust.'

Diaz continued to stare at me with the cloudy eyes, then frowned at Pardy like he was spastic.

'You saw the crosses he had all over himself? It's not a stretch to imagine he's some kind of religious freak, is it?'

Pardy grunted, but still looked unconvinced.

'When we're done here, have Cole go over everything each girl told him. When you talk to them, see if you get the same answers. Maybe you'll catch one of them in a lie. Right now, you should put out a BOLO on the car. That's a good description. Some traffic cop might pick it up while we're here dicking around.'

Pardy left to file the BOLO, and Diaz watched him go.

'You gotta tell him every goddamned thing, one slow-motion step at a time. And they say Mexicans work slow.'

'That what they say about you, Diaz?'

Diaz laughed, then took the medical examiner's reports from me and flipped through the pages.

'You don't have to read all this, Cole. Here's what you need –'

The pages she handed back were the faxed correspondence from the Penzler Surgical Orthopaedics Company of East Lansing, Michigan, to Beckett.

Dear Mr. Beckett,
Per our conversation regarding #s HSO-5227/HSO-5228.

Units are matched (bilateral reversed) femoral support appliances manufct on 16 Oct 46 by this company. (See attch descript.) Our records indicate the following assignments:

Units assgnd: Andrew Watts Children's Hospital
1800 Mission Boulevard
San Diego, California

Surg assgnmt: Dr. Randy Sherman
Andrew Watts Children's Hospital
1800 Mission Boulevard
San Diego, California

Pat assgnmt: George Llewelyn Reinnike
15612 L Street, NW
Anson, California

Pat cond: Legg-Calve-Perthes
minor m, func. +, adv.
surg. 6/20/47/AWCH/Sher
(see attch)

This is the extent of company records. Please do not hesitate to call if I can be of further assistance.

Sincerely,

Edith Stone, M.D.
V.P. Sales

I copied Reinnike's address, as well as the names of the doctor and hospital. A second page gave a brief explanation of Legg-Calve-Perthes Disease that read like a company brochure. LCP was a degenerative ball-joint disease that caused the femur to weaken in young children. Appliances were screwed into the femur to support the bone and maintain the integrity of the joint.

Diaz let me read the M.E.'s report while we waited for Pardy. The cause of death was a single gunshot wound to the left chest that resulted in two broken ribs, a cracked vertebra, and two ruptured arteries. George Llewelyn Reinnike had drowned in his own blood. The bullet was a copper-jacket .380, and had fragmented upon impact with the vertebra. The M.E. had found no traces of semen in the urethra, colon, or stomach, and no semen or vaginal residue present on the penis, indicating the victim had not had a recent sexual encounter. Blood-screen results were to follow, but the M.E. noted no overt evidence of drug use other than a moderate cirrhosis of the liver, indicating the victim had been a drinker. Reinnike hadn't gone into the alley to buy drugs or sex. He had gotten a phone call, cut short his prayers, and almost certainly gone downtown to meet someone. I felt certain whatever happened in the alley was not a chance encounter.

Pardy returned as I finished reading, and perched on the edge of the desk.

I said, 'One other thing. The girl who was with Reinnike on the night he was murdered said he got a call when she was with him, and he cut short her visit. He got the call on a cell phone. Did you guys find a cell with the body?'

Pardy and Diaz looked at each other, and Diaz shook her head. Pardy shrugged.

'Maybe he left it in his car. We'll see when we find it.'

Diaz leaned forward, then stood.

'Okay, I don't need to be here for the rest of this. I got my own cases to work. Pardy, you know what you have to do?'

'Sure. I'm going to bust a killer.'

I said, 'Just so everyone understands, what we now have is a two-way flow of information, right? No one has a problem?'

Pardy's jaw rippled again as it had in the elevator.

'Cole, I'm here for the murder. So long as you don't do anything that interferes with my case, help yourself. If you turn something that helps me out, so much the better.'

Diaz arched her eyebrows at me.

'You happy?'

'Thrilled. And I appreciate it.'

'I'm gone. Just remember, if you kick up anything, you keep us in the loop.'

She left us sitting at her desk. Pardy slid off the edge, then stepped around me and sat in her chair.

'Okay, Cole, tell me what the whores said.'

I gave him a detailed report. While we were talking, I thought about Diaz. I had wanted to ask if she found the witness she had been searching for, but I knew she probably hadn't. Sometimes you never find them. Sometimes, after you search long enough, you realize the person you've been chasing was nothing more than a dream.

CHAPTER 21

Nightmare

Frederick fought down the shiver of rage that crept up on him. *Payne betrayed us, and now he will have to deal with me.* He picked up the pay phone outside a 24/7 minimart across the street from the Home Away Suites. A man answered with an irritated voice as if he resented answering the phone.

'Home Away, Toluca Lake.'

It was difficult to hear with the passing traffic.

'Uh, I'd like to speak with, uh, a Mr. Payne Keller, please. He's staying with you, uh, but I don't know the room number.'

'I'll see.'

'I don't know which room –'

'We have no guest by that name.'

'Uh, well –'

'Can I help with something else?'

Frederick read the man's impatience, but didn't know what to say.

'Uh, Payne –'

'Sorry, we have no guest by that name.'

Frederick put down the phone, then bought a super-size Diet Rite and returned to his truck. Earlier, he had cruised the Home Away parking lot, but had not seen Payne's car. Frederick guessed that Payne had registered under another name, but he didn't know whom to ask for.

The Home Away Suites sat across from a Mobil station. Frederick pulled up to the pumps. He went into the service bay, and considered the service technician who was changing the oil filter on a Sentra.

'Hey, you got an old box? I need a little cardboard box about this big.'

Frederick held his hands eight or ten inches apart.

The technician gave Frederick a discarded air-filter box, and didn't even charge him. Frederick dug around under his seat, fishing out a broken water pump and a work shirt he used to wear before he tore the pocket. The shirt didn't say Mobil or Payne's Car Care, but it was dark blue, grease-stained, and had a nice professional pinstripe. His name was stitched on the right breast: *Frederick*.

Frederick put the water pump in the box, changed shirts, then drove back to the motel. He carried the box into the lobby, and smiled at the desk clerk, a young guy with an inflamed rash of pimples on his chin. His name tag read *James Kramer*.

Frederick set the box onto the counter with a clump.

'I'm Frederick from over at the Mobil. I got a rebuilt pump here for the guy with the crosses, I don't remember his name. He said I should let him know.'

Frederick made his eyes vague as he waited to find out whether or not Kramer would recognize the man with the crosses.

Kramer said, 'Did he pay you?'

'Uh-uh. Not yet.'

'You're screwed. That guy was killed. The cops been all over us.'

Frederick stood motionless, smiling, giving the good ol' Frederick face with the simple, open eyes.

'What did you say?'

Kramer made his hand into a gun and clicked his thumb.

'That was Faustina with the crosses, but that wasn't his real name. He got dropped. It's a big deal, man; we've had cops, CSI, even private detectives.'

A rush of overlapping voices filled Frederick's head. They sounded like the sea at night. Kramer was saying something, but Frederick didn't hear. He didn't know how long Kramer had been talking before he focused again.

' – here all day yesterday and said they'd be back, but it didn't look anything like that TV show, *CSI*.'

Frederick said, 'Payne is dead?'

'Who's Payne?'

'What was the name you called him?'

'Herbert Faustina, with the crosses. Someone murdered him. The cops asked us to put together a list of everyone who spoke with Faustina or came to see him, so you should talk to them.'

Frederick had trouble controlling his thoughts. He saw himself walking through the lobby with his shotgun. He pictured himself shooting Kramer in the head, then pointing the muzzle up under his chin and blowing his own face off; all of it seen from outside himself, watching it happen until something Kramer was saying brought him back.

' – the one guy, he was pretending to be a cop, but I recognized him right away. Remember that mercenary thing last fall with all the shootings in Santa Monica? It was him. He comes in here pretending to be a cop like no one would know.'

'He was looking for Payne?'

'Faustina. He got here even before the cops, and they didn't like it. The one cop, I could tell he was pissed off. He asked as many questions about Cole as he asked about Faustina.'

'What was his name?'

'Pardy, something like that.'

'Not the policeman – the one he was asking about.'

'That was Cole, as in Elvis. I bet he changed his name from something else. Remember the shootings? He hammered some guys before Halloween last year. Remember?'

Frederick left the box, and went out to his truck. A low sigh hissed between his teeth. It started deep inside him and made a noise like a soft whistle, but the pressure that drove it didn't lessen. It seemed to build – like he had swallowed the air hose at the station, the one he used to put air in tires, and he was being filled with cold gas. His eyes filled and his chin quivered, and he bawled, sobbing until he hiccuped. He felt alone and frightened, and he wanted Payne here RIGHT NOW so badly his stomach clenched like a fist. He slapped at the steering wheel and the seats, and blubbered and spit, blowing snot and tears; he kicked at the floorboards, and swung hard at the dash, and wrapped his arms over his head, and wailed. After a while, he felt better. He looked down at himself. His shirt was in shreds, and his chest and belly were bleeding. He realized he had torn at himself, but had no memory of it.

Frederick was scared, but he was angry at the same time. He wondered if the private detective had killed Payne. Private detectives didn't work for free; they were bought and paid to do someone's dirty work. Somehow Cole had identified Payne (probably through that rotten priest) and baited him into Los Angeles.

Frederick suddenly burned with a panic that Payne had talked before Cole killed him, maybe spouting prayers to Jesus as he begged Cole for mercy, Frederick seeing it as vividly in his head as if it were happening in front of him, Payne finally after all these years popping under their secret weight like a blood orange crushed under a boot – *spurt!* – squirting seeds and pulp as –

Frederick's head filled with the strange buzz that left his brain tight and cloudy, like he had swallowed the air hose again. He pressed his fingertips into his eyes as hard as he could. He rolled his knuckles across his temples, then grabbed his ears. He pulled his ears so hard that the pain was blinding, then released; pulled, then released.

The buzzing faded.

Cole had obviously been hunting them for years. Somehow he had identified Payne, and made contact, but Payne probably hadn't ratted him out, else Cole would have gone straight to Canyon Camino instead of dicking around here at Payne's motel. Cole had been hired to find them and kill them, and he had killed Payne. Now he was trying to kill Frederick.

Frederick Conrad couldn't imagine it any other way: They were being executed. They were paying the price

Payne always said they would pay. He felt the sudden sharp panic of wanting to blast south out of town, burning rubber off all four tires all the way into Mexico, but –

Elvis Cole had killed Payne.

Frederick wondered if Cole had mutilated Payne's body. He imagined Payne screaming in pain as he prayed for forgiveness. Cole probably got paid extra for this kind of stuff. Frederick started crying, and he suddenly saw it happening right there in the truck through the blurry prisms of his tears – Payne was sprawled naked across the seat, his loose, old man's flesh ugly and bleeding as a towering gray shadow ripped away long strips of skin with a pair of pliers. Payne screamed horribly as Cole tore his skin.

Frederick covered his ears.

'Stop it. Stop screaming like that.'

Payne and Cole went away, but it took a while for Frederick to calm. He was scared and sickened by what Cole had done to Payne. Frederick wanted to run, but he couldn't leave with an assassin like Cole on his trail. Cole wouldn't stop unless you stopped him. Frederick had to stop Cole right now, and he had to make him PAY FOR PAYNE.

Frederick didn't give it another thought. He considered going back into the Home Away Suites to punish that smart-mouth kid, but instead he changed shirts again, then drove back across the street to the 24/7. He used their pay phone to call information.

'What city?'

'Los Angeles.'

'Listing?'

'Elvis Cole.'

'I don't show an individual by that name, but we have the Elvis Cole Detective Agency.'

'That will do.'

Frederick's heart calmed as he copied the information. Having a clear purpose made him happy. So did the thought of avenging Payne's murder.

CHAPTER 22

The late-afternoon traffic inched out of downtown L.A. Poorly marked one-way streets fed – with all the organization of a nest of snakes – into infrequent (and poorly marked) on-ramps. The feeder streets were stop-motion parking lots, advancing one frame at a time. Pedestrians moved faster; cyclists blew by at warp speed. So much for life in the fast lane.

I felt an edgy, just-on-the-other-side-of-the-door hope in knowing Faustina's true name, and in having an original address. I was anxious to follow up, even though I knew the odds were slight that they would lead anywhere. But still I thought about it, and maybe that's why I did not see the man approaching.

'Dude, hey, what's going on?'

He was buffed out with muscles, a shaved head, and hot-chrome wraparound sunglasses. He had approached from the rear on my blind side while I simmered in the motionless traffic, just another pedestrian going with the flow before he stepped off the curb. He was smiling, so the people in the surrounding cars would think we were friends. First glance, he appeared to be carrying a paper bag. Then I realized his hand was inside the bag.

He made sure I clocked the bag, then opened the door with his free hand, and slipped in beside me. The bag pointed at me, down low in his lap so the surrounding motorists couldn't see. He was still smiling.

'Keep both hands on the wheel, motherfucker.'

They say 'motherfucker' when they're tough.

'It's a four-speed. I gotta shift.'

He glanced at my shifter. His smile wavered, like his whole line about me keeping my hands on the wheel was ruined.

'So one hand on the shifter, one on the wheel, smart man. You know what's in this motherfucking bag?'

'Your hand?'

'A fuckin' atom bomb. You do anything but what I say, it'll pop in your guts.'

'One on the wheel, one on the shifter. I hear you.'

'Look in your mirror. See the white Toyo two back?'

A young woman in a green Lexus was directly behind us, but I could make out a white Toyota behind her. Two men were in the Toyo.

'Are they with us?'

'Brother, they are *so* with us they got beachfront up your ass. If you even *think* about fucking with me, they will cook off their caps. You understand the word?'

I glanced over at him, and wasn't impressed. He acted tough with his shaved head and gym-rat muscles, and maybe he was, but he came across like an actor who won fights without sweating because he lived in a make-believe world where every woman was last year's Miss June.

I said, 'How could I not understand, them having

beachfront up my ass? Now that I'm scared, who are you and what do you want?'

'Golden's computer.'

I glanced in the mirror again. Neither of the men in the Toyo appeared to be Golden, but I couldn't be sure.

'Do you think I have it with me here in the car? I don't have it.'

'Where is it?'

'With a friend in Culver City. I gave it to him for safekeeping.'

'Fine. We'll pick it up from your friend.'

'Did Golden send you?'

'Don't worry about it.'

'Is he in the Toyota?'

'Let's go see your friend.'

He flicked the atom bomb to remind me it might go off, so I shrugged.

'Okay. If that's what you want.'

We didn't bother with the freeway; we dropped south out of downtown, and used the surface streets. It was a lot faster. Only an hour and twenty minutes.

When we reached Culver City, I approached the back of the shop through a residential area and an alley with our escorts close behind. I didn't want them to see where we were going until it was too late.

'Where are we going?'

'He has a little business nearby. They're closed now, but he'll still be there with the computer.'

'What's this asshole's name?'

'Joe.'

'If he makes any trouble, we'll cook his ass.'

'I understand. Hey, you're the man with the gun.'

'Remember it.'

I turned down the alley behind the row of stores where Joe Pike has his business and pulled into the delivery spot directly outside the back door. Joe's gleaming red Jeep was to my left and a highly polished Chevy truck was to the right. The white Toyota pulled up behind us, blocking me in. A small gray peephole stared out at us from the door.

'Okay,' I said. 'This is it.'

He glanced at the door. A sign hung above it saying:

FIREARMS
ARMED RESPONSE UNNECESSARY

'What the fuck, a gun store?'

'Yeah, this is his. He has several businesses.'

I tapped the horn twice, and the man with the bag lurched, jerking the bag up toward me.

'Fuckin' asshole! What the fuck?'

'Take it easy. He won't answer the door after business hours. I have to let him know to come to the back. C'mon, you want to get the computer or not?'

I waited with my hands in place until he waved with the bag for me to get out. I got out my side as he got out his, and then we went to the door. I stood at the door, but he stood to the side so if anyone looked out the peephole they couldn't see him. Pike had made the same positioning move when we went to see Golden.

I said, 'Okay to knock?'

'Hurry up, fuckin' knock.'

'You've done things like this before?'

'Knock, asshole.'

He knocked for me. He pounded hard on the door three times with his free hand – BOOMBOOMBOOM – while he kept the bag trained on me with the other.

On the third boom, Joe Pike raised up behind him as if he were rising from the earth. Pike pushed the bag straight up in the air while twisting the bag hand to the outside farther than it was ever meant to twist. Then Pike pushed him over and down face-first into the Chevy truck's fender. It sounded like a cantaloupe dropped from the roof. The two men who work at Pike's shop had the clowns from the Toyota proned out on the ground. Both men had black Sig .45s, and both men could clear the LAPD Combat Shooting Range in competition-level times. Both men had.

I picked up the bag, and showed Pike what I found. A nifty little .38 snub-nose.

I said, 'Golden.'

Pike said, 'Uhn.'

Pike peeled his boy off the truck, then turned him toward me. His face was a mess. He was trying to cradle his broken arm, but Pike still had it. I squatted so we could see eye to eye, and now his tough eyes looked scared.

'What's your name?'

'Rick.'

'Okay, Rick. These men are professionals. You're just some asshole. You understand the word?'

He nodded. I think he was trying not to cry.

'What was supposed to happen after you had the computer? You supposed to call, just bring it over, what?'

'Call.'

'He's waiting to hear from you?'

'Yeah.'

'Let him call, Joe.'

We found a silver Samsung in Rick's pocket and let

him speed-dial Golden. He got a signal and a ring right away. Everyone gets a signal but me.

When Golden answered, I took the phone.

'You cover these guys' health insurance?'

'Who is this?'

'Two of these idiots are tied up on the ground, and Rick has a broken arm. I think his nose is broken, too. Do I need to come see you about this?'

He understood who I was. Silence filled the phone as he thought it through.

'You said you'd give back my computer.'

'After the girls cooperate with the police and their stories check out. When I'm satisfied that everyone has been straight, you'll get it back.'

'I'm out of business without the computer.'

'Live with it. Stephen, you could be punished for this. Do you understand that?'

'I understand.'

'What would Detective Pardy do if he knew you sent these turds to assault me?'

'They weren't supposed to assault you. They were supposed to get the computer.'

'They didn't get it.'

'I'm losing money without that computer. Look, you want a few bucks? I'll buy it back from you. How much you want?'

I shut the phone, and shook my head. Amazing.

Pike said, 'What do you want to do?'

We took their guns, their photographs, and their driver's licenses, and then we let them go. When they were gone, Pike stood with me by my car. The sky was deepening, and I was anxious to go home.

Pike said, 'Let me ask you something.'

I waited.

'How'd a lightweight like Rick bring it this far?'

I filled him in on my meeting with Pardy and Diaz, and what I had learned about George Reinnike. Rick had brought it as far as he had because I hadn't been paying attention; I had been thinking about Reinnike.

Pike didn't say anything. He studied me, and some small part of me was left feeling ashamed.

CHAPTER 23

Predator

The information operator gave Frederick the address and phone for the Elvis Cole Detective Agency on Santa Monica Boulevard. Frederick didn't call; he was worried that calling might somehow tip off Cole, so he just drove over. He found a spot on a side street two blocks away, then walked back with his shotgun. He carried the shotgun in its case, walking along with it tucked under his arm like a stubby package. No one seemed to notice. Frederick enjoyed believing that the people who noticed the case dismissed it as a musical intrument, a pool cue, or a fishing rod. People were so predictably stupid.

Cole's office was located in an older five-story building with Spanish styling. A narrow lobby opened off the street, having stairs and a rickety elevator as access to the upper floors. A directory hung across from the elevator. Cole's office was on the fourth floor.

Frederick got into the elevator. When the door closed, he unzipped the end of his gun case. The door opened on the fourth floor. Frederick stepped off, then hesitated. His heart pounded, and his neck prickled. He took a fast step back onto the elevator, but held the door. He wondered whether or not Cole would recognize him. If Cole saw him first, Cole might be able to get the drop on him. Frederick thought it through; he would have to move fast and kill Cole before Cole realized what was happening, but there was a problem –

Frederick didn't know what Cole looked like.

Frederick stood frozen in place on the elevator, his heart hammering, seeing an entire room filled with men. How would he recognize Cole?

Frederick stepped off the elevator and moved down the hall. He didn't decide what to do so much as know it – he would kill everyone he found in Cole's office.

Frederick passed an open door, and heard a woman talking. The open door made him uncomfortable. He found Cole's office, and stood facing the closed door, breathing hard. He slid his right hand into the gun case and put his finger on the trigger. He made sure the safety was off. He gripped the knob with his left hand. It felt slick and wet.

The woman said, 'He's not there.'

Frederick clutched the knob and tried to turn it, but his wet palm slipped.

'He doesn't come in anymore, not since all that mess.'

Frederick twisted and jerked the knob, pulling and pushing, but unable to open the door.

She said, 'Excuse me.'

Frederick realized someone was talking to him. A neatly dressed young woman with long fingernails stood in the open door across from Cole's. Frederick could see an older woman at a desk behind her. Frederick slipped his hand out of the case, and managed a smile.

'Oh, hi. I'm supposed to deliver this to Mr. Cole.'

'He's hardly ever here anymore. You could leave it with us if you want.'

'Oh, thanks, that's really nice, but I couldn't. Will he be here later?'

Frederick didn't like it that she glanced at the gun case, as if she was trying to figure out what was in the package.

She said, 'I haven't seen him in weeks. I know he's been here, but he doesn't keep regular hours.'

'Ah-huh, okay, well – he doesn't have a secretary or anything?'

'No, there's just him. You can leave it with us, though. We've done that before.'

Frederick considered his options. He could probably find Cole's home address in Cole's office. He wanted to kick down the door, but couldn't very well do it with all these people across the hall. He would have shot Cole, but that would be that and he wouldn't mind if they saw; but if they saw him breaking into Cole's office, Cole would be tipped off.

Frederick said, 'Where does he live?'

A frostiness rimed the woman's eyes.

'I wouldn't know.'

Frederick said, 'Well, I could just bring it up to his house. That would probably be okay.'

'I'm sorry. I can't help you.'

Frederick could see the stiffness as she turned away. Bitch. He tried Cole's door again, then returned to the elevator. He would come back later when everyone was gone. Then he would find out where Cole lived.

CHAPTER 24

It was a quarter after seven by the time I got back to my house and searched the Triple-A map of California to find Anson. It was a tiny red dot on Highway 86, southeast of the Salton Sea. I called information, told the operator I wanted a listing in Anson, then asked if he had any Reinnikes. I spelled it for him.

'No, sir, I don't show any listings for that name.'

The nearest two towns were Alamorio and West-morland.

'How about in Alamorio and Westmorland?'

'Sorry, sir.'

I went to the next town.

'Calipatria?'

'Here you go, Alex Reinnike in Calipatria.'

He punched me off to the computer before I could ask for more, so I copied the number, then called information again. This time I told the operator I wanted to check several towns, and asked her not to hand me off to the machine.

Three minutes later, we had covered six more outlying

towns, and I had one more name, Edelle Reinnike, who was listed in Imperial.

I looked at the two names and their numbers, then went into the kitchen for a glass of water. I drank it, then went back to the phone. At least it wasn't gin. My hands were shaking.

I dialed Alex Reinnike first because Calipatria was closest to Anson. Alex Reinnike sounded as if he was in his thirties. He listened patiently while I explained about George Reinnike from Anson, and asked if he was related.

When I finished, he said, 'Dude, I wish I could help, but I only moved here last April when I got out of the navy. My people are from Baltimore. I never heard of this guy.'

I thanked him, then called Edelle Reinnike.

Ms. Reinnike answered on the fourth ring with a phlegmy voice. Her television was so loud in the background that I could hear it clearly. *Wheel of Fortune.*

She said, 'What is it? Yes, who is this? Is someone there?'

I shouted so she could hear me.

'Let me turn this down. It's here somewhere. Where is it?'

She made a little grunting sound like she was reaching for something or maybe getting up, and then the volume went down.

She said, 'Who is this?'

'Edelle Reinnike?'

'Yes, who is this?'

'My name is Cole. I'm calling about George Reinnike from Anson.'

'I don't live in Anson. That's up by the lake.'

'Yes, ma'am, I know. I was wondering if you know George Reinnike.'

'No.'

'Are there other Reinnikes in the area?'

'They're dead. We had some Reinnikes, but they're dead. I got two sons and five grandchildren, but they might as well be dead for all I see them. They live in Egypt. I never knew an American who lived in Egypt, but that's where they live.'

You hear amazing things when you talk with people.

'The dead Reinnikes, did any of them live in Anson?'

She didn't answer, so I figured she was thinking.

'This goes back a while, Ms. Reinnike. George lived in Anson about sixty years ago. He was a child then, probably younger than ten. He had surgery on his legs.'

She didn't say anything for a while.

'Ms. Reinnike?'

'I had a cousin who had something with his legs. When we all got together, he had to sit with his parents and couldn't come play with the rest of us. That was my Aunt Lita's boy, George. I was older, but he had to sit.'

'So you did know a George Reinnike?'

'Yes, the one with the legs. That was them up in Anson. I didn't remember before, but that was them.'

'Does George still live there?'

'Lord, I haven't seen him since we were children. We weren't close, you know. We didn't get on with that side of the family.'

'Would you have an address or phone number for him?'

'That was so long ago.'

'Maybe in an old phone book or a family album. Maybe an old Christmas card list. You know how people keep things like that, then forget they have them?'

'I have some of Mother's old things, but I don't know what's there.'

'Would you look?'

'I have some old pictures in one of those closets. There might be a picture of George, but I don't know.'

She didn't sound thrilled, but you take what you can get.

'That would be great, Ms. Reinnike. Would it be all right if I come see you tomorrow?'

'I guess that would be fine, but don't you try to sell me something. I know better than that.'

'No, ma'am, I'm not trying to sell anything. I'm just trying to find George.'

'Well, all right, then. Let me tell you where I live.'

I copied her address, then hung up. I was still standing by the table. My hands were still shaking, but not so badly.

I studied the map of Southern California. Anson was in the middle of nowhere. What would have been the odds? My mother had vanished for days and sometimes weeks when I was a child. I never knew where she went, but Southern California was so far from where we lived it was unlikely she had gone so far. Still, I didn't know. She had vanished again and again. More than once, my grandfather hired someone to find her.

Ken Wilson
Miami, Florida

Wilson sat in the dark on his porch, feeling old and disgusted as he listened to the frogs squirming along the banks of the Banana River. Moths the size of a child's hand scraped against the screen that was the only thing saving him from the clouds of mosquitoes and gnats that filled the night with a homicidal whine. Wilson figured all he had to do was punch one finger through the screen and so many goddamned monsters would swarm in they could suck him dry before sunrise. He thought about doing it. He thought it would be pretty damned nice to be done with the whole awful mess of his life.

He took a sip of watered Scotch instead, and spoke to his dead wife.

'You should've never left me. That was damned lousy, leaving me like this, just damned awful of you. Look at me, sitting out here by myself, just look at me.'

He had more of the Scotch, but didn't move, alone with himself on the porch of his little bungalow that felt so different now with her gone.

Wilson had buried his wife three weeks ago. Edie Wilson had been his third wife. It took three times for him to get it right, but once he found her they had stayed together for twenty-eight years and he had never once, not once, well, not in any meaningful way, regretted their marriage. They didn't have children because they were too old by the time they hooked up, which was a shame. Wilson's first wife hadn't wanted children, and his second marriage hadn't lasted long enough, thank God. Such things hadn't seemed important back then, him having the concerns of a younger man, but a man's regrets changed as he grew older. Especially when he got into the Scotch.

Wilson drained his glass, spit back a couple of wilted ice cubes, then set the glass on the floor at his feet.

He said, 'Come to Papa.'

He took the .32-caliber Smith & Wesson from the wicker table and held it in his lap. It had been his gun since just after Korea, purchased for five dollars at a pawnshop in Kansas City, Kansas; silver, with a shrouded hammer and white Bakelite grips that had always felt a little too small for his hand, though he hadn't minded.

He put the gun to his temple and pulled the trigger. *Snap*.

Sixteen years ago, Wilson sold his investigation business and retired. He and Edie had packed up, moved to south Florida, and bought the little place on the river, her liking it more than him, but there you go. The day they packed, he unloaded the gun, and had never seen a need to reload it; those days being gone, him needing 'a little something' on his hip in case events grew rowdy, long gone and done. The gun had been unloaded for sixteen years.

But that was then.

Wilson had a nice new box of bullets. He opened the box just enough, shook out some bullets, then put the box down by his glass. Those .32s were small, but they had gotten the job done. He pushed the cylinder out of the frame, carefully placed a bullet into each tube, then folded the cylinder home until the axle clicked into place. He grinned at the sound.

He said, 'Well, that calls for a drink, don't you think?'

He put the gun down on the wicker table, went inside for another one-and-one Scotch, and was heading back outside when the phone rang. He thought about not answering, then figured what the hell, it was late and might be important, though later he would think it was Edie, taking care of him.

He answered as he always had even though Edie had hated how he answered, complaining, 'Goddamnit, Kenny, this is our *home*, not an office, can't you say *hello* like a real person?'

But, no, Wilson answered like always.

'Ken Wilson.'

'Mr. Wilson, this is Elvis Cole. You remember?'

Of course he remembered, though it had been a few years since they last spoke. The boy's voice cut clear and bright through the years, riding the backs of memories like a pack of greyhounds exploding after the rabbit.

'Why, hell, how are you doing, young man? Jesus, how long has it been, eight or nine years, something like that? We got a good connection. You sound like you're across the street.'

'I'm in Los Angeles, Mr. Wilson. I know it's late there. I'm sorry.'

'I wasn't sleeping. Hell, I was talking to myself and drinking Scotch. You get to be my age, you don't have a helluva lot else to do. How you doin', boy? How can I help you?'

Wilson decided he wasn't going to tell Cole about Edie, not unless the boy came right out and asked after her, and even then Wilson thought he might lie, might ladle out some bullshit like, oh, she's sleeping right now, something like that. If he explained about Edie, Wilson would start crying, and he didn't want to cry any more, not any more, not ever again.

Elvis said, 'I want to ask something about my mother.'

Well, there they were, right back where they started.

'Okay, sure, go ahead.'

'You know where the Salton Sea is out here?'

'Out by San Diego, but inland, just up from Mexico, isn't it?'

'Yes, sir, pretty much dead center between the ocean and Arizona.'

'All right. Sure.'

'Does the name George Reinnike ring a bell, George Llewelyn Reinnike?'

Wilson mouthed the name to cast a bait for his memory, but it settled in the dark waters of his past without a stir. Many names swam in that dark pool, but most swam too deep to rise.

'Nope, nothing springs to mind. Who's that?'

'George Reinnike was from a small town near the lake called Anson. He came to L.A. a few days ago to find me. Two nights ago, he was shot to death, but before he died, he made a deathbed statement. He told a police officer he was my father.'

Ken Wilson didn't answer right away. The boy's tone was as matter-of-fact as a cop reciting case notes, but a familiar hopeful energy pushed the boy's words out. Wilson hadn't heard the boy sound that way in years.

Wilson answered slowly.

'Why are you calling, son?'

'You knew my mother.'

'Uh-huh.'

Wilson didn't want to commit himself.

'You knew her better than I ever did.'

'I wouldn't say that.'

'I would, Mr. Wilson. I knew some of her, but you knew the parts I couldn't have known. So I want to know if it's possible. Could my mother have come to Southern California? Is it possible they met?'

Wilson thought how much he admired the boy. All

these years later, and the boy was still chasing his father.

'Mr. Wilson?'

'Lemme think.'

Wilson had been hired to find the boy on five occasions. Each time, the boy had chased after a carnival featuring a human cannonball because the boy's loony mother – that bitch was crazy as a bedbug on Friday night – filled his head with nonsense about Cole's father being a human cannonball. But on seven other occasions – four even before the boy was born – Elvis's grandfather had hired Wilson to find the boy's mother. Each time, she had run off without telling anyone where she was going or why, just up and disappeared, and they'd wake to find her gone without so much as a note. Most times, she'd return when she was ready, acting as if she had never been away, except for those times when Wilson found her. Then, per her father's instructions, Wilson would make sure she was safe, call the old man to report her whereabouts, then wait for the old man to come fetch her. There never seemed any plan or motive in her journeys; she'd feel the urge to go, so she'd go – like a dog that slips under a fence for a chance to run free. She'd hitchhike in whatever direction the cars were going, back and forth across her own path on misshapen loops that went nowhere, living with beatniks or hippies one night, or with co-workers another if she'd gotten herself a waitress job and promoted a place to stay. Her wanderings had always seemed aimless, but she had gone pretty far a couple of times, not so far as California, but close. Who was to say she hadn't been there and back before Wilson found her, or took a trip Wilson knew nothing about? Wilson had been involved only when the old man hired him.

He said, 'I don't remember so good anymore, so you can take this for what it's worth – I don't have a recollection of that name or that little town. Your mother never mentioned them to me, and I never tracked her out that way, but all of that was a long time ago.'

'I understand.'

'She went pretty far a couple of times, so she could have gotten out there if she set her mind. I'm not saying she did. I don't know if she got out there, but you asked if it's possible, and I guess I have to tell you it is.'

'I understand. I need to ask one more thing –'

'Ask as much as you like.'

'I always thought she didn't know who he was, my father I mean. I guess I figured he didn't even know I existed –'

Wilson knew where the boy was going, but let him get there in his own way.

'I guess what I'm wondering is, could they have been in touch with each other after I was born? That's the only way Reinnike could have known my name.'

Wilson thought about it, and thought it through hard because he was wondering the same. He answered slowly.

'Your grandfather, he used to go through your mother's things all the time. He had to, you know – don't think poorly of him for that – he was always scared she'd up and disappear one day and get herself murdered, so he used to look –'

'You don't have to apologize for him, Mr. Wilson. I know what he went through. I went through it, too.'

'He would have told me if he found letters from anyone. Your aunt, too – she always had an eye out – but they never told me about finding anything like that. I think they would have told, especially when you started running off, but –'

Cole interrupted.

'It's possible.'

'When two people want to get hold of each other, I guess they can do damn near anything. I don't think it's likely, her being the way she was, but –'

Wilson wanted to say more, but anything else would be a lie. God knows, the boy had enough of those.

'– I don't know.'

A silence filled the empty space as the boy mulled that over.

'Okay, Mr. Wilson, I understand. I just needed your opinion. Like always.'

Wilson felt warm, hearing the boy say that.

'I wish I could be more help.'

'You help. You always have.'

'This guy, Reinnike, he have any proof, anything that links him to your mother or you?'

'No.'

'Was he a human cannonball?'

Elvis Cole laughed, but it was strained at the edges.

'I don't know. I'll find out.'

'Well, I guess you could have one of those tests, the DNA.'

'I've been thinking about it. They have to locate the next of kin first. You have to get permission.'

'Well, we both know there are ways around that. Old as I am, I could get around that one.'

'I'd better get going here, Mr. Wilson. Give Mrs. Wilson my love.'

Ken Wilson's heart squeezed tight in his chest. He felt the tears come and looked at the little .32.

He said, 'Call more often, goddamnit. I miss talking with you.'

'I will.'

Wilson fell silent; here he was, on the Banana River, talking to a man he had known from a boy, and this man was as close to a son as Wilson would ever have.

'I've always been proud of you, the way you turned yourself around – you rose above yourself, son. Every man should, but most folks don't even try. You did, and I'm proud of you. Whatever that's worth.'

'I'd better go.'

'It's time for me to go, too. You take care.'

He was putting down the phone when he remembered one last thing.

'Elvis?'

'Sir?'

He'd caught the boy just in time.

'It doesn't matter who your father was. You're still you. You hear what I'm saying? There's no such thing as a dead end – not in this game. You keep looking. You'll find what you need to find.'

'Thanks, Mr. Wilson.'

'Good night.'

''Night.'

The line clicked, then Wilson put down his phone. The frogs and moths were suddenly loud again, and his screened porch was once more a dark cage. His little shack on the Banana River had seemed brighter while he spoke with the boy, but now the brightness was gone.

'Why in hell did you have to go?'

He had a last sip of the Scotch, then picked up his pistol, pushed open the cylinder, and shook out the bullets. He left all of it on the little wicker table, and went inside to his bed. He fell asleep thinking of Edie, and of the ways he had failed her, and of all the ways he had failed himself, but with a final dim hope that he had done right by the boy.

CHAPTER 25

Invasion

Frederick loitered outside Cole's building until cars bled from the parking garage, then hustled up to the fifth floor, where he hid in the men's bathroom until almost eight o'clock. When Frederick sensed everyone was likely gone, he crept down to the fourth floor and back to Cole's office. He worried that a security guard or cleaning crew might find him, so he used the direct approach – he pried open Cole's door with a jack handle. Cole would immediately know that someone had broken into his office (as would a passing security guard), but Frederick moved quickly. He scooped up Cole's Rolodex and blew through the desk for bills, letters, and other correspondence. He grabbed anything that could even possibly contain Cole's home address, then ran back down the stairs, and out to his car. He had worn gloves. He didn't take the time to go through the things he stole until he was safely at home. It had been a helluva bad day, so he was relieved to be home. He enjoyed sleeping in his own bed. He felt safe. Best of all, the third bill he inspected was addressed to Cole's home. He dreamed about Cole that night. He dreamed about what he would do. He dreamed about Cole's screams.

CHAPTER 26

At three-thirty that morning the traffic moved with professional grace. That time of day, big-rig truckers who knew the rules of freeway driving moved cleanly, content to let me drift among them. The city thinned and the eastern sky lightened as I reached the Coachella Valley and curved south between the jagged shoulders of the mountains.

The Salton Sea was the largest, lowest lake in California, filling the broad, flat basin of the Salton Sink like a mirror laid on the desert floor. It was shallow because the land was flat, and surrounded by barren desert and scorched rocks like some forgotten puddle in Hell. When the periodic algal blooms died, it smelled like Hell, too. During the worst of summer, the temperature could reach one-thirty on the lake's shore, but now the air rushing over me felt cool and good, and the smell was clean.

I dropped down the west side of the lake past pelicans and fishermen lining the rocks for tilapia and corvina. The valley floor rose quickly when I passed the lake, cut by irrigation canals and small farming roads without many signs, and dotted with small towns that all looked the same. At six-fifty that morning I entered Anson. Imperial was another twenty miles south, but I wanted to find George Reinnike's original home first. A neighbor might have maintained contact with his family.

Anson was a sleepy collection of hardware stores, video rental shops, and small businesses. Eighteen-wheelers laden with tomatoes and artichokes lumbered through town, kicking up enormous clouds of dust that covered buildings and cars with a fine white powder. No one seemed to mind.

I stopped at a gas station where an overweight man behind the counter nodded past a burrito bulging with beans and eggs and cheese.

I said, "Morning. I need a local map. You have something like that?'

He shoved the burrito toward a tattered map taped to the glass. He didn't put down the burrito. Once you get a grip on something like that, you can't set it down.

'Right up there. Help yourself.'

The map was from the Bureau of Land Management, and had been taped to the glass so long its colors were bleached.

'Do you have one I can take with me?'

'Nope. You can try the Chamber of Commerce. They might have something.'

'Okay. Where's that?'

'Second light down next to the State Farm office, but they don't open for another two hours. I could probably tell you how to get wherever it is you want to go.'

I gave him Reinnike's address. He studied the map, then tapped L Street with his knuckle.

'Well, this here's northwest L Street, but there ain't nothing out there but fields. No one lives out there.'

'Is there another L Street?'

'Not that I know of, and I've lived here all my life. You passed it on the way in.'

I used his rest room, bought a cup of coffee, then followed his directions back out of town. L Street was at the three-mile marker, just as he told me. I turned left onto the northwest side and drove until I reached a county sign that said END. Two silver tanks stood quietly near the horizon, but they were the only structures I saw. Fields planted with brussels sprouts extended to the horizon in every direction. Mechanical irrigators rolled along on spindly wheels, mindlessly squirting water and chemicals on individual plants so as not to waste money on unused soil. No one lived there, and no one had likely been there for a very long time. The Burrito Man was right – the houses that once stood on L Street had long since been razed for agribusiness.

I worked my way back to the highway, and headed south to Imperial.

Edelle Reinnike lived in a simple stucco house just off the main highway at the southern edge of Imperial. The houses were white or beige, with white-rock roofs to reflect the heat. Most had trailers or trucks parked in their yards. Mrs. Reinnike opened her door as I got out of my car. It was eight-thirty that morning; still early, but hot.

'Mrs. Reinnike, I'm Elvis Cole. Thanks for seeing me.'

'I know who you are. Don't mind this dog. She won't bite unless you get fancy.'

Edelle Reinnike was eighty-six years old, with the dry desert skin of a golden raisin. Her dog was a fireplug-shaped pug with enormous eyes bulging on either side of its head. It looked like a goldfish. I couldn't tell what the dog was looking at, but it growled when I approached. Maybe it had radar.

Mrs. Reinnike said, 'Margo, shush! You don't fool anyone.'

She invited me in, showed me to her couch, then went into her kitchen for coffee. I didn't want more coffee, but it always pays to be friendly. Margo planted herself in front of me. Mrs. Reinnike called from the kitchen.

'She likes you.'

'Did you have a chance to look through your mother's things?'

'I did. I found an old picture of George, but only the one. Mama couldn't stand Aunt Lita, and they had an awful falling-out. Lita was George's mother. She said Lita was loud. If Mama thought you were loud, well, that meant you were trash.'

Mrs. Reinnike came back with two cups of coffee, and sat in a recliner at the end of the couch. She put on a pair of reading glasses, picked up a crumbling photo album from beside the chair, and opened the album to a page marked with a strip of tissue. She turned it so I could see.

'Here, this is Lita and Ray – Ray was Daddy's younger brother – and this is George. Look at the way Lita was carrying on even when her picture was being taken. They were nasty people.'

Great. Just what you want to hear about people who might be your family.

The picture showed a man, a woman, and a boy with a triangular head in front of a Christmas tree. It was George. He was propped on crutches, and looking past the camera as if he was not expecting the picture to be taken. His father was a soft man with uncertain eyes, and his mother had close-set features that made her look irritated. I could see George's features in Ray. Like father, like son.

'This was before George had the operation. Lita wouldn't have sent a picture after. Ray asked Daddy for money to help with the operation, but Mama said we had our own family to feed. Well, Lita wrote the most awful letter you can imagine, and that was the last we saw of them.'

I gave back the album.

'So you didn't stay in touch after that?'

'Lord, no. Mama would have had a fit. I haven't seen nor heard from George since, oh I had a family, so he would've been in high school. You never told me why you're looking for George.'

'George is dead. He was murdered four days ago.'

She stared at me with no expression for a moment, then dropped a hand down alongside the chair. Margo hobbled over and snuffled her fingers.

'Well, that's just terrible. What a terrible thing.'

'How about your brothers and sisters? You think they stayed in touch with George?'

'Well, I can't know, but I doubt it. Both my sisters and my brother are gone. I was the youngest on my side.'

'How about your children?'

She made a little snort, and Margo stopped snuffling.

'They don't even come to see *me* – they wouldn't bother with George. George had run off by the time they were old enough to give a damn.'

'What do you mean, run off?'

'George got some gal pregnant, and dropped out of school. Mama said the apple doesn't fall far from the tree, Lita being loud the way she was and Ray a drinker. Mama said that boy would come to no good, gettin' some girl pregnant, and now here he is murdered. I guess Mama was right.'

I sipped the coffee and made a tiny scratch on my pad. A tiny black line that disrupted the perfect order of the blank yellow page.

'Pregnant.'

'Low-class people will do that.'

She arched her eyebrows and made a nasty smile. I made another mark on the pad.

'This girl, do you know who she was?'

My hands were damp when I asked. I rubbed them on my thighs, and tried not to be obvious.

'No. That all might have been just talk, anyway. If George had a girl, I sure never saw her and don't know anyone who did.'

'That year when George ran off, did any of the local girls move away?'

Mrs. Reinnike laughed.

'Not for anything like that. That was 1953, son. When a girl had a problem like that, she bee-lined it down to Mexicali and was back the next day. We called it the one-night-stand shuttle.'

She cackled again, as if she had known more than one or two who had taken the shuttle.

'Do you recall what people were saying about her? If she wasn't a local, was she a stranger? Maybe from out of town?'

'You sound like you know who she was.'

'Just trying to help you remember.'

She made a shrug like she couldn't be sure either way.

'What's all this have to do with finding his next of kin?'

So much for not being obvious.

'The child would be his next of kin, and the child's mother might know where George was living.'

'Well, that's true. I wish I could help you with that, but I don't know, and I can't imagine anyone still living who might. George wasn't a likable boy. He took after Lita that way. I guess it might have been his legs, leaving him bitter and angry, but I don't remember anyone having anything good to say about him. He got in fights and was always in trouble and lorded his money. No one wanted to be around someone like that.'

Lording money didn't jibe with the cheap furnishings in the Christmas picture, and Ray and Lita asking Edelle's parents for help to pay for George's operation. I asked her about it.

'Oh, George had plenty of money. That hospital botched up his operation, and had to do it again. Ray and Lita got some kind of fancy settlement. Well, they didn't get the money, but George did. He got a check every month, right on the dot.'

'He got monthly payments?'

Mrs. Reinnike looked smug.

'That was the judge. The judge took one look at Ray and Lita, and gave the money straight to George. I guess he figured if George got the money little by little, Ray and Lita wouldn't be able to spend it.'

'This was the hospital in San Diego?'

'Well, I guess. I don't really remember, but I guess it had to be.'

If George had been getting a monthly payout, the hospital or their insurance company would have a record of his addresses. I checked the time. It was still before noon, and I could probably make it to San Diego in less than two hours.

I thanked Edelle Reinnike, and the two of us walked to the door. I wanted to ask another question, but had to work up my nerve. I stepped out into the heat, then turned back to face her.

'Mrs. Reinnike, do I look familiar to you?'

'Nope. Should you?'

The sun burned bright in the clean desert sky, and bounced off the white dust as if it were snow.

CHAPTER 27

The Andrew Watts Children's Hospital looked like a grim Iberian citadel perched in the El Cajon foothills, one of those imposing stone and cast-cement fortresses that architects built when they hoped their buildings would last forever. I paid five dollars for visitor parking, then entered the main lobby and wandered around for ten minutes trying to find the reception desk. If the outside looked like a citadel, the inside looked like Grand Central Station.

A nursing aide gave me directions, but I got lost and had to ask someone else. On my third try, I found the right hall, and stepped through double glass doors to another receptionist.

I said, 'Hi. Elvis Cole to see Mr. Brasher. He's expecting me.'

'You can have a seat if you like. I'll let him know.'

After two hours in the car I didn't want to sit. I drifted back to the glass doors and stared out into the hall. Chairs and padded benches lined the wall, but no one was sitting in them. Two women walked by, laughing. One of them glanced at me, and I smiled, but she went about her business without smiling back. I imagined a little boy on crutches hobbling into the building. The boy's father smelled of whiskey and his mother was loud. I wondered if he had been scared. I would have been scared.

Behind me, a man said, 'Mr. Cole, I'm Ken Brasher. C'mon back to my office and I'll show you what we have.'

Ken Brasher was a neat, balding man in his mid-thirties with dark-framed glasses and a businesslike handshake. I had phoned ahead from the car, figuring it would be a smart use of the two-hour drive. I had been in the middle of nowhere just a few miles north of the Mexican border, but my cell reception was flawless. Maybe I should move to the desert.

After we shook hands, Brasher glanced at the receptionist.

'Would you tell Marjorie he's here and ask her to come down, please.'

The receptionist touched her phone as I followed Brasher into another hall.

'Our legal-affairs people want to be in on this. I hope you don't mind.'

'Not a problem. Were you able to reach the medical examiner?'

'Yes. He faxed down the death certificate.'

'Is there going to be a problem with me getting the addresses?'

'I don't think so, no, but I'll let Marjorie handle that. Marjorie is our legal-affairs officer.'

When we spoke on the phone, Brasher confirmed that the hospital had a legal agreement with Reinnike, but wouldn't divulge the details until he had confirmation of Reinnike's death and discussed it with their attorneys. I gave him Beckett's number at the coroner's office, and asked that he call. Apparently, he called. Apparently, Beckett told him that I was for real.

Brasher made an abrupt right turn into a small, windowless office and went behind the desk. A small square of construction paper was pushpinned to the wall facing me. The paper was filled with yellow and blue lines that might have been a cat or a tree, and a red message written in a child's hand: I LUV U DADY.

He smiled at me nicely.

'Do you mind if I make a copy of your identification? Marjorie will want it for our records.'

I gave him my DL and investigator's license. He placed them on a copy machine behind his desk, and pushed a button. He smiled at me some more as the machine made its copies. The smile made him look like a guy who wanted to sell me aluminum siding. I didn't like all the smiling.

I said, 'Is everything all right, Mr. Brasher?'

'Marjorie will be right down.'

That wasn't the answer I wanted to hear, and I suddenly had the feeling Marjorie wasn't anxious to share her information.

'You spoke with Beckett. I'm sure he told you he's trying to locate the next of kin.'

'Oh, yes. Marjorie spoke with him, too.'

'The man was murdered. He was living in a motel under an assumed name with no way to trace him until now. You guys were sending him checks. If the police can find out why he was using an assumed name and why he came to Los Angeles, it might give them a line back to who murdered him. Someone at the receiving end of his checks might know those things.'

Brasher glanced at the door, but Marjorie still hadn't arrived. The smile faltered as if he wouldn't be able to hold out much longer without her.

'We intend to cooperate to the full extent of our legal responsibility, but there are issues to be resolved.'

'What issues?'

He glanced at the door again, and suddenly looked relieved. The aluminum-siding smile returned.

'C'mon in, Marjorie. This is Mr. Cole. Mr. Cole, this is Marjorie Lawrence from our legal department.'

Marjorie Lawrence was a short, humorless woman in a blue business suit. She nodded politely, shook my hand, then pulled a chair as far from me as possible before she sat. She was carrying a thick file that looked dingy and old.

She said, 'We were told Mr. Reinnike made a dying declaration that you were his son. Are you?'

She stared into my eyes, and I let her. I felt awkward and surprised, but I didn't want her to know it. I hadn't mentioned that part of the business to Brasher because I didn't know and it didn't seem relevant. Beckett must have told them.

'He did, but I have no reason to believe I am. I never met the man.'

She nodded, and everything in her body language said that all the power in the room was hers.

'Regardless. I'm sure you can understand our position, you possibly being an heir.'

They thought I had come to chisel. I looked from her to Brasher, then shook my head. An heir.

'All I want is to know where the checks were going. I'd like to get that information from you now because that will speed things up, but if you don't share it with me, you know you'll have to give it to the police, and I'll see it then. If you'd like me to sign something releasing you from any claim by me, I'll sign it.'

She glanced at Brasher, and Brasher shrugged.

Marjorie had already prepared the paper. She slipped it out of the file, and I signed it on Brasher's desk. While I was signing, he gave back my licenses. When I finished, we went back to our seats. Easy come, easy go.

She opened the file again, studied the top page, then looked up at me.

'In 1948, this hospital – through our insurance supplier at that time – entered into a settlement agreement with Ray and Lita Reinnike – George Reinnike's parents – in their son's name. Rather than a lump-sum payment, we agreed upon a monthly payment in the patient's name that would span thirty years. The payments would have ended in nineteen seventy-eight.'

'Seventy-eight.'

'Yes.'

I felt a dull sense of defeat. If the payments had ended in nineteen seventy-eight, then the most recent address they had would be almost thirty years old.

'Just because I'm curious – why did I have to sign a release? Any money would have been long gone.'

'Mr. Cole, it's a bit more complicated than that.'

She opened the file again, fingered out another sheet, and handed it to me. It was a payment record for George L. Reinnike showing addresses, check numbers, and dates of payment. It was cut-and-dried bean-counting except for a stamp affixed at the bottom that didn't seem part of an accountancy record: EXHIBIT 54.

'You can see for yourself that checks were sent to Mr. Reinnike at three addresses, the first being the original home address with his parents in Anson, California –'

She leaned closer to point out the Anson address at the top of the sheet. I was still thinking about the exhibit number.

'Why is there an exhibit number here?'

'Checks were sent to Mr. Reinnike at the Anson address until 1953 when he filed a change of address to Calexico, California, where he received checks for five years and seven months before moving to –'

Her finger traced down the page.

' – Temecula, California. He filed an appropriate change of address, and his checks were redirected to Temecula, where the checks continued until 1975, at which time we discovered that a theft was taking place and terminated the payments.'

I looked up, and discovered Marjorie and Brasher watching me.

'What theft?'

Brasher said, 'Reinnike moved in 1969, but failed to file a change of address. A man named Todd Edward Jordan moved in, and banked Reinnike's checks –'

Marjorie interrupted. She was guarding the hospital's liability base like a Gold Glove third baseman.

'If Mr. Reinnike had filed a change of address as was required, or contacted us to inquire about his payments, we would have acted immediately to resolve the problem. We were as much the victims here as Mr. Reinnike.'

Brasher went on.

'Right, so we continued sending the checks to Temecula, only Reinnike wasn't getting them. Jordan got them. Jordan forged Reinnike's name, and deposited the money into his own account. People do this kind of forgery with Social Security checks all the time. We discovered the theft in 1975, and that's when we terminated the payments, and contacted the police.'

'Reinnike just moved away?'

'So far as was known, yes. All we know is what we've read in the file, Mr. Cole. None of us were here at that time.'

Marjorie said, 'I was in junior high.'

I stared at the page as if I were studying it, but mostly I was giving myself time to think. George Reinnike would have gotten a check every month for another nine years, but he had walked away.

Marjorie Lawrence opened the file again, and this time she took out a bound collection of newspaper clippings.

'These were in our files. They're news clippings of Jordan's arrest and prosecution. Maybe they will help you, Mr. Cole.'

Marjorie Lawrence brought me to an empty conference room, and left me with the file.

CHAPTER 28

The file contained eleven yellowed newspaper articles, all clipped from the San Diego *Union-Tribune* and filed by date. The first piece reported that an unemployed electrician named Todd Edward Jordan had been charged with theft, forgery, and mail fraud for cashing insurance-settlement checks intended for a former tenant of the house Jordan rented. The facts were light, indicating that the reporter had filed his piece before he knew of Reinnike's disappearance. The next story was more interesting. Investigators had been unable to locate George Reinnike, and sources within the Sheriffs Department suggested that Reinnike was a possible homicide victim. Some of the speculations read like lurid *noir* potboilers.

The next story stopped me cold –

FORGERY VICTIM STILL MISSING

by Eric Weiss
San Diego Union-Tribune

Six years ago, George Reinnike disappeared from the modest home he rented on 1612 Adams Drive in Temecula. According to his former landlord, Reinnike told no one he was moving. Reinnike not only abandoned a house – he left behind a small fortune in monthly disability payments. Foul play is suspected.

Todd Edward Jordan, 38, has been charged with forging Reinnike's name to cash the monthly checks. Jordan, an unemployed electrician, moved into the house several weeks after Reinnike disappeared in May of 1969. When Jordan discovered Reinnike's mail included a monthly disability payment from the Claremont Insurance Group, Jordan cashed the check. He continued to cash the monthly checks for the next six years.

Sheriffs investigators do not believe Jordan had anything to do with Reinnike's disappearance.

'Mr. Jordan responded to an ad in a local paper, and rented the house. We don't believe he ever met Mr. Reinnike,' said Detective Martin Poole of the San Diego County Sheriffs Department.

Reinnike's landlord at the time, Charles Izzatola, knew nothing of the forgery.

'Todd was a good tenant. He was polite, and his rent was on time.'

According to Izzatola, Reinnike moved out without informing him.

'The rent was late, so I went to ask about it. The house was empty. They left without saying a word.'

Reinnike, who was a single parent with a teenage son, was not well liked by neighbors.

'The neighbors complained about George and his kid. They even called the cops a couple of times.

Maybe one of the neighbors got fed up and ran them off.'

According to Poole, Sheriffs investigators tried to locate Reinnike when Jordan was arrested, but by then Reinnike had been missing for six years.

Poole said, 'A man doesn't walk away from free money like this. Reinnike could have filed a change of address or notified the insurance company. He did neither, and he never came back for his money. I'd like to know what happened.'

Anyone with knowledge of George Reinnike or his son, David, 16 at the time of their disappearance, should contact Det. Martin Poole of the San Diego County Sheriffs Department.

I walked the length of the conference room, and listened to the silence. It was a lovely conference room with lush carpet and richly upholstered chairs. The kind of conference room where important decisions were made.

Anyone with knowledge of George Reinnike, his son, David, 16 . . .

I went back to my chair.

Reinnike had lived as a single parent with a teenage son, and that son was not me. I turned to the next article.

The next three stories recounted more or less the same details as Jordan's prosecution proceeded. Jordan initially denied forging the checks; bank records indicated a steady deposit history of like amounts into Jordan's account; Jordan's handwriting matched the endorsements on the checks; Jordan claimed no knowledge of Reinnike and had never met the man; local homicide detectives failed to establish a connection between the two men. Jordan was convicted. A final sidebar piece appeared with the crime reports, accompanying the story that reported Jordan's conviction –

NO ONE WAVED GOOD-BYE

by Eric Weiss
San Diego Union-Tribune

George Reinnike and his son, David, 16, lived on a quiet street on the outskirts of Temecula for almost ten years. Reinnike, a single parent, kept to himself, paid his rent on time, and often argued with neighbors about his unruly son. Then, one spring night six years ago, the Reinnikes packed their car, drove away without a word, and neither have been seen nor heard from since.

'People move all the time,' said Detective Martin Poole of the San Diego County Sheriffs Department. 'But this one has us baffled.'

The police might be baffled, but when George Reinnike and his son moved away, most of their neighbors breathed a sigh of relief.

After ten years in the small rented house on Adams Drive in Temecula, the Reinnikes had made no friends, and seemed not to care. Many of the problems seemed to stem from Reinnike's son, David.

'George was sullen and unfriendly, and I tried to avoid David,' said Mrs. Alma Sims, 48, the Reinnike's next-door neighbor. 'I wouldn't let my children play with him.'

She recalls the time David Reinnike, then twelve,

was walking in the street as she was bringing her own children home from soccer practice.

'David was walking in the middle of the street and he wouldn't move to the side. When I beeped my horn, he started making faces at me, but he still didn't get out of the way. I tried to go around him, but he stayed in front of the car, calling me the most terrible names. He was out of control.'

That night, when Mrs. Sims' husband, Warren, went next door to discuss the matter with Mr. Reinnike, Reinnike allegedly threatened him.

Mrs. Sims said, 'George was defensive and belligerent when it came to David. No matter what David had done, if you tried to say something, George would act threatening.'

According to neighbors, the younger Reinnike was in trouble often. Stories of vandalism, fights with other children, and bizarre behavior were common.

'Someone broke windows in every house on this block one night,' said Pam Wally, 39. 'Everyone knew it was David, but no one could prove it.'

Neighbors believe David broke the windows, because only the Reinnikes' house was spared.

Karen Reese, 47, described a similiar incident. Her two sons had gotten into an argument with David. The following day, when Mrs. Reese was driving her sons home from school, they passed the Reinnike home where David waited at the curb.

Said Mrs. Reese, 'As we passed, he threw a hammer at us. It was the strangest thing, because he didn't care if we saw him or not. The back window shattered and glass was everywhere. Thank God no one was hurt.'

Mrs. Reese summoned the police, but no charges were filed. Mr. Reinnike agreed to pay for repairs.

'I'm not sure the boy even went to school,' said Chester Kerr, 52, who lived across the street. 'It would be midday during the school year, and you'd see him running around.'

Tabitha Williams, 44, the mother of two small children, tells a slightly different story.

'David had a learning disability and was being home-schooled. I never had any problems with David or George. It was hard for both of them without David's mother.'

The absence of David Reinnike's mother was a mystery, too, because George Reinnike gave differing explanations. At different times, Reinnike told neighbors his wife was deceased, had abandoned them when David was an infant, or had remarried and lived in Europe with her new family.

Now, the whereabouts of George Reinnike and his son, David, are as mysterious as that of David's mother. Though police are suspicious of the circumstances surrounding the Reinnikes' disappearance, they have no evidence of foul play, and have cleared Jordan of any involvement.

'It could be the guy just wanted to live somewhere else and didn't think enough of his neighbors to tell them,' said Det. Poole. 'There's no law against moving, but we'd still like to know.'

If you have any information about George or David Reinnike, please contact Detective Martin Poole of the San Diego County Sheriffs Department.

*

After the cold facts of the crime reports, the sidebar article made the Reinnikes real.

I compared what I knew with what was reported. Neither the Sheriffs nor the neighbors mentioned George Reinnike's tattoos or any sort of religious zeal. The tattoos were of such a dramatic nature that this omission indicated Reinnike had not been tattooed when he lived in Temecula. The tattoos coming later suggested a significant change in Reinnike's emotional state. The police had suspected foul play in Reinnike's disappearance, but thirty years later I knew that Reinnike had not been murdered at that time; it took another thirty-five years for someone to kill him. A rational person might not walk away from the insurance payments, but an emotionally troubled man might, and so might a desperate man. It had been the sixties. A lot of people dropped out, and plenty of them had good reasons. Maybe Reinnike felt a radical change would help his son. Maybe he walked away from the checks because they were a monthly reminder of everything he had hated about his earlier life. Maybe he needed to escape himself to heal, and the tattoos and prayers were part of the process. And thirty-five years later, he had come to Los Angeles with the belief he had fathered a child named Elvis Cole. Maybe he was crazy.

After a while I grew tired of thinking about it. I gathered together the clippings, found Marjorie Lawrence, and asked for copies of the articles. I also asked if I could use her phone. She was happy to let me do so.

I called Starkey. I could have called Diaz and Pardy, but Starkey worked the Juvenile desk. If David showed only a Juvie file, his record would be more difficult to find. Juvenile records are often sealed or expunged.

Starkey said, 'Hey, dude, where are you?'

'San Diego. I found something down here maybe you can help me with.'

'Oh, I live for that. You've made my day, adding more work to my load.'

I gave her the headline version of Reinnike's disappearance, and told her about David Reinnike.

She said, 'The guy had another son?'

'That's not funny, Starkey.'

'Oh, hey.'

'Will you check it out for me or not?'

'Yes, Cole, I will check it out for you. Don't be so snippy. Listen, those newspaper articles, do they name the investigating officers?'

'Yeah. The lead was a guy named Poole. San Diego County Sheriffs Department.'

'Are you coming back tonight?'

'Yeah, I'm going to leave in a few minutes.'

'I'd like to see the articles. With all this happening thirty years ago, having the names might help me out.'

'Okay, sure.'

'Well?'

'Well what?'

'Seeing as how I'm going to so much trouble, maybe I should come up to your house tonight and you should feed me dinner. An invitation would be nice.'

Starkey made me smile.

'How about eight o'clock. I should be back by then.'

'Eight o'clock. Don't get killed driving home.'

Starkey always knew what to say.

I found my way back to the freeway. It had been a long, difficult day, and I had logged a lot of miles. I had more miles ahead of me, and all of it would be grudging.

My head buzzed with a remote ache from all the thinking about George Reinnike, and what he might mean to me, or not. If Reinnike believed he had a child named Elvis Cole, why did he wait so many years to get in touch? I tried to make sense of what I knew, and nothing good came to mind. Anything was possible. Reinnike might have lost both his son and his mind, then convinced himself I was a long-lost replacement. Dial-a-Child, at your service. My picture had been in the newspapers, magazines, and on television. Maybe David Reinnike looked like me; the two of us interchangeable American males, brown, brown, medium, average. George Reinnike might have seen me in the news, convinced himself I was the long-lost 'other,' and swept me up in his madness. Here I was, driving in traffic, thinking about a total stranger named George Reinnike, and Reinnike had become real to me. He had flesh and weakness, and his tortured path had somehow crossed mine. Even if he was not part of my past, he had begun to *feel* like my past. When I remembered my mother, he was now in the memory like a transparent haunt. All through my life those memories had been a puzzle with a missing piece, but now George Reinnike filled the hole. The picture was complete. Daddy was home whether he was real or not.

Three hours later I slipped between the trees along Mulholland Drive, heading for home. It had been a long day. The sky had grown smoky, and the dimming light purpled the trees.

I turned onto my street and saw a tan car parked outside my house. The last time I came home to a car, it was Pardy. I decided that if Pardy was waiting in my house again, I would scare the hell out of him.

I pulled into my carport, took out my gun, then let myself in through the kitchen. I didn't try to be quiet. I pushed open the door.

CHAPTER 29

Starkey

Starkey put down the phone after Cole hung up, and kicked back in her chair with a wide nasty grin. She was pleased with herself for jamming Cole into dinner. It would have been nicer if the idiot had thought up the idea himself, but beggars couldn't be choosers.

'That must've been your boyfriend Cole on the phone.'

Starkey's grin floundered. Ronnie Metcalf was watching her from his adjoining desk. Metcalf was a D-2 with Hollywood Robbery, which had to share office space with the Juvenile Division. Metcalf tapped his mouth.

'I can tell by the grin.'

He pursed his lips and made puckered kissing sounds. Starkey didn't flinch, flush, or turn away.

'You're an asshole.'

Metcalf laughed, then got up and sauntered over to the coffee machine. Starkey turned back to her desk, but now her mood was soured. She didn't like Metcalf eavesdropping on her calls. She could get in trouble for using LAPD resources for an outside party, and a dick-head like Metcalf might use it against her. Starkey considered the repercussions, then realized her irritation had nothing to do with getting in trouble. She resented that her feelings were obvious. What she felt about Cole – or anything else – wasn't anyone else's business. She would have to remember not to smile so much when she thought about Cole.

Starkey swiveled around to her computer and entered David Reinnike's name into the State of California Criminal Information Center's search engine. If David Reinnike had been arrested as an adult, his listing would appear. A case number was required, so Starkey used a number from one of the sixteen cases she currently worked, and punched in her badge. Fuck Metcalf.

Starkey watched the little wheel spin for a few seconds, then the search was complete. David Reinnike had no adult criminal record.

Like it should be easy.

Starkey considered what Cole had told her. San Diego P.D. had responded at least once to a complaint about the boy, but that didn't mean he would have an accessible juvenile record. Cops and courts were usually lenient with minor offenders, and their records were often expunged or sealed. But juveniles with chronic behavior problems were sometimes assessed by officers with special training, especially if the child manifested bizarre or unusual behaviors, and those records were usually maintained in the files of the local police.

Starkey went to the large map of California that hung on the wall. She searched for Temecula, and found it on I-15, just north of Fallbrook.

'Hey, Starkey.'

Metcalf was still by the coffee. He opened his mouth in an O, and pushed out his cheek with his tongue.

Starkey turned back to the map.

Temecula patrol officers had probably responded to the call, but Temecula would have been too small for its own Juvenile Division. They had probably laid off the case on the San Diego County Sheriffs, so the Sheriffs station would have the records, if they existed. Starkey had been on Juvie for only a few months, and had no clue in hell how she could get someone down there to look for thirty-year-old juvenile records. But Gittamon probably knew.

Starkey walked over to Gittamon's cubicle and rapped on his wall. Dave Gittamon, who was Starkey's sergeant-supervisor, had been on the Hollywood Station Juvenile desk for thirty-two years and had solid relationships with pretty much every senior juvenile officer throughout the southwest.

Gittamon glanced up at her over his reading glasses. He was a kindly man with a preacher's smile.

She said, 'Dave? Do you have juice with anyone down in San Diego County?'

Gittamon answered in his calm, reassuring voice. He was the most understated man Starkey had ever met.

'Oh. I know a few folks.'

Starkey described the situation with David Reinnike and told Gittamon she wanted to find out if a record existed. She did not mention Cole.

Gittamon cleared his throat.

'Well, you're talking about a minor child, Carol. You might need a court order. What are you going to do with this?'

Starkey noted his choice of the word: *Might*.

'If this kid was arrested, his file could show a person or persons who can give me a line on finding him. That's all I'm looking for here. They disappeared, Dave. They changed their names and vanished.'

'But you don't know that he was arrested?'

'No.'

'So you don't know that a file exists.'

'No.'

'In Temecula.'

'That's right.'

Gittamon grunted, thinking about it, so Starkey pressed on.

'I guess what I'm looking for here is a personal favor, Dave. Like if I had a file, and someone with a legitimate reason wanted to see it, I'd let them take a look, no harm, no foul, no paperwork. Cop to cop. You see? No court orders, nothing like that.'

'How do you spell his name?'

Starkey knew she was in.

'The sooner the better, Dave.'

Gittamon picked up his phone like it was the easiest thing in the world.

'Oh, I know a few people down there. Give Mr. Cole my best.'

Starkey felt herself flush as she walked away.

CHAPTER 30

The kitchen was dim and silent, but a single lamp burned in the living room. The glass doors to the deck were open. I crept forward, feeling the muscles in my shoulders tighten, but then I smelled her scent, and knew who was waiting. The long day and hard miles were gone.

She must have heard me. She stepped in from the deck, and I felt my heart swell.

'I let myself in. I hope it's all right.'

'Of course it is, Lucy.'

George Reinnike vanished, and the world was at peace.

Lucy Chenier saw the gun, and looked away. When we were first together, she would have made a joke, but now the gun represented the violence that drove her away. I hadn't spoken to Lucy in weeks. I hadn't seen her in almost two months.

I unclipped the holster from beneath my shirt, seated the gun, then put it out of sight above the refrigerator.

'I've had a problem with mice.'

Her lip curled in a forgiving smile. She wore a

234

fall-orange turtleneck sweater over jeans, the sweater perfect for her golden skin and auburn hair. The best color money could buy, she liked to joke.

She said, 'Here, I brought you a Care package.'

Two bricks of Community Coffee Dark Roast, two bags of Camellia red beans, and a six-pack of Abita beer were on the dining table. Baton Rouge staples. It couldn't have been easy, bringing all that from Louisiana. I took her effort as a good sign.

'CC Dark – this is great, Lucy. Thanks.'

'I hope you don't mind my being here like this. Joe said you were on your way home, so I let myself in.'

'C'mon, you know better than that. This is a great surprise. What are you doing in L.A.? How's Ben?'

Nothing in her body language warned me away, so I gave her a polite kiss, then stepped back to let her know I respected the boundaries she had imposed. Her lips smelled of raspberries.

'Ben's doing really really well. You're the class hero, you know – everyone at school has to hear about Elvis Cole.'

I laughed, but only because she expected me to be pleased. Picturing Ben Chenier telling his ten-year-old buddies about me caused an ache in my chest. I wanted to tell her how much I missed them, but I didn't want to make either of us feel guilty. I changed the subject instead.

'Hey, would you like a drink? You want something to eat?'

'Yes to both, but let me see your hand. How is it healing?'

She turned my right hand palm up to inspect the puckered scar that sliced across three fingers and part of the palm. I had been cut when it went down with Ben. Forty-two stitches and two surgeries, but they said I would be ninety-five percent, no problem. So long as I didn't mind chronic pain.

'It's fine. They put in bionic motors and steel cables – I'm like the Terminator now, me and the governor.'

She studied the scar, then folded my fingers, and gave back my hand. She pushed out a smile we both knew was fake.

'How about that drink?'

'Coming up.'

She had flown out to meet with the prosecutors about Ben's part in his father's trial. Though I had been cut, Richard had been shot, and almost died. He probably would have been happier if he had. Richard Chenier had hired three mercenaries to kidnap his son, and five people had died before it was over. Richard had not personally pulled a trigger, but because he had set the kidnapping in motion, he was an accessory before the fact and a de facto accomplice. Under California law, Richard could be and was charged with the murders. He currently resided at the County-USC Medical Center, where he awaited more surgeries and, eventually, the trial. Lucy told me as she sipped her drink.

'The judge agreed to hear Ben's testimony on videotape, but I wanted to be sure they understand that's as far as I'll go. I will not bring him to court, and I will not allow him to take the stand.'

'Why doesn't Richard save everyone the trouble and plead out? That would be easier for Ben.'

She had more of her drink.

'This is part of the process. He's facing two first-degree counts and three in the second, but his lawyers want a reduction to negligent homicide on the firsts and a pass on the rest.'

Lucy stared at nothing for a moment, then sipped again and shrugged.

'They'll probably end up at two counts of manslaughter if they can agree on the sentence. Richard has to do time. I'm sorry he was hurt, but he has to pay for this.'

She finished her drink with a tinkle of ice, then looked at the glass as if its being empty was just another of life's inevitable disappointments.

She said, 'You know what? I'm tired of being nice. I'm only sorry for Ben and what this is doing to him. Richard deserved everything that happened to him.'

I reached for the glass.

'Here. I'll make another.'

She held out her glass, and our fingertips laced. Neither of us moved. We were locked together like two grappling wrestlers frozen by tensions neither could overcome or escape –

– then Lucy dropped her hand, and pretended nothing had happened. I should have pretended that, too.

'When are you going back?'

'Tomorrow afternoon. I have to see the D.A. again in the morning, then I'm flying out of LAX.'

Tomorrow afternoon. I turned away to make the drink. I filled her glass with fresh ice, then cut a wedge of lime and sprayed it over the ice. I tried to pretend I was calm, but my hope was probably obvious. I stopped messing with the drink, and looked at her. Tomorrow left the night to be filled.

'Would you stay with me tonight?'

She shook her head without even considering it, but her voice was kind.

'Just make the drink, World's Greatest. And tell me what I can help cook.'

We were both on uneasy ground. You take great care on the thin ice. Go slow, and you just might make it across. I smiled, sending word that we were okay again and I would not pressure her. I freshened her drink instead.

'How about spaghetti with a putanesca sauce?'

She waved her hand, looking pleased with my choice.

'Bring it.'

'I've got Italian sausage in the freezer. We could grill it, chop it in the sauce.'

Waved the fingers again.

'Bring it all.'

CHAPTER 31

The Watcher

Frederick worked his regular shift, opening the station as usual until he handed the pumps off to Elroy that afternoon. Elroy bitched about not having heard from Payne, and it was all Frederick could do not to string up the skinny bastard on the hydraulic lift and stab him in the eyes, but Frederick was too practiced for that – he pretended to be exactly the same Frederick that Elroy expected – unaware of Payne's fate, and unaware of the terrible vengeance that had been visited upon Payne by Elvis Cole, and the even more terrible vengeance that would soon be visited upon Cole in return. If Elroy suspected anything else, he gave no indication. Nor did Elroy see the pair of vise-grip pliers that Frederick lifted from the service bay as he was leaving. Frederick planned to torture Cole just as Cole had tortured Payne – by tearing away his skin with the pliers.

Frederick returned to Los Angeles that afternoon. Cole's house was a vicious crouched spider clinging to the edge of a cliff, all mean angles and shadows. The carport was empty, and two women were walking a dog past Cole's house, so Frederick continued on. He parked at a nearby construction site, then hunkered down behind an olive tree to keep an eye on Cole's house.

A few minutes before six that evening, a car parked outside Cole's front door, and a woman got out. She didn't knock or ring the bell; she let herself into Cole's house with her own key, which gave Frederick pause. A woman might be named Elvis as easily as a man. Maybe Elvis Cole was a woman. Then he remembered that James Kramer had spoken of Cole as a man, so Frederick decided she was probably Cole's wife. He was deciding whether or not to murder her, too, when a dirty yellow Corvette came around the curve and turned into Cole's carport. It was one of the old Corvettes from the sixties, what they called a Sting Ray. Frederick sensed this was Elvis Cole; more than sensed it, he knew it, and knew that Cole was wearing a disguise as perfect as Frederick's own; the dirty car, the jeans and knock-around running shoes, and the stupid Hawaiian shirt with its tail hanging out were a pretense. Cole was pretending to be a regular man to hide his true self – a relentless killer-for-hire with a heart of hot ice.

Frederick's suspicions were confirmed in the next moment when Cole reached under his shirt, pulled out a pistol, and let himself into the house. Frederick tipped forward, expecting gunfire, but no shots rang out.

Now Frederick didn't know what to do. He had planned on killing Cole as soon as Cole arrived, but Cole was armed and expecting trouble. If Frederick went to the door, Cole might shoot him on sight.

A little while later, a third car appeared, this one also driven by a woman. She parked across Cole's driveway. When she got out of her car, Frederick saw a badge clipped to her waist. Frederick wondered if she had come to arrest Cole, but when Cole answered the door, he let her in with a beaming smile.

CHAPTER 32

I was searching the freezer for sausage when I remembered about Starkey. Starkey was coming over. She was probably on her way.

'Hey, you remember Carol Starkey? I forgot. She's coming over tonight.'

Something like interest flickered in Lucy's eyes, but then she smiled.

'I guess you forgot, all right.'

'It's nothing like that, Lucille. Starkey's tracking a juvie file on someone I'm trying to find. I have to get these articles to her, so I invited her for dinner. No big deal.'

The articles were still on the counter.

'I'm serious. Is it better if I leave?'

'Absolutely not. If I'd known you were going to be here, I wouldn't have asked Starkey. She'll understand.'

Lucy and I were thawing the sausage when Starkey knocked.

I said, 'That's Starkey.'

'Ask her to stay. I mean it.'

I called out that I was coming and went to the door.

When I opened it, Starkey flipped away a cigarette, blew a geyser of smoke toward the trees, and came in with a square pink bakery box.

She said, 'Whose car is that?'

Lucy stepped out of the kitchen as Starkey came inside. Lucy was holding the package of sausage and a knife. She smiled nicely.

'Hello, Detective. It's good to see you again.'

Starkey stared at Lucy as if she couldn't put a name to her face.

I said, 'Ben's mom.'

'I know who she is, Cole. Ms. Chenier. How's your little boy?'

'He's well, thank you. He's doing very well.'

Lucy gestured with the sausage, and went back to the kitchen.

'I have to get back. I'm dripping.'

When Lucy was gone, I lowered my voice.

'Lucy was here when I got back. I didn't know she was in town.'

Lucy called from the kitchen.

'Ask her to stay.'

I lowered my voice even more.

'Starkey, look, you mind taking a rain check? She's only here for –'

Starkey pushed the box into my hands.

'Fruit tarts. Don't worry about it, Cole. Give me the stuff and I'm gone.'

I brought the dessert box into the kitchen, and told Lucy that Starkey was leaving. When I scooped up the articles, Lucy followed me back to the living room. Starkey was still fidgeting by the door. She hadn't come three steps into my house.

Lucy said, 'Please, Detective, have dinner with us. At least have a drink.'

'I don't drink – I smoke.'

Starkey snatched the articles from me, folded them, then tried to slip them into her outer pocket.

'I ran Reinnike's name, Cole. He doesn't have an adult record, so you're shit out of luck with that. I'll let you know if I find something in Juvenile.'

Lucy said, 'Please – stay for a while. We can visit.'

'I gotta get going.'

Starkey kept pushing the articles at her pocket, but they wouldn't go in. The paper had folded outside her pocket.

I said, 'The paper's bent.'

Starkey pushed harder.

'Jesus fucking Christ.'

I said, 'You're making it worse.'

Starkey gave up on the pocket and turned for the door.

Lucy said, 'It was good seeing you, Detective.'

'Tell the little boy I asked after him.'

Lucy smiled nicely, clearly touched.

'I will. Thank you.'

Starkey stopped at the door, looked at me as if she was going to say something, but glanced back at Lucy.

'He misses you.'

Lucy's jaw tightened, but she made no other response as Starkey went out. I stood in the door until Starkey was in her car, then returned to the kitchen. Lucy was searching through my cupboards. She saw I was back, and smiled brightly.

'Okay, boss, let's get this going. I'm starving to death.'

'I'm sorry she said that about me missing you. It's none of her business.'

Lucy put two large cans of chopped tomatoes on the counter, and set about opening them as if nothing was wrong. Her eyebrows arched.

'She likes you, Mr. Cole.'

'Not the way you mean.'

Lucy considered me, then shook her head, and went back to opening the cans.

'You can tell me what she's helping you with while we cook.'

I watched her for a moment, wondering what to say and how to say it. Lucy softened me. Maybe it was the warmth of her hair (the best color money can buy) or the curve of her cheek or the determined intelligence in her eyes; maybe it was her scent or the way one front tooth overlapped the other or the faint lines gathered at the corners of her eyes. The whole of her gave me a peace I had not known without her. The knots in my neck and upper back loosened; the strained buzzing in my chest calmed. I did not tell her about Reinnike. I told her I was working a missing-persons case, and let it go at that. A man and his son had disappeared, and I was trying to find them. I didn't lie to her; I just didn't tell her everything. I didn't tell her the important things. Maybe I was tired of the drama, or maybe I didn't want to spoil our evening.

We cooked together as if she had never been away, and I only remembered we were no longer a couple when I wanted to touch her, but couldn't. I wanted everything to be as it had once been, but I respected her choices, and knew her choices weren't easy for her, either. She was doing what she felt she had to do. She was doing what she thought was right for her child. Maybe I could appreciate those choices more than other people, or maybe I was just drunk. In my fantasies, my own mother loved me as much; my own father cared. That Lucy gave up so much for her child left me loving her more and wanting her more and willing to sacrifice anything to nurture her love. What she gave Ben was everything I had wanted for myself; what she was to him was everything I had been denied by my own parents.

We cooked, and ate, and after a while we sat together in the silence of my house, the two of us on the couch, sitting close, her hand in mine. My home felt warm and alive; not just wood and glass and tile, but something more. I knew she would leave soon. She knew it, too. Maybe that's why we were silent.

After a time, Lucy whispered, softly.

'I have to go.'

I whispered back.

'I know.'

Neither of us moved. I believed she still loved me, else she would not have come to my house. I had asked her once to stay, and thought that if I pressed her again, she might. I could have brushed her ear with my lips, and whispered the gentle words. Maybe some part of her wanted me to convince her, but I knew if I did the difficult choices she had made would be even more difficult to bear. I didn't want to force her. I didn't want to make it harder for her.

She whispered, 'I'm going.'

She still did not move.

It was up to me.

I kissed the back of her hand, then smiled, trying to tell her I begrudged her nothing.

'I'll walk you out.'

If something I hoped was disappointment flickered in her eyes, I ignored it.

She found her wallet, then walked with me out to her car. The sharp night chill hooked at the skin around my eyes and made me blink. That's right – the chill. She kissed my cheek, then slipped behind the wheel.

She said, 'I'm glad you came home.'

I wanted to say the same, but couldn't.

Her taillights disappeared around the curve. They flickered in the trees, then disappeared again. I stood in the street, watching, hoping for one more glimpse, but after a while I knew she was gone. Ken Wilson told me there was no such thing as a dead end, but I feared he was wrong.

CHAPTER 33

Archangel Love

When the female police officer drove away, Frederick decided to kill Cole and the other woman. It was full-on dark by then, and no neighbor would be able to see Frederick approach the house. Cole might have a gun, but Frederick was even more concerned by the presence of the police. The policewoman – obviously Cole's minion – might have helped murder Payne, and she might even be helping Cole identify Frederick. So ten minutes after she drove away, Frederick slipped the shotgun from its case and readied himself for the killing.

Lights swung around the curve, and a car appeared. It slowed, and Frederick recognized the female police officer. She slowed, but she did not stop, and continued past Cole's house. Frederick didn't like it that she had returned, but didn't know what to make of it.

Frederick decided to wait. Maybe Cole would come outside to put out his trash and Frederick could shoot him from the trees. Maybe Cole and the first woman would go for a walk.

Twenty minutes later, the same female police officer cruised past again. She was patrolling Cole's house!

Frederick grew worried she might become suspicious of his truck. He pictured her calling in his license plate and alerting Cole he was in the area. She might be calling for more of Cole's minions at that very moment!

Do it, Frederick! Do it RIGHT NOW!

Frederick felt trapped between his need to avenge Payne and his fear of the police –

Do it, Frederick!

All he had to do was run to the door, kick it in, and crash into Cole's house. If he took them by surprise, he could shoot down Cole and his wife where they stood.

The police officer drove past again, and in that moment everything changed. Frederick grew convinced she knew he was in the area. That's why she was patrolling Cole's neighborhood – they knew he was here! They were looking for him. Even as he had been stupidly hiding in the trees, Cole's masked minions were probably closing in, surrounding him as silently as smoke; they would surround him, trap him, then hold him down so Cole could use a long thin knife to slit his throat just as he had killed Payne.

That monster, Cole.

Frederick lurched up from behind the trees and hurried back to his truck, desperate to get away before the officer reappeared, and before her assassins trapped him.

CHAPTER 34

I turned on the television to put noise in the house, then returned to the deck, wondering why I hadn't been able to tell Lucy about George Reinnike. The hillsides were sprinkled with their inevitable lights, following the canyon like a twinkling river to the city. High over the lights, a flashing red crucifix climbed toward the east; a jet out of LAX with red strobes on its wingtips and tail. They take off toward the sea, but turn across the city for a final good-bye. Lucy would fly that route tomorrow.

I went inside, made a cup of instant coffee, and stood in the living room. The television showed a news promo during a commercial. The Red Light Assassin had added another victim to the traffic signal body count. As part of the promo they showed a traffic camera's view of cars blowing through an intersection. I wondered if the Home Away Suites had a security camera in the parking lot. Gas stations, convenience stores, and supermarkets had cameras watching their parking lots, so maybe the Home Away Suites did, too, and Reinnike's car had been captured on tape. If their tape showed Reinnike's car, it might show his license plate.

I brushed my teeth to cover the gin, locked the house, and drove back to the Home Away Suites. It was better than brooding about Lucy.

Traffic was light, and Toluca Lake was quiet when I reached the motel. The parking lot was well lit, but not so bright that it would disturb the residents in the surrounding apartments. I got out of my car, but didn't go inside right away. I walked between the cars, looking for surveillance cameras on light poles and outside the motel, but I didn't find anything. Maybe they were hidden.

I went inside to the front desk and identified myself. The night clerk was a middle-aged woman who grew irritated when she learned what I wanted, and why.

She said, 'I don't know anything about that business. They brought me down from Bakersfield because of all this.'

The regular night manager had been relieved when the corporate office learned that prostitutes had visited the motel. She resented coming down from Bakersfield, and didn't think it fair that the regular manager had been fired.

'I want to ask about the parking lot. Do security cameras cover the parking?'

She pointed to the corner of the ceiling where a small camera hung from a metal bracket.

'We only have the camera inside. The police already asked for the tape, but it wasn't working. Now the home office is flying in and more people are going to lose their jobs. All for nothing, if you ask me. They buy these cheap things, then blame the managers when nothing works.'

'The police were here about the cameras? Do you remember which officer?'

'I wasn't here. That was the day manager.'

'All right. I'm going to walk around the building and the parking lot for a few minutes. I just wanted you to know what I'm doing.'

'We'll have to put armed guards in our motels now, everyone's making such a big deal. You would think that poor man was murdered right here in the lobby. It's absurd.'

I left before she could go on.

The Home Away Suites did not have outside security cameras, but the surrounding apartment houses and businesses might. Thomas said Reinnike had been parked in a spot directly across from the motel entrance, which was on the north side of the motel. I walked to the street, then looked back at the parking lot. A Mobil station was directly across the street to the south on the southeast corner, and a strip mall featuring a liquor store sat kitty-cornered across the intersection on the southwest corner. Both the Mobil station and the liquor store would have security cameras, but the angles wouldn't show the Home Away parking lot.

A 24/7 convenience store sat directly across Cahuenga Boulevard from the motel. The 24/7 would have cameras, too, and the angle might be better.

I trotted across Cahuenga. Two cars were tanking up at the pump island out front, with a heavy bass line booming from a little Toyota.

Inside, I joined three people in line at the counter. The clerk was a young guy with a neatly trimmed beard wearing a faded Mall Rats T-shirt. He checked out each customer mechanically and without interest. *How are you today? . . . That will be six dollars and forty-two cents. . . . Have a good evening.* He had an unobstructed view of the Home Away parking lot. A security camera hung from the ceiling behind the counter, with a second camera at the back of the store. They almost certainly had cameras outside the store.

When it was my turn, the clerk said, 'How are you today?'

'I'm investigating the murder of a man who was staying across the street. I have a couple questions for you.'

'Wow. That's not something I hear every day.'

I asked if their exterior security cameras showed the Home Away's parking lot.

'Sorry, dude, the cameras don't point that way. If you lean over here you can see what I mean.'

He realized I wouldn't be able to see much by leaning, so he told me to come around behind the counter. A security monitor was set up on a shelf beneath the cash register. It showed grainy black-and-white views of us, the aisles, and the outside area between the gas pumps and the front door. The clerk pointed at the monitor.

'You see? The outside camera doesn't show the street. You can't see the motel.'

We couldn't see the motel, but we clearly saw the cars at the pumps. Reinnike might have bought gas here, and his tag number might show on their tape.

'How long do you hold the recordings?'

'Twenty-four hours. It's not tape anymore – it's digital. The pictures stream to a hard drive, but the memory buffers out at twenty-four hours unless we put in a save.'

'And you only put in a save if something happens?'

'Yeah, like if the store is robbed or an alarm goes off or whatever.'

Reinnike had been murdered more than seventy-two hours ago. Twenty-four hours wasn't enough.

He folded his arms and looked at me curiously.

'I saw police cars over there last night. Was that what it was about?'

'One of their guests was murdered three nights ago.'

'Right in the motel?'

'He was murdered downtown, but he was staying there.'

I showed him the morgue shot. He studied the picture, then shook his head.

'They all kinda blend together. I couldn't tell you what my last three customers looked like.'

'He was driving a brown Honda Accord with a bad dent at the left rear wheel. Maybe he bought gas.'

'Sorry, dude. If their credit card clears, I don't even bother to look.'

'He would have paid cash.'

'A lot of people pay cash. I don't remember.'

A construction worker grimed with white dust came in. He ordered two hot dogs, plain with nothing on them, and a large coffee with four sugars. I stood out of the way while the clerk took two hot dogs off the rotisserie and filled a large Styrofoam cup with coffee and sugar. The wall behind the counter was lined with a soft-drink dispenser, a coffee machine, a frozen-yogurt dispenser, and the rotisserie, but I didn't see an espresso machine. Nothing said 'mocha.'

When the construction guy left, I said, 'Is there a coffee shop in walking distance?'

'Starbucks, up Riverside. It's ten or twelve blocks, though. We got coffee. What do you need?'

'It's not for me. A witness at the motel told me he crossed the street for a mocha. I was wondering where he got it.'

'I get you. He could have come here. We got mocha, vanilla, and hazelnut – they're bullshit instant mixes, but we sell it. You know that stuff is mostly sand? You mix it with hot water.'

The clerk's eyebrows suddenly arched with interest.

'Hey, was that the black dude?'

Just like that. You interview people, you never know what they're going to say, or why; sometimes, you kick over a stone like the thousand other stones you've kicked, and something glitters in the soil.

I said, 'I don't know. Describe him.'

'It was –'

His lips moved soundlessly as he counted on his fingers.

'– five nights ago. Big guy, buffed out and kinda fierce, with his hair high and tight?'

Five nights ago was the night Dana had prayed with Herbert Faustina.

'You remember every mocha you sell?'

He made a self-conscious smile.

'Not hardly. I remember this guy because of his chick. Dude, she was *hot* –'

He cupped his fingers to indicate the size of her breasts. Thomas hadn't said anything about Dana having a mocha.

'Did she have a mocha, too?'

'He came in alone. The Lakers were playing, and he's killing time, but he keeps looking outside. I'm thinking, what's this dude looking for, is he going to rob me? But then he says, shit, there's my chick, and turned so fast his drink splashed all over his hand. Ouch.'

'Ouch.'

'Right. This chick was *smoking*. I would've spilled my coffee, too.'

'Un-huh.'

'Anyway, he beat it back across the street. I just stared at the chick. She had a serious case of the floppies when she ran. It made my night.'

He cupped his hands over his chest again, and bounced them up and down.

'Why was she running?'

'They got into his car, but then she got out again. She ran over to see some guy –'

Thomas hadn't said anything about Dana getting out of the car. No flopping had been described.

The door chimed as an Armenian couple with a small baby came in. The woman was sultry, and beautiful. The clerk stared at her and lost his train of thought. I touched his arm.

'Describe the man she ran to see.'

'I wasn't looking at the dude, bro – I was watching her bags; they were hopping.'

'An older man? Thin, with badly dyed hair?'

'You mean the guy in the picture?'

'You tell me.'

The clerk glanced at the woman again, watching her walk, then sighed when he turned back to me. Fantasy interruptus.

'I didn't see the dude's face. I guess he was kinda old, but I couldn't swear to any of this. She almost knocked him over when she hugged him.'

It had to be Reinnike. Reinnike had come outside, and Dana had gone to see him. Thomas hadn't mentioned that part, and now I wondered why.

'What about the black guy? Did he go see the guy, too?'

'He kinda ducked down like he was hiding. I thought that was weird. I think he took a picture.'

'Why do you think he took a picture?'

'I saw his camera –'

He lifted his hands to either side of his face as if he was aiming a camera. As he demonstrated, the Armenian man asked if they had concentrated milk. The clerk told him to check the last aisle.

I said, 'You sure it was a camera? Maybe it was a cell phone.'

'Dude, I know a camera. Not one of those dinky little things, either; a real camera with a long lens.'

He pointed out a white car on the street-side row of cars in the Home Away parking lot.

'See the white sedan . . . four, five, six spots from the entrance, right here by the street? They were parked where that white sedan is. I saw the camera.'

'How long was she with the other man?'

'Coupla minutes. Maybe not that long.'

'Then what happened?'

'They left.'

'Did they follow the other man?'

The clerk was beginning to look annoyed.

'Dude, I don't know if they followed him. They just left.'

The Armenian family brought two cans of condensed milk and a jar of applesauce to the counter.

The clerk said, 'I gotta get back to work.'

'Me, too.'

I thanked him for his help, then ducked under the counter and went out to my car. The air was cold, but I didn't feel it. It was ten fifty-three when I called Joe Pike.

I said, 'I need you to meet me.'

Pike didn't ask why; he only asked where. I gave him Dana's address.

Ken Wilson was right. Dead ends don't exist. Lucy had gone, but she would return.

CHAPTER 35

People lie. Half the people in jail were arrested because they lied even though they hadn't done anything wrong. A cop asked where they were Tuesday night, and they didn't say they were having a beer at the Starlite Lounge; they said they were in Bakersfield. Next thing they knew, they were popped for a Bakersfield stickup because they matched a description. They suddenly remembered they were at the Starlite, but then it was too late. They had lied, been arrested and booked, and by the time the detectives figured out they were telling the truth about the Starlite, the detectives had also found an outstanding warrant for failure to pay child support or skipping a court appearance. All because they lied about having a beer. Many people are like that. Lying is their automatic reaction.

Thomas and Dana probably lied because they had something to hide. I didn't see how their lies had anything to do with Reinnike's murder, but I wanted to see their pictures.

Dana's street was well lit in a small-town way, with gold light softening the cheap stucco buildings to make everything seem nicer than it was. Cars lined both curbs like too many puppies crowding their mother. It was after eleven as I crept past Dana's building; the neighborhood had settled for the night.

Pike's Jeep was blocking a drive two buildings beyond Dana's. Pike was a motionless black smudge masked by black shadows. His window was down.

Pike's low voice came quietly from the darkness.

'I couldn't tell if they're home. The drapes are pulled and everything's quiet.'

'You could've kicked in the door.'

'Waiting for you.'

'Okay. Let's see.'

I told Pike how I wanted to play it, then walked down the drive to Dana's apartment. Behind me, Pike slipped from the Jeep. The interior light did not come on when his door opened.

I went to Dana's door, listened, then rang the bell. Her apartment was dark. The windows were cheap aluminum sliders with spring-loaded handles serving as clip locks. I tried to slide the glass, but the latches held firm. I padded the muzzle of my gun with my handkerchief, pressed the muzzle to the glass alongside the handle, then smacked the butt hard with the heel of my hand. The muzzle popped through the glass, leaving a jagged hole the size of a tennis ball. I opened the window, hoisted myself inside, then closed the drapes.

'Hello?'

I flipped on the lights, then checked the bedroom and bath to be sure no one was hidden. Like lying, people often hide, and then you don't see them coming. It can ruin your whole day.

When I visited their apartment two days ago, a camera

260

with a big lens was on the dining room table beside the computer. Now, the camera was gone. The desk was cluttered with papers, a cordless phone, and dust bunnies, but a clean new LAPD business card stood out. Detective Jeff Pardy. I smiled when I saw the card. Pardy might be a flathead, but he was doing his job. It made me feel better about him.

I went back to the living room, sat on the couch, and waited. It was eleven twenty-six when I started waiting. At twelve-seventeen, voices approached. I went back to the dining room, turned the chair to face the front door, and made myself comfortable.

A key ground into the deadbolt lock.

Outside, Dana said, 'But I turned off the lights.'

Thomas stepped inside, not seeing me because he was looking at Dana. He was carrying the camera. He didn't see me until Dana stepped inside past him, but by then it was too late.

Thomas said, 'You –'

Pike came in behind Thomas fast, and hooked his left arm tight around Thomas's neck. He turned Thomas's right hand high behind his back and lifted him inside. Thomas made a gurgling sound, and the camera hit the floor with a clunk.

Dana said, 'Hey! What are you doing? Stop it!'

Pike let Thomas's weight ride the bent arm. Thomas tried to reach Pike with his free hand, but Pike was out of reach. Thomas kicked and twisted, but Pike lifted higher and cut off Thomas's air. You can't get much leverage when you're hanging by your neck with your tongue turning purple.

I closed the door behind them, then brought Dana to the couch.

'He's okay. You sit here and don't get up.'

I picked up the camera and sat beside Dana. It was a professional-grade Sony digital with ports for extra memory chips and buttons I didn't understand. I gave the card and phone to Dana.

'Here, hold these, okay?'

'What do you want? Why do I have to hold this?'

'Pike, you good?'

'Perfect.'

'Okay.'

The camera had a view screen for reviewing shots. I turned it on, then pressed a button labeled REVIEW. The screen filled with the picture of an ordinary street. It was the picture Thomas had most recently taken. A bright yellow bar across the top of the picture showed the number 18. Eighteen pictures were stored in the memory. I pressed the review button again to see the seventeenth picture, and clicked back through the remaining pictures one by one. The first four pictures were ordinary shots of ordinary things, but the fourteenth picture showed a dimly lit room through what might have been partially closed curtains. The image was small and orange, but I made out what seemed to be a woman's back and a man's legs. They were stretched out on a bed, and the woman was hunched over the legs. The only clear shot of Dana was when she first entered the room and was still on her feet. The angle showed a clear view of her face. None of the shots showed the Home Away Suites or George Reinnike, aka Herbert Faustina, but as soon as I saw them I knew what Thomas and Dana were hiding.

I said, 'This is sweet. Thomas here takes pictures of Dana with her johns. Why do you suppose he does that?'

Pike said, 'Blackmail?'

Thomas thrashed as he kicked at Pike's legs, but Pike did something to the bent arm, and the thrashing stopped. Dana didn't try to get up. She seemed embarrassed.

I said, 'You and Mr. Three Strikes left something out of your story the other day. Herbert Faustina's real name is Reinnike. An eyewitness saw Thomas take a picture of you and Reinnike outside the Home Away Suites. I want to see it.'

Dana said, 'We didn't take any pictures. Whoever said that was lying.'

'Tell you what, I want you to call Detective Pardy for me. You have his card and the phone. Let's see how it works for Thomas when he's booked for blackmail, extortion, and suspicion of murder.'

Thomas stiffened again, and his eyes widened. Dana held the phone.

'Dana isn't helping, Thomas, so I'll have to dial. We'll tell Pardy you don't just pimp tricks for your girlfriend, you take pictures to blackmail her johns. Then we'll see if Stephen rats you out to save himself.'

Pike said, 'Oops. Strike three.'

Dana suddenly pushed up from the couch, and dropped the phone.

'It's Stephen. It isn't us. We don't blackmail anyone – it's Stephen!'

Thomas made a grunting sound to warn her to shut up, but she shouted at him.

'I'm not the one who told him about the car! I wasn't gonna say anything, but you had to say about the car!'

I waited for Thomas, and watched the resignation settle into his eyes.

'You going to talk to me if he lets go?'

Thomas croaked a sound like a yes. Pike released the pressure, and Thomas staggered sideways, coughing, with his right arm hanging limp. Dana kept shouting.

'You hadda say! You hadda tell him about the car!'

Thomas glared at Dana, but there was more hurt in his eyes than anger.

'It was my ass with the three strikes! Stephen already *told him* we were there. That bastard gave'm our *names*. I hadda give the man somethin', else they'd think we were holdin' out!'

I said, 'Show me Reinnike's picture.'

'I can't. I sent those pictures to Stephen.'

Those pictures. More than one picture of George Reinnike. More than one chance to see his license number.

I picked up the phone and punched in Pardy's number.

'Listen, I'm telling you the truth. I sent'm to Stephen. After I sent them, I deleted them. *He* has them. I don't keep incriminating shit like that on my computer.'

I lowered the phone. I studied him, then glanced at his computer. Thomas was probably telling the truth, but I couldn't be sure.

'What does Stephen do with the pictures?'

'A lot of johns use credit cards, and expense the charge to their companies. Stephen's girlfriend has a brother works at a credit bureau, something like that, so he can get contact information. These guys go home, a few weeks later they get a copy of the picture. A lot of them, they cough up an extra grand to make Stephen go away. Stephen doesn't push it; he don't ask for too much or keep after them. Stephen ain't no hardcore badass; he's just looking for an easy dollar.'

'Reinnike paid with cash.'

'Here's this dude with all this cash, hiring all these girls – Stephen said it was worth a shot. I didn't get any sex stuff. Just them out in the parking lot. That was all I got, and I ain't even got that anymore. I sent'm to Stephen.'

I walked over to his computer. A screen-saver pattern had appeared. A ball slowly bounced between the four sides of the screen, the ball trailing an expanding wake that overlapped and consumed itself. Thomas might be lying, but I believed he was telling the truth.

'Here's my problem, Thomas. Those pictures could be sitting right here, and I couldn't find them. The experts at LAPD can turn this thing inside out.'

'I'm telling you they won't find nothing. I pick out the best shots, send them to Stephen, then get rid of the evidence. I don't keep that shit on my computer.'

'You e-mailed the pictures to Stephen?'

'I sent the best three. The rest weren't so good. He got them. I know he got them – he wrote back and said.'

Pike said, 'When?'

'Five days ago, I guess. It hadda be five.'

Dana said, 'The day after I saw him.'

I glanced at Pike, and Pike nodded. We were both thinking the same thing.

I said, 'Have you gotten an e-mail from Stephen in the past three days?'

'No.'

Pike's mouth twitched. Stephen had been working at a laptop when we saw him three days ago. It was the only computer we saw, and we took it. George Reinnike's picture was in my car.

*

I pushed Thomas's computer out of the way, put Stephen's laptop on the table, and turned it on. Thomas came over to see.

'If you had Stephen's computer, why didn't you just ask him for the goddamned pictures?'

Pike said, 'Shut up.'

The screen filled with a dark blue desktop. The DESKTOP FILES icon opened the hard drive, but revealed nothing more than a long list of files with meaningless names. I knew the list of call girls and business records were somewhere in the files, but nothing was labeled BLACKMAIL or JOHNS. We would have to make Stephen show us, but Stephen had already told his lawyer that we had taken his computer. If Stephen turned up beaten to death, the lawyer would probably suspect.

Pike said, 'Anything?'

'Nothing obvious. We'll have to go back to Stephen.'

Thomas said, 'Let me ask you something. What's so important about me taking his picture? What you expect to see?'

'Reinnike's license plate.'

Thomas seemed vague for a moment, but then his right eye flickered. Thomas was working on something.

'I think I got that. You can see the back end of his car pretty good in one of the shots I sent.'

I said, 'Do you know his password?'

'You think he wants me checkin' his mail? Would *you*?'

I waited. I didn't have to wait long. Thomas saw a way out and he was spooling up to make his offer.

'I send him these pictures, he's gotta download them, right? He's gotta save'm, print'm, make copies, whatever, so he can use'm to shake down the johns. If he downloads them into a file, then we don't need his password to get into his e-mail; all we gotta do is find the picture files, right?'

'Get to it.'

'I figure you got three ways to get'm. You take that thing to the police like you was gonna do with mine, and maybe they find'm and maybe they don't. The other way is you pack it back to Stephen like you said, hope he's home, there aren't any witnesses, nothing like that, then put a gun in his mouth and hope he don't delete'm while you're looking the other way.'

'What's the third way?'

He stared at me without expression in a way that made me feel obvious. I felt myself flush.

'What?'

'Whatever you're after is important to you. You've been here twice now, and you're in a hurry. You don't want to wait for the police and you don't want to mess around with Stephen. I'm not saying I can find those pictures, but I got an idea how, so maybe I can save you some time.'

He let it hang. I knew what he wanted.

'When I send Stephen the pictures I give each of them its own name. If Stephen didn't change the names, I might be able to find them. Save you all that time. But I gotta get a pass on the crimes. I got the three strikes.'

Pardy might go for it. He told me he wasn't interested in sex crimes, but this was a slam-dunk blackmail and extortion conviction, and it was a major case. If he wouldn't go for it, Diaz would go for it. I thought I could deliver the deal.

267

'Show me the pictures.'

'You gotta get me a deal.'

'I'll get you the deal.'

Thomas sat at the laptop. He opened and closed several scrolls until a window appeared, asking which file he wanted to find. He typed DANA1.JPEG, then clicked a button to initiate the search. A tree chart showing files within files appeared with the DANA1. JPEG at the bottom.

Thomas suddenly laughed as the tension blew out of him.

'Be damned.'

The tree chart showed that DANA1.JPEG was in a file called DUMMIES, which was in a file labeled ASSOCIATES, which was tucked within another file called ED'S VACATION, which had been stored in yet another file with the innocent name COVER LETTERS, which was located on the hard drive. Thomas copied the names, then closed the finder window to open the hard drive. He opened each file in reverse order, beginning with COVER LETTERS, then ED'S VACATION, then ASSOCIATES. Each time he opened a file, Dana and I leaned over his shoulders, trying to pick out the next name in a jumble of other files. When Thomas finally opened DUMMIES, the screen filled with a list of tiny file names in alphabetical order –

ALLIE1.JPEG
ALLIE2.JPEG
ALLIE3.JPEG
ANGELA1.JPEG
ANGELA2.JPEG

There were hundreds of JPEGs. Maybe a thousand. Many of the names showed more than one series –

```
BARB1.JPEG
BARB2.JPEG
BARB3.JPEG
BARB2/1.JPEG
BARB2/2.JPEG
```

I said, 'Why the different series with some of the names?'

'Different johns.'

'You took all these?'

'Uh-huh.'

Pike said, 'You're a piece of shit.'

Thomas knew better than to glance up. He knew better than to crack wise or give with an attitude.

I pulled Thomas out of the chair and scrolled down the list. Dana had been photographed with seven different men. When I opened the first series, it showed a milky night shot of Dana outside a bar with an overweight man in a business suit. The angle of the picture suggested it had been taken from the opposite side of the street, and the pale colors indicated some sort of electronic light enhancement had been used instead of a flash. It was obvious by the man's expression he didn't know he was being photographed.

The next series showed Dana, a second young woman, and two older men on a sleek white boat in Marina del Rey. Dana and the other woman were wearing thong bikinis and nose zinc. The angle and graininess indicated the picture had been taken with a long lens, probably from one of the restaurants or apartments that lined the marina.

I opened the first picture in the last series, and saw George Reinnike. The photograph had the same milky quality as the other night shots – the colors bleached with a too-bright wash from the optical enhancer. Reinnike was wearing a plaid, long-sleeved shirt with the cuffs buttoned, but no jacket, and a set of car keys was clearly visible in his right hand. Dana was kissing his cheek, but he looked surprised and embarrassed, as if he didn't want this kind of attention in a public place. They were standing by the tail end of a brown Honda Accord, though the way they were standing I couldn't see the dent or the license plate.

Thomas said, 'Go on to the next one. I know you can see the plate in one of'm.'

The next picture was wider, revealing more of the surroundings. Dana was approaching Reinnike, but had not yet reached him. He was leaning toward the motel, as if caught in the awkward moment when he was deciding how to respond. His dubious expression suggested he was worried she was going to make a scene or ask for more money. I could see the top edge of the license plate, but it was blurry and unreadable.

Thomas said, 'Goddamnit, I know I had it. I got one more here. Open it.'

The third angle was the widest. Dana was on her toes, with her arms around Reinnike's neck. The dented left rear wheel well and the missing hubcap were obvious. Thomas hadn't remembered the car from a fast glance; he had studied the pictures to choose the best shots for Stephen. The entire license plate was visible, but blurry and unreadable, like a face in the fog.

Thomas leaned closer.

'Shit. I can't read it.'

It appeared to be a California plate, but I couldn't be sure.

'Can you bring this into focus?'

'Dude, that's *science*. I found the pictures. We got the deal, or what? You said we had a deal.'

I concentrated on the blurred license plate. It did not clear. A computer-graphics technician might be able to tighten the image. They can work miracles with this stuff. But not always. I closed the file. George Reinnike vanished.

I tucked the laptop under my arm, then nodded at Pike. He went to the door and waited. I turned back to Thomas.

'I'll set it up with Pardy. You'll have to testify against Stephen, but I'll make sure they cut you a deal. If you try to weasel or get funny, our deal is off and I'll let them have you. We clear on that?'

'We're clear.'

'They get your testimony about the prostitution, the blackmail, all of it. We clear?'

Dana said, 'Yes.'

They looked like rabbits caught in the headlights when Pike and I left.

We walked back to Pike's Jeep, both of us silent until we reached the street.

He said, 'Close.'

'I'll find someone to sharpen the image. There has to be a way to do that. Maybe Chen.'

I left Pike at his Jeep and continued toward my car, thinking about it. Close, but still out of reach, like an imagined image of my father.

When I got home that night, I put Stephen's laptop in my front closet, covered it with a raincoat, then drank a glass of milk. I ate a banana, took a shower, then tried to go to sleep, but I kept seeing the long line of names on the list. I was worried that Pardy wouldn't go along and I wouldn't be able to leverage the deal for Thomas and Dana even though I had given my word. I was worried that I would not be able to read Reinnike's license plate and would never know the truth. I stared into the darkness gathered at my ceiling thinking these things until I grew angry with myself, and got out of bed.

I turned on all the lights in my house, then brought Stephen's laptop to my dining room table. The cat came in as I worked, and sat silently, watching me.

I opened the files one by one as Thomas had done, until I found the long list of JPEGs. I scrolled down to the three pictures that were named VICTORIA, whose real name was Margaret Keyes. I deleted them.

I still had Margaret's cell phone number. I called her, even though it was two in the morning. I did not expect her to answer, but she answered on the fifth ring. From the background, she was at a club or restaurant with other people. Or maybe it was just the TV.

'Hello?'

'This is Elvis Cole. You don't have to say anything. Just listen.'

She hesitated, and I wondered if she, too, was awake at this hour because of the anger and pictures in her head. She answered guardedly. Because of the other voices.

'Yes. Oh, sure. I understand.'

She tried to make her voice light and conversational, as if she had gotten a call from a friend.

'You told me Stephen had something on you. Were you talking about the pictures?'

She didn't answer.

'Yes or no, Margaret. You don't have to say anything more than that.'

'That's right.'

'He had pictures of you having sex that he used in a blackmail scam, and he threatened to implicate you unless you continued to work for him. Yes or no.'

'Yes.'

'Those pictures no longer exist. You're free.'

I hung up without waiting for her to respond. I put down the phone, then went back upstairs to bed.

After a while, the darkness was not so foreboding. I slept.

CHAPTER 36

Starkey

Starkey suffered a miserable night after she woke from the dream; she sucked down a cigarette, then tried to go back to sleep, but every time the shadows took shape, she startled awake. Once, she glimpsed Sugar; another time, Jack Pell; but mostly it was Cole, the same terrible dream again and again. When Pell came to her, he smiled with bright bulging eyes and pointed at something behind her, but Starkey didn't turn fast enough and woke in the darkness before she could see. Finally, Starkey told herself to stop being stupid. She got out of bed.

Starkey glugged down a hit of antacid that tasted like mint-flavored snot, then made a cup of hot chocolate. She hadn't been able to drink coffee since the bomb. She missed it, but coffee fired the scars in her stomach like alcohol poured on a fresh cut. Her stomach was a mess.

Starkey sat at her kitchen table, smoking as she thought about Cole, up there right now with Little

274

Miss Honey-dipped Southern Comfort. Starkey was in love with the goofy doofus, that's all there was to it, and hadn't been able to shake it off. It was so bad she thought up reasons to call him, cruised his house in the middle of the night, and even called Pike, thinking maybe she could get to Cole through Man's Best Friend. The whole damn mess left her feeling like a degenerate.

Starkey made up her mind. She had to sit down with Cole, and lay it out: *Look, Cole, I'm in love with you, okay? I want to be with you. What do you think?*

Starkey saw the scene in her head, playing it through, then jabbed her cigarette into the chocolate. She didn't have the guts. Here she was, the same woman who used to defuse bombs, and she knew she wouldn't have the courage to risk his answer. What a frigging mess.

Starkey lit a fresh smoke, pulled the heat deep, and coughed. Thank God she had cigarettes.

Carol Starkey sat at the table, smoking, and did not sleep again that night. Here she was, scared to death by a dream.

THE FENCING MASTER

In Starkey's dream, she hides in darkness beneath the stairs in a great stone tower that belongs to a beautiful princess. Starkey has never described the dream to her shrink because the players are embarrassingly obvious. The first time she woke from the dream, she thought, jesus, you don't have to be Sigmund to understand that. Starkey is ashamed by what she believes the dream reveals.

275

In her dream, he is the fencing master. He never arrives nor leaves nor has a story to tell, but is forever trapped in the moment of her dream. She has never seen his face, but he has the build and grace of a dancer, clad in leather tunic and tights. He carries himself with the pride of his past as he was once the King's Hero, known for his bravery and valor. Now, he visits the tower each day to teach the fencer's art to a beautiful princess. The princess deserves no less than the King's Hero. He deserves no less than a princess.

Starkey hates this fucking princess.

The princess, too, has no face, but Starkey – glumly – knows the fucking bitch is hot. Honey-colored hair cascades over flawless golden shoulders, and a rich velvet gown drapes a body that is strong, athletic, and perfect.

Starkey, meanwhile, wears burlap rags, has dirty feet, and has smudges on her cheeks. She has somehow made her way into the tower, somehow hidden herself beneath the stair, somehow watched their endless lessons from her secret place, and through it all has fallen hopelessly in love with him.

Every time, the dream begins the same:

Starkey, hidden, watches as:

Great stone walls rise high around them, lit by the copper flickers of torches and candles. Tapestries hang on the walls; a fine rug muffles the stone floor. To one side, a heavy oaken door leads to the princess's chambers; to the other, a similar door leads to the outside. The room is empty, like a ballroom; its details missing, like a dream. The fencing master and the princess thrust and parry in perfect unison, back and forth, eyes locked in total concentration on the other. Their *foils gleam with bursts of light, the steel tinkling like chimes. He thrusts, she parries, she counters, he denies, back and forth until sweat runs from their brows and their breath is quick –*

Starkey, after she wakes, will roll her eyes and think, 'I get it! They're FUCKING!'

But not now –

Now, in the dream, her breath quickens with his. She wants to be the one on the floor with him; she wants his eyes on her, seeing only her. She wants to rush from the shadows to take her rightful place –

– but she does not.

She wears burlap, not velvet.

She is flawed, not a princess.

Then the moment shifts as moments will in a dream:

Darkness presses down on her. Starkey is suddenly aware that all has changed beyond the tower walls. An invading army swarms the city. The cry of cleaved men rides the clang of battle-axes and the scream of dying horses. Demons are coming. Starkey can't see any of this, but, hell, it's a dream – she knows it's happening just out of view.

The fencing master stands alone in the round fortress room. The princess peers from her door, frightened. He tells her to escape down the back stairs. She flees –

Starkey, trapped in her hiding place, silently screams, 'CHICKENSHIT BITCH!'

Something heavy booms at the far door. The fencing master turns.

Starkey screams silently –

'FUCK THE STUPID BITCH! SAVE YOURSELF! RUN!'

But, like Starkey, he is trapped in the dream, too.

The heavy door shatters. Monstrous warriors spill forward, giants with heavy muscles and broadswords, each bigger than the last.

'RUN, YOU STUPID NOBLE MORON!! RUN!!!!'

Starkey cannot know that he wants to run. She cannot know that he is scared. But he is all that stands between them and the princess, so he calmly raises his foil. Like Starkey, he has no choice. It is his place in the dream, to give his life for the princess.

'RUN!'

He glances in slow motion over his shoulder at the empty doorway where once the princess stood. A tear fills his eye. His lips move. Starkey sees the words.

I love you.

He once more faces the enemy, and his blade flicks like lightning. He dodges, weaves, and darts among them. Their bodies mount before his skill and rage. He is the fencing master, the King's Hero, known for his bravery and valor.

But finally they are too many.

Their steel finds him.

His body parts.

Starkey is his witness.

His tear-filled eyes.

His glance toward the princess.

His undying love.

His inevitable death.

Part Four

HIS INEVITABLE DEATH

CHAPTER 37

The morning broke clean and bright, filling the glass peak of my A-frame with an amber glow. I opened the doors to my deck, hoping for a breeze. The scent of the garlic and tomatoes Lucy and I cooked were still sweet. I liked it, even when I realized Lucy had not told me where she was staying. If I didn't know, I couldn't call. Maybe that was best.

I scrambled three eggs, drank the Community coffee, then got ready for Diaz and Pardy. I jotted a list of the people I interviewed in Anson and San Diego, then made copies of the newspaper clips and articles about the Reinnikes. When I finished with the copying, I called Diaz at her office.

She said, 'So, World's Greatest, have you solved the case yet?'

'I have something that might help. Did you get a hit on the BOLO?'

'C'mon, nothing is ever that easy.'

'I need to talk about something with you and Pardy. I have a digital picture of Reinnike and his car. You can see his license plate, but it's blurry –'

She interrupted me.

'What does that mean, blurry? Can you read the digits?'

'You can't read it, but we might be able to have it enhanced. It's a pretty good picture, but it doesn't come free –'

She interrupted me again.

'Waitaminute. Is anyone else in the picture?'

'One of Golden's outcall girls.'

'Where was it taken? Can you recognize the location?'

She was looking for other witnesses.

'It's not like that, Diaz. It was taken outside the Home Away Suites three nights before his murder.'

She fell silent, so I plowed ahead.

'Listen, that's what we have to talk about. Golden's operation isn't just outcall. He's running a blackmail scam, and you have to clear the field for the people who took the picture. They were involved in the blackmail.'

'Bring it around and let's see what you have.'

'They need the pass. Is Pardy going to go for it?'

'Pardy will go with whatever I say.'

I picked up Golden's computer from the hall closet, then let myself out through the kitchen. When I opened the kitchen door, an unsealed manila envelope was propped against the door. I looked inside, then tipped out a thin stack of faxed pages. The cover page was addressed to Sgt. D. Gittamon regarding David Reinnike. The letterhead showed the pages had been faxed from the San Diego County Sheriffs Department, North County Station, Juvenile Intervention Bureau. No other note was enclosed.

I knew Starkey must have dropped it off earlier that morning, and probably hadn't left a note or knocked because she was pissed off about dinner. Realizing that Starkey was pissed off left me feeling badly. I went back inside, and got her voice mail when I called her cell.

'Starkey, it's me. Listen, I want to apologize about last night. I didn't know Lucy was in town and I guess I was abrupt with you. It was rude. I got the stuff you left. I'll read it now, and talk to you later.'

I hung up, but I didn't feel any better.

David Reinnike's Juvenile arrest file was nine pages long. The first page was a form showing general information like the arrestee's name, address, date of birth, and description. Under that was a box containing the subject's record of arrests. The newspaper articles I read at the hospital indicated that the Reinnikes' neighbors had called the police about David at least twice and possibly three times, but only one arrest was listed. David had been taken into custody at the age of fifteen, a little more than ten months before he and his father disappeared. The charges were for threatening the life of another and animal cruelty, but the file was marked NF. The NF notation meant the case officer had decided not to forward the case to the Juvenile Division Court.

Two reports were attached to the cover. The first was the arresting officers' report. It was hand-typed, and only a page and a half.

Submitted by:
Ofc. Carl Belnap, #8681
Ofc. Gregory Silias, #11611

Arrest of David Reinnike, 15, minor male, 9/12
Chrg: Penal Code 16-7218a

Offcrs on routine patrol were dispatched to 1627
Adams, a residence, at 1640 hours on 9/12.
Complainant (Mrs. Francine Winnant, 46, female)
answered the door in an emotionally distraught
condition. Present with Mrs. Winnant was Mrs. Jacki
Sarkin, 42, female, who identified herself as a neighbor. Mrs. Winnant directed ofcs. to a side yard where
an adult collie dog was observed dead with what
appeared to be a wooden stake or spear in its chest.

Mrs. Winnant stated that David Reinnike, 15, a
minor male, of 1612 Adams, had threatened to kill
her dog. Mrs. Sarkin confirmed that Mrs. Winnant
told her of this threat three days prior, when both
agreed it occurred. Mrs. Winnant stated she had
found David Reinnike urinating on her front lawn
and told him to leave. She stated his response was
the threat to her dog.

Mrs. Sarkin stated she witnessed the confronta-
tion from her house, but could not hear the threat.
She stated she later spoke with Mrs. Winnant, who
told her of the threat.

Mrs. Winnant and Mrs. Sarkin both stated that
David Reinnike had commited acts of vandalism
and exhibited bizarre behavior in the past.

During these statements from Mrs. Winnant
and Mrs. Sarkin, Mrs. Sarkin observed that David
Reinnike was currently at his residence in the open
garage.

Ofcs. proceeded on foot to the Reinnike residence.
They identified selves as police officers, and asked

the minor teenage male to identify himself. He stated, 'David Reinnike.'

It was ascertained that no adult was present, both by David Reinnike's statement and by knocking and ringing the bell. No vehicle was present in the garage or drive.

David Reinnike was questioned as to Mrs. Winnant's statements regarding the dog. David Reinnike denied her statements, then grew unresponsive. He appeared to have trouble concentrating. He denied being under the influence of drugs or medications.

Mrs. Winnant and Mrs. Sarkin came out of their house and approached. Ofc. Silias went to ask them to return to their home.

David Reinnike became agitated. Ofc. Belnap attempted to calm him, but Reinnike's agitation increased. He shouted foul language at Mrs. Winnant and Mrs. Sarkin and made as if to approach them. Ofc. Belnap restrained him in the garage. At this time, Reinnike shouted at Mrs. Winnant, 'I'm going to kill you.'

Reinnike was placed under arrest and taken into custody on the charge of threatening the life of another, pending investigation by Juvenile Division and Animal Control in the matter of the dog. Reinnike was delivered to Juvenile Division, North County Station. No guardian or adult parent was present at the time of arrest or at the writing of this report.

(signed)
Ofc. Carl Belnap, #8681
a/o/9/12/68

I put the first report aside. The second report was written by a Juvenile Division detective named Gil Ferrier. It opened with two pages describing Ferrier's investigation, then concluded with his summary and recommendation –

David appeared calm, but appropriately concerned regarding his situation. He expressed regret regarding his outburst toward Mrs. Winnant, but denied knowledge of the dog's death. He explained his outburst was provoked by her accusation, which he states is untrue and unfair, and by a series of similar accusations by the Winnant family. He stated he has been repeatedly blamed by Mrs. Winnant for acts done by her son, Charles. According to David, Charles, who David states is two years older, has bullied David since David moved to the neighborhood. David admits that in response to one such occasion several years ago he struck Charles Winnant with a baseball bat. David states that since that incident the Winnants have regularly harassed, accused, and threatened him.

David's father independently confirmed the antagonistic relationship between his son and the Winnants, and explained the baseball bat incident. Mr. Reinnike stated his son had a bed-wetting problem at that time. He stated that in an attempt to cure his son, he hung his son's soiled sheets on the clothesline in their backyard, and that the other children, instigated by Charles Winnant, ridiculed David for many months. He stated that on the day in question, Charles Winnant was once more ridiculing David for being a bed wetter when David struck the older boy with a baseball bat. Charles Winnant was not seriously injured and required no stitches or hospitalization. George Reinnike assumed full responsibility for creating the situation. He stated that he personally apologized to the Winnants, but that they had been frightened of his son and had spread stories about his son ever since.

David Reinnike appears bright, but is given to inappropriate behaviors and extreme swings of emotion. He is being raised by his single father, George Reinnike, who is disabled and unemployed. George Reinnike states that David's mother abandoned them soon after David's birth. She has no contact with her son, and her whereabouts are unknown.

Neighbors both involved and uninvolved with the charges at hand allege David Reinnike has demonstrated violence, vandalism, and bizarre behaviors. No record of these allegations exists in police files. David Reinnike has no prior arrests.

George Reinnike admitted that David has committed two acts of vandalism, but stated these incidents have not recurred. He denies the other incidents. The neighbors making the allegations were re-questioned as to when these incidents allegedly occurred, and admitted the incidents were not recent.

Though Mrs. Winnant's allegation that David Reinnike threatened to kill her dog is credible, no witnesses or evidence exists that David Reinnike did in fact kill the dog. It is clear that much hostility exists between several neighbors and the Reinnikes. This hostility is apparent in their statements.

It is my opinion that prosecution of David Reinnike in this matter would be unsuccessful. It is further my opinion that David Reinnike would benefit from appropriate counseling. George Reinnike stated he would submit David for such counseling.

My recommendation is that the charges against David Reinnike not be forwarded for prosecution.

(signed)
Gil Ferrier, Detective
#1212
9/14/68
JD/SDCSD

When I finished, I copied Ferrier's name and badge number, and the names and numbers of the two arresting officers. I didn't expect the A.O.s to remember, but it was clear that Ferrier was thorough and concerned, and might have stayed involved in David's case. Thirty-five years was a long time ago, but he might even know what happened to the Reinnikes after they left Temecula.

The image of the dead collie was hard to erase, and left me feeling unnerved. The incident with the dog happened almost a year before the Reinnikes disappeared, and the file contained no record that the police had rolled out again, but I believed the neighbors. David Reinnike had been a seriously troubled child, and troubles like that didn't vanish with leaving a house. Maybe George had gotten David into counseling, and David had straightened out, but I doubted that, too.

I went back to the phone, and got Starkey's voice mail again.

'Hey, I just read this stuff. I'm on my way to see Diaz, but I want to talk to you about it. I'll call you later.'

I headed for Central Station.

CHAPTER 38

Twenty minutes later I left my car in the same parking lot I had used before, checked in at the front desk, and waited another ten minutes before Diaz came down. I started to outline Golden's operation as we rode up in the elevator, but Diaz cut me off.

'Let's see if the picture helps us before we get into all that.'

The squad room was busy. Almost every desk was occupied with detectives working their phones. Pardy was the only detective in the room who didn't look busy. He was slouched at his desk on the far wall, staring at nothing with his arms crossed. The dark blue murder book was open on his desk, but he didn't seem to be looking at it. Diaz called out to him, and waved toward her desk.

'Hey, Sherlock. Come see.'

Pardy considered her for a long time before he got up. He was probably getting tired of her put-downs. He closed the murder book, checked his pager, then made his way over. He pulled up a chair as far from us as he could get.

I said, 'You making any progress?'

'I'm working a few leads. You know.'

'Got any ideas?'

'I'm not looking for ideas.'

Diaz said, 'Okay, Cole, let's see it. What do you have here?'

While the computer booted up, I gave them the page with Edelle Reinnike's and Marjorie Lawrence's names and numbers. I gave them the copies of the newspaper articles and told them what I had learned. Diaz glanced at each item, then passed them to Pardy. Pardy looked up when I told them about David Reinnike.

'I guess that leaves you out, Cole. Unless you were separated at birth.'

Diaz flushed like she was pissed off.

'The one doesn't have anything to do with the other. How about you run the name and see if we get a hit?'

'I'm just saying. Why would Reinnike think Cole was his son if he already had a son? It doesn't make sense.'

'Why would he tattoo crosses all over himself and pay hookers to pray? We'll find out when we find some people who really knew the guy.'

I found the photo file, and opened the picture. Reinnike and Dana filled the little screen, standing beside Reinnike's brown Accord. The license plate was a blurry rectangle in the lower right corner of the screen. Pardy stood closer.

'She has the boyfriend, Thomas Monte.'

'That's right.'

Pardy looked disappointed.

'Not bad, but not great. It's blurry.'

Diaz said, 'SID might be able to pull it out. We could snatch the registration with just a couple of digits.'

Pardy went back to his chair.

'I'm not getting my hopes up. That backlog is a bitch. If we have to wait months to get a gun checked, how long will it be before they get around to this?'

I interrupted them.

'I can help you with that, too.'

Pardy said, 'What, you have your own private Walk-in Wednesday?'

So much crime was committed in Los Angeles that the LAPD lab was backlogged for months. Priorities were given to hot cases and cases going to trial, but the backlog was still so great that LAPD set up an experimental program called Walk-in Wednesday. Every Wednesday, detectives could hand-carry evidence to the lab on a first-come first-served basis to cut through the red tape. But there were still so many cases that the waiting rooms were crowded with loitering detectives.

I said, 'Something like that. I have a friend at SID who owes me a favor.'

'The little creep who worked with the key card?'

'Yeah, Pardy, him.'

The little creep. Chen would love it.

I explained how Thomas came to take the picture, and that a couple of hundred pictures just like it were in the computer. Diaz and Pardy listened as I went through the terms of the deal, then Diaz arched her eyebrows at Pardy.

'You'd have to turn it over to Southwest Bunco, but it would still look good. I think we should go for it.'

'Do whatever you want.'

Diaz stared at him, and was clearly annoyed.

'Listen, Pardy, don't drop the ball here. This could turn into a major investigation with the Feds. You should get a piece of that. You should develop the case to see what you have before you hand it off. That way, you get more of the credit.'

Pardy had resumed his slouch, and stared at her with sleepy eyes.

'I'm busy. You develop it if you want.'

Diaz looked as if she was going to say something more, but turned back to the laptop and angled the screen for a closer look.

'Okay, fuck it. We get this cleaned up, it might be good for a registration. I want to get this over there right away.'

'Are you good with the pass for Thomas and Dana?'

'We're good, but not if they had anything to do with the murder. Everything about this killing stinks like sex to me. If it turns out they had something to do with the murder, all bets are off.'

Pardy said, 'It wasn't about sex.'

He was slouched back in the chair with his arms crossed and his legs out, looking like he was about to fall asleep. Diaz's mouth tightened with irritation.

'Okay, genius, what do you think it was?'

'A straight-up murder.'

Diaz swiveled to face him, and Pardy went on.

'I haven't been sitting on my ass, Diaz. A witness ID'd Reinnike at Union Station about an hour before he was killed. Described the tats on his hands, and picked his face from a six-pack.'

'What witness?'

'Homeless dude I know from Metro. Reinnike was hanging around, he said. My guy hit him up for a hand-out, and Reinnike came across. I'm thinking if Reinnike was at Union Station, he was meeting someone.'

Maybe Pardy looked sleepy because he had been working the case all night.

Diaz said, 'Then what? Someone picked him up, and they drove to an alley in the middle of nowhere? Why the alley? Why *that* alley?'

Pardy stared at her, and seemed absolutely confident in his answer.

'Because it was in the middle of nowhere. Because whoever brought him there intended to kill him. They might have even murdered him somewhere else, and the alley is just a body dump. We didn't find a shell casing. We didn't find the cell phone Cole said he had. A lot of things are missing.'

Diaz frowned, but I was liking how Pardy was putting it together.

She said, 'Beckett found no evidence the body was moved.'

'If he wasn't moved far and he was moved right away, there wouldn't necessarily be anything to find.'

I said, 'How about the car? Did your guy see the car?'

'No, but it had to be nearby or someone gave Reinnike a ride. That alley is a long walk from the station. I walked it myself. Reinnike couldn't have made the walk in an hour.'

Diaz studied Pardy as if she had never seen him before. A deep smile slowly split her face, but Pardy didn't smile back. Diaz fingered the little heart necklace.

'Well, now, that is outstanding police work, Detective. That is truly excellent work.'

Pardy nodded, and Diaz went on.

'Have your wit bring you around to his friends. Talk to them, too.'

'Already in the works.'

Diaz smiled at him a little bit longer, but Pardy didn't return her smile.

'Okay, Cole, you're going to talk to your boy, Chen?'

'I'll bring it over now.'

Pardy roused himself from the chair and picked up Stephen's computer.

'I'll bring it. I want to meet your pal, Chen. Maybe I can get my own private Walk-in Wednesday.'

Diaz said, 'Give Cole an evidence receipt.'

'Sure. I can do that.'

Pardy filled out a receipt for the computer, signed it, and then they told me to leave.

CHAPTER 39

Frederick

Frederick did not open Payne's gas station that morning. He had spent most of the night sick to his stomach with the growing certainty that he would not be able to escape. The army of forces aligned against him was enormous, and might be anyone – Cole, a policeman, the priest, any random motorist who pulled to the pumps; everyone who crossed his path might be a tentacle employed by the beast that was trying to find him. Frederick imagined a dozen scenarios, all of them ending with his own terrible death, until finally he locked his trailer, brought the shotgun out to his truck, and drove back to Los Angeles to see if the police were still guarding Cole's house.

CHAPTER 40

John Chen was out of the office that morning working a homicide near Chavez Ravine. I left word on his voice mail explaining about Golden's computer, and asked him to call. After I left word for Chen, I called Starkey.

'Detectives. This is Starkey.'

'It's me.'

'Oh. Hey.'

She sounded uncomfortable. I was uncomfortable, too.

'I feel bad about last night. I didn't mean it to play that way.'

'What are you talking about? I didn't think twice.'

'I could've played it better, is all. I should've asked you to stay. Lucy was all for it.'

'Cole, please, you're making too much out of this. You had to adjust your plans. I'm cool with that.'

'Okay. Listen, I want to talk to you about David Reinnike. Can you meet me at Musso's? We could have a late breakfast.'

'Look, Cole, what is this, a mercy meal? You don't

have to feed me today to make up for last night. It's not like I don't have a life.'

'I'm not trying to make it up. I still need a way to find Reinnike, and I want your opinion.'

She hesitated.

'C'mon, Starkey. Please.'

'Begging is good, Cole. Begging, I like. I'll meet you in twenty minutes.'

She hung up before I could say something smart.

Musso & Frank Grill on Hollywood Boulevard was a five-minute walk from the Hollywood station. It's been in the same location since 1938, hunkered down behind glass-paned doors that have kept the restaurant safe since Hollywood's early beginnings when movie stars and studio heads filled the back tables. They've served pretty much the same menu since 1938, too. When other restaurants in L.A. went light with nouvelle cuisine, Musso's piled on butter and salt. Hollywood declined in the sixties when street people, prostitutes, and crime sprouted on the boulevard. The city decayed into a crime-ridden slum, but Musso's survived all that, and flourished. Maybe because of its history, or maybe because of the tough old men who served as the waiters and simply refused to let such a good thing die. It was and always has been one of my favorite restaurants. I liked it that they refused to change. The world caught up to them again. It was a good place to eat.

I parked in the back lot and made my way inside. Diners lined the counter, and most of the red-leather booths were already filled with the typical Musso cross-section of businessmen, studio flacks, musicians, and bookies. Starkey was already seated in a narrow booth in the center aisle, set up with water and a couple of menus. I put Reinnike's file and the news clips between us as I took the bench across from her.

'Hey. Thanks for meeting me.'

Starkey looked uncharacteristically pleased with herself.

'Don't try to feel me up or anything, Cole. I don't put out on the first date.'

Starkey's comment left me feeling awkward, especially when three women in the next booth glanced over.

'Look, I'm sorry if we had a misunderstanding. I didn't mean for last night to be a *date* date. It was just dinner.'

'I was teasing you, Cole. You're so fricking easy to tease.'

Starkey popped two antacid tablets when the waiter took our orders. I went with a Denver omelet; Starkey ordered a tongue sandwich. When the waiter left, Starkey glanced at the reports and articles.

'I don't know what I can tell you about this.'

'If Chen can't pull the registration, I'm out of ways to find George. Finding David might be as good as finding George.'

I tapped David Reinnike's file.

'Did you read it or just pass it along?'

'I read it. That kid had problems.'

'Yeah, he did, but there was only this one arrest in his record. The newspapers said the neighbors called the police three or four times on this kid.'

Starkey shrugged.

'It's newspapers, Cole. Newspapers get everything wrong. But even if it's true, the police roll out, somebody agrees to pay for somebody else's broken window, everyone calms down, and that's the end of it. The cops could have rolled out a dozen times – two dozen – and we wouldn't know.'

'I'm not looking at it that way, Starkey. I'm coming at it from the other direction. The detective who covered this case, Ferrier, recommended counseling. I'm thinking the counseling helped – that's how this kid was able to stay out of trouble. Can I find out who the counselor was?'

'Not from the police records. What's here is here.'

'Would Ferrier know?'

Starkey glanced at the three women, then shook her head.

'Ferrier retired in eighty-two and died in eighty-nine. I checked. I figured you might want to talk to him.'

I didn't know what else to say. I drank some water, then looked at the three women, too. George Reinnike wasn't in the database, only this single file existed about David, and there didn't seem any way to go forward with it.

Starkey fingered the pages one by one.

She said, 'Let me tell you something I learned on the Bomb Squad – you have a bomb, that bomb is going to explode.'

'What does that mean?'

'Just because this kid wasn't arrested again doesn't mean he was a model citizen. This boy was acting out violence and aggression over a significant period of time. I see kids like this all the time. Let me tell you, man, their arrests are just the tip of the iceberg – they get popped for one thing, there could be thirty or forty other incidents they get away with.'

'You don't think someone can change? You must see kids change all the time.'

'Yeah, I see change. I just don't expect it.'

She suddenly pushed the pages aside, and seemed embarrassed.

'Cole, look, I don't know why anyone does anything. I chased bomb cranks four years after I left the squad. These freaks were the sickest, most mentally fucked-up degenerates you can imagine. You know the difference between them and everyone else? Real people get the urge to do something weird, they don't do it. Assholes get the urge, they just do it.'

'No impulse control.'

'This kid had no impulse control. I see kids with no impulse control every day. That's why they have to deal with me; they get in trouble. But this isn't just some unhappy kid acting out a bad home life –'

She fingered through the report and articles, looking for examples.

'Assaulting this kid with a bat, pissing in this woman's yard – this is showing a lack of impulse control. But here where he throws the hammer at this car – she says he stood there laughing? – and here where he's in the middle of the street talking to himself? This is getting into psychosis.'

Starkey glanced up, and her eyes were serious.

'I've been thinking about this, Cole. Here you have a kid with this history, and he and his father up and disappear, leaving behind all this money? All right, no evidence was found linking their disappearance to a crime, but the Sheriffs were investigating check fraud and forgery – they thought the Reinnikes were victims. They weren't investigating a kid who would spear a collie with a garden stake. I'm thinking you should check out the unsolved violent crimes in their area just before they left.'

I nodded. It was a slow nod, but Starkey made sense. I could see it happening that way; George was protective of David, and defensive about him. He had gone to bat for David again and again, but had also made excuses for his son's behavior that bordered on denial. George might well have left to protect his son. He might have abandoned the money and never looked back.

'That's a good idea, Starkey. That's a really good idea.'

'Of course it is, Cole. It's also a long shot and totally unlikely, but it'll give you something to do in your spare time.'

I thought about it. George probably wouldn't have abandoned his money unless David had done something so bad that George was afraid David would go to prison or be taken away from him. It would have to be something serious; arson, or a crime against persons, like rape, armed robbery, or homicide.

I said, 'If I wanted a list of the open major crimes that occurred in Temecula between certain dates thirty-five years ago, could I get it?'

Starkey pouched out her lips, thinking, then opened her cell phone.

'Lemme make a couple of calls. I can find out.'

Starkey's cell phone worked perfectly, which left me annoyed. You try to be big about these things, but still. I thought she was calling Gittamon, but she phoned her former boss at the Criminal Conspiracy Section, instead; a lieutenant named Barry Kelso. CCS detectives investigated bombs and bombings, which is what

Starkey did after she left the Bomb Squad. She copied a number Kelso gave her, then called someone on the Sheriffs named Braun.

'Barry Kelso told me you could help. This is Detective Carol Starkey, LAPD Bomb Squad.'

When I arched my eyebrows at her, Starkey covered the phone.

'You say Bomb Squad, it gets people's attention.'

She asked Braun if he could provide a list of unsolved felony crimes that had occurred in and around the city of Temecula in the fourteen days prior to the Reinnikes' disappearance thirty-five years ago. Braun must have asked why she wanted the information. Starkey's voice grew frosty.

'All I can tell you is it involves bomb components and national security. Don't ask any more than that.'

Braun must have been impressed. They spent another ten minutes on the phone, with Braun asking questions designed to narrow the search. When they finished, Starkey covered the phone again to ask my fax number, then passed it to Braun.

She said, 'Okay, I'm going to give you my home fax number. You can fax the information to me here.'

That was it. She closed her phone and looked at me.

'We'll see. He isn't sure what he can come up with. It might take a couple of days.'

I said, 'Thanks, Carol. Really.'

She nodded, but pursed her mouth again as if she still had something to say. She stared at the women in the next booth again, then glanced back at me. She laid her hand on Reinnike's file. She placed her palm carefully, as if she were touching something delicate. She shook her head.

'You don't believe this clown is related to you, do you?'

'No.'

'George isn't your father. That would be absurd, thinking George was your father. Everything you've told me says it doesn't add up. You see that, don't you?'

'I realize that. I know.'

'I don't care what he thought or that he had those clippings with him; he was delusional.'

I wanted Starkey to stop talking about it. I glanced at the three women.

'I know what you're saying.'

'Then why don't you stop this nonsense?'

Starkey was hunched forward on the table, staring at me. She did not look away. I didn't look away, either.

'George went into that alley with pictures of me. He went in thinking I was his son. Maybe he even went in thinking I would be there. I don't know why he had the pictures and did that, but I want to know. The only way I can find out is to find someone who can tell me. I don't want to just write him off as crazy because then I'll never really know; not *really*. I need someone to tell me. I need to see it for myself. Do you see that?'

'I just don't want you to get hurt with this stuff.'

I nodded, and made a little smile. That was nice of her to say.

She said, 'In the alley, when Diaz told you and you saw the clippings – before you knew all this other stuff – did you hope it was true? Did you want him to be your father?'

The answer to that one was easy.

'Someone is. Somewhere.'

Starkey laid her hand on mine. She gave me a squeeze.

'I gotta get back to work.'

She slid out of the booth, but I didn't get up. Starkey bent to kiss my cheek. When she leaned to kiss me, her hair fell forward. I had never seen Starkey from that angle. She was pretty.

CHAPTER 41

When I left Starkey at the Musso & Frank Grill, I thought about swinging past my office, but didn't. My office was close to Musso, and dropping in would have been easy, but I didn't; I was anxious to hear from Braun and Chen, so I blew off the office and hurried back to my home. I should have gone to my office. Everything would have played out differently if only I had gone to my office.

But my instinct to go directly home paid off in its way – a fax was waiting in my machine by the time I reached home. The cover letter was addressed to Starkey, recapping that Braun had limited the search to unresolved Crimes Against Persons occurring thirty miles or less from Temecula, resulting in twenty-seven entries. Braun had worked fast thanks to Starkey's magic words: Bomb Squad.

I brought the pages to my couch, and read through them. The individual entries were each no more than a few lines written in an abbreviated shorthand that read like code –

SDC#R4123; 05/12/70; rsp. 1120hrs; AGR. ASLT/RBY;
1255 Park Dr/Murrieta/prv.res;VIC Ronald L. Peters,
wht, 41; aslt w/entrg hm/weap.red brick.RAS/DNS
aslnt;no wit;no arr; no sus. Ofc #664.

The first entry described an aggravated assault and
robbery that had taken place in Murrieta, California,
which I knew to be five or six miles north of Temecula.
The victim was a forty-one-year-old white male named
Ronald Peters, who was assaulted while entering his
home by an unknown assailant wielding a brick. The
brick was recovered at the scene, but Peters did not
see his assailant, no one else witnessed the crime, and
the police had no suspects. The Reinnikes probably
hadn't disappeared to flee assault and robbery charges.
Peters had probably flashed too much cash in a bar, and
been followed home in what amounted to a crime of
opportunity.

Most of the entries were assaults and armed robberies like the first, but I found two rapes that gave me
pause. The rapes occurred on consecutive nights about
a week before the Reinnikes disappeared. The first
happened ten miles south of Temecula, the next
twelve miles east. Both victims were abducted by two
masked assailants driving a white van. I wondered how
I could find out if George Reinnike had a white van at
the time he lived in Temecula. I made a note about it
and moved on.

The next several entries were lightweight armed
robberies and assaults, but then I reached a homicide.
Kenneth Dupris had been murdered in Sun City, eight
miles south of Temecula, and nine days before the
Reinnikes disappeared. He had been murdered at home.

The cause-of-death abbreviation was MLTP KNF/HD – an unknown subject had repeatedly stabbed Dupris in the head. The entry noted that Dupris's dog had also been stabbed. I made another note.

When I read the eighth entry on the third page, the context of everything changed –

SDC#H5009; 05/22/70; rsp. 1915hrs; HOM (MLP - 3); 625 Court Ln/Temecula/prv.res;VIC H. Diaz, m, mex, 36; VIC M. Diaz, f, mex, 32; VIC R. Diaz, m, mex, 12MC; COD BFT; aslt in hm/weap.bbbat/RAS;WIT K. Diaz, f, mex, 4MC;no arr; no sus. Ofc(s) #716, 952. DME#FG877-2.

A family had been beaten to death with a baseball bat nine days before the Reinnikes disappeared. The ages and genders of the victims indicated they were a father, mother, and son. The only surviving member of their family was a four-year-old girl, who was also the only witness. The victims were named Diaz. The surviving child was K. Diaz.

I went into the kitchen, drank a glass of water, then read the entry again. K. Diaz. I checked the dates, then did the math. K. Diaz would now be about the same age as Kelly Diaz, but the name Diaz was as common as Smith or Johnson. The L.A. general directory contained thousands of people named Diaz.

I was still thinking about it when my phone rang. It was Chen.

'That guy Pardy is a prick. He said I had to do for him like I do for you. He said if I don't help him out, he'll report me for doing outside work on LAPD time.'

'John, I will cover you, okay? Did you get a chance to look at the image?'

'Yeah, yeah – I got all seven digits. The vehicle shows to a Payne L. Keller in Canyon Camino. That's by Magic Mountain.'

Canyon Camino was a small community north of the San Fernando Valley, twenty minutes away.

'Is it stolen?'

'Not even an outstanding ticket. Either Keller loaned Reinnike the car, or Keller was another alias like Herbert Faustina.'

Chen gave me the address on the registration. I asked if he had told Pardy.

'Yeah, he told me to call him first, that prick. I gotta call Beckett, too. Beckett has to notify the next of kin, so they'll be calling up there.'

'Thanks, John. Thanks for the good work. I appreciate it.'

'That isn't you, is it? His next of kin?'

'No, it isn't me. I just got a little carried away.'

Chen sounded awkward.

'Okay. Well. I'm sorry.'

'Don't be.'

I put down the phone, feeling torn between Keller's address and Braun's letter. Braun had included two phone numbers. I reached him at his office and tried to sound businesslike. Payne Keller would have to wait.

'Mr. Braun, my name is Cole. I'm working with Detective Starkey on the matter you discussed.'

'That's right. Did she get those faxes?'

'That's why I'm calling, sir. We have an interest in learning more about one of these cases. We'd like to see the file.'

'Those files would be in storage. What I sent were computer summaries.'

'We have an urgent interest in one of these files. Could you tell us where it is located?'

'Are you with the Bomb Squad, too?'

'I can't discuss my agency, sir, but our interest is urgent.'

'All right, well, okay. What's the file number? I have to get to my desk.'

I read off the file number while he went to his desk, and then he told me how to find the file. I could have taken five minutes longer before leaving my house. I could have used the bathroom or fed the cat or washed a few dishes. It all would have worked out better if I had killed a few minutes, but I didn't. I was in a hurry. I left.

CHAPTER 42

Frederick

Frederick returned to Cole's house. The carport was empty, and just as when he arrived the previous day, no one appeared home. Frederick left his truck around the curve at the same construction site, then sat in the same olive trees to watch Cole's house, but neither Cole nor the police officer who was guarding him appeared. After thirty minutes, Frederick didn't hesitate.

He walked straight out of the trees, up the street, and knocked at Cole's front door. No one answered. He tried the knob, but the door was locked. He walked through the carport around the side of the house, and found a likely window.

Frederick popped Cole's kitchen window, hoisted himself up with a grunt, and shimmied over the sill into Cole's kitchen. Once he was inside Cole's house, he took the shotgun from its case.

Cole had to come home sooner or later. Frederick decided to wait.

CHAPTER 43

The Sheriffs kept their records in a five-floor gray building south of the train yards at Union Station. A long train rumbled past the parking lot as I parked. The ground trembled with the strain of steel crushing into steel like a slow-motion earthquake. I waited for the caboose, but cars kept coming in a steady line. A low mist of dust was kicked up in the parking lot by the tremor. I trembled, too. I waited, but more cars came, and the line didn't end. I finally went inside.

A middle-aged woman was seated behind a narrow counter like the service counter at an auto-parts store. They don't let people walk in off the street to search their files; a sworn officer had to provide a badge and case number, then wait while the clerk found the file. I had convinced Braun that time was crucial. He had been kind enough to call ahead.

I said, 'Long train.'

'You get used to it.'

'My name is Cole. Sergeant Braun called to request a file.'

She peered at me, then went to a wire shopping cart

that was parked beside her desk. She took out a dingy black file box and brought it to the counter. The file number was handwritten on the box's spine.

'That's right. I brought it up, but that file is not available. Someone checked it out, and didn't return it. That happens sometimes.'

I could tell the box was empty by the way she placed it on the counter and spun it toward me. She flipped open the lid to show me. Empty. The Diaz file was missing.

I said, 'Is there a sign-out log?'

'Oh, sure, there should be.'

She took a yellowed card from a sleeve attached to the outside of the file box. Everyone who requested the files had to sign for them, like an old-fashioned library card. She glanced at it, then placed it on the counter.

'These people must think they're all doctors, the way they write.'

Three people had requested the file since it turned cold. The first two names were Alvarez and Tolbert, both of whom had revisited the file on separate occasions more than twenty years ago. A third entry was scrawled and difficult to read, but I could make out enough of the letters. Det. K. Diaz. Diaz had taken the file almost eight years ago, and never returned it.

I thanked the clerk, then went back to my car. The train was gone. The earth no longer shook with its enormous rolling weight, but somehow the parking lot and train yard seemed smaller without it. I called Diaz on her cell, but her message picked up. I asked her to call, then phoned her office. A duty detective named Pierson answered.

'She isn't here.'

'When do you expect her?'

'Got no idea, man. You want to leave word?'

'How about Pardy?'

'Pardy isn't here, either.'

I left word they should call, then hung up. Police officers never list themselves in the phone book. They stay unlisted so the criminal sociopaths they arrest can't shoot out their windows. But Diaz had given me her cell number, and cell accounts have billing addresses. I called a friend of mine at the phone company. She used the number to identify Diaz's cell provider, from whom she obtained the billing address. A cop would need a court order for something like this, but Dodgers tickets work even better.

I looked up the address on my Thomas Brothers, then went to see what I would find.

Diaz lived south of Sunset Boulevard in Silver Lake, on a winding street that had once been crowded with Central American refugees. The bottom half of her duplex had recently been painted a bright turquoise blue, but the tiny front lawn was nappy from poor care. I parked on the upslope, then went to her door. I knocked. The building was so small the pounding must have filled the little apartment.

'Diaz, it's Cole.'

I tried the door, then stepped back and studied the up-stairs apartment to see if anyone was home. I couldn't tell. I knocked again.

'Diaz?'

A horn honked behind me. I turned, and saw Pardy idling in the street. I wondered if he had been watching the house or following me. He tapped his horn again, and waved me over.

'What are you doing here, Cole?'

I hesitated. I wanted to tell him about the murder book, but I also wanted to see what was inside her house.

'I dropped by to see her. How about you?'

Pardy glanced toward the apartment like he knew I was lying, and ignored my question.

'Is she home?'

'She didn't answer.'

'Didn't answer her phone, either. C'mon, get in.'

'I'm okay.'

'It's too hot to stand out there. C'mon, sit where it's cool.'

I went around the tail of his car, and got in. He studied me, and I wondered what he was thinking.

He said, 'Diaz never told me you were friends. How do you know where she lives?'

'She gave me her address.'

'Was she expecting you?'

'I just dropped around. I wanted to talk about Reinnike.'

Pardy nodded, but didn't comment, and I wondered again why he was here.

'How about you, Pardy? Are you close to making an arrest?'

'I'm working on it.'

'So you came over to talk about it with Diaz.'

'That's right.'

'Why not just talk at the office?'

Pardy checked his rearview mirror, then studied her apartment as if he expected to see something new. He made no move to move the car.

'Let me ask you something, Cole. Did you find anything that explains why Reinnike had those clippings?'

'No.'

'Nothing that connects you to him?'

'Nothing.'

Pardy stared at me, and I stared back. He glanced at her apartment again, and I was sure we suspected the same things. He just couldn't bring himself to say it.

'Now I have a question for you, Pardy. What if I said a cop killed him? What would you say to that?'

'I'd say you'd better have your facts together and your ass covered. I'd say you better have a slam-dunk case with every *i* dotted and *t* crossed. If you don't, you'd damned well better keep your mouth shut until you do.'

'Did you talk to Chen?'

'Yeah, about the registration. I spoke to the sheriff up in Canyon Camino a couple of hours ago. Keller owns a gas station up there. So far as the sheriff knew, Keller never said anything about a son. He said Keller lived alone.'

'Do they know why he came to L.A.?'

'Didn't even know he was missing. They're going to try to locate a next of kin.'

'Did you tell them about the arrest you're thinking about?'

Pardy put the dark eyes on me again.

'Why would I talk out my ass like that?'

'You not being able to dot the *i*'s and cross the *t*'s.'

'That's right. I'm going to work on it right now. I'm going to take off, and I won't be back, but I'll be nearby. Maybe you and I will talk later.'

He stared at me steadily when he said it, and I knew he was giving me the green light to go into her house. We were both thinking that Kelly Diaz had something to do with Reinnike's death.

I got out of his car.

'Okay, Pardy. I'll see you.'

He leaned across the seat and held out his card.

'Take my cell. You might need to call me.'

CHAPTER 44

I watched Pardy drive away, then walked around the side of Diaz's apartment to a cracked cement courtyard overgrown with bougainvillea. A small balcony hung out from the second floor with wooden steps going up to a narrow door. A similar door was tucked beneath the balcony. It took eight minutes to pick the locks.

Diaz had a small place, with one bedroom and a bath sprouting off the kitchen and living room. The furniture was mismatched and spare, with the temporary quality of a resident hotel, as if Diaz was only passing through on the way to somewhere else.

The murder book was on her dining table. She hadn't hidden it, or even attempted to hide it. Like every other murder book, it was a dark three-ring binder. Her family name was written on the binder's spine. Diaz.

I walked through her apartment because you always have to walk through, looking for bodies or lurkers, then returned to the table. I sat with the murder book just as she must have sat. I opened it.

The pages felt thin, but weren't yellow or brittle. The first document was a standard form stating the

318

facts of the crime. The lead detective was identified as Detective-Sergeant Max Alvarez, but the form was signed by Detective Korvin Tolbert. Leads often left the paperwork to their partners.

At 1915 hrs on 22 May 69, RO/s Padilla (#1344) and Bigelow (#6191) entered private residence at 625 Court Lane, Temecula, in response to summons by neighbors. Upon entering residence, RO/s observed three deceased (see below) and surviving minor child (see below). RO/s secured scene. Detectives M. Alvarez (#716) and K. Tolbert (#1952) arrived 2025 hrs. At that time, Coroner's Office pronounced victims dead of apparent homicide.

Photo ID (DL) found at scene and vis. ident. by neighbors (see below) provided prelim. identification of victims as Herman Eduardo Diaz, age 36; his wife, Maria Diaz, age 32; their son, Richard Raul Diaz, age 12. Confirmed ID pending Medical Examiner. Initial indications were the three suffered severe blunt-force trauma to the head. A 30-inch Louisville Slugger baseball bat was recovered at the scene, and has been submitted for tests. Bat evidenced blood, tissue, and hair. (See below.)

Neighbors identified unharmed female minor child as Kelly Louise Diaz, age 4, the daughter of Herman and Maria. No attempt was made to question child at scene. Child was taken into custody by Children's Services pending next of kin.

When I saw the little girl's full name, my breath hissed out in a soft low sigh. Kelly Diaz's family had been bludgeoned to death with a baseball bat twelve-point-two miles from the Reinnikes' house, nine days before the Reinnikes disappeared. Kenneth Dupris's dog had been stabbed to death two days earlier. David Reinnike had been accused of stabbing a collie, and had once attacked another child with a baseball bat. Thirty-five years later, LAPD Detective Kelly Diaz had been the only one present when David Reinnike's father, George, was murdered in an alley.

The first report was only three pages long. Tolbert had written it on the morning after the murder, so his initial facts were spare, but later that day he attached reports written by the responding officers, and statements from neighbors. The victims were discovered by a neighbor who had gone to ask if her children could stay with the Diaz family that night while she visited a hospitalized friend. She believed them to be home because their cars were in the drive. No one responded to her knocking, but the door was ajar, so she pushed it open and announced her presence. That's when she saw Maria Diaz lying on the blood-saturated carpet.

A sketch followed the initial statements, showing the location of the bodies and the baseball bat. Each body was a little stick figure with initials written beside it. Tolbert noted that the premises had not been vandalized, the vehicles had not been stolen, and nothing appeared to be missing. Robbery was not considered a motive, but would not be ruled out until further investigation.

The next pages contained photographs of the crime scene. The first showed Maria Diaz facedown behind a couch. Her head was a red mass of hair and tissue. She was wearing shorts and a black T-shirt emblazoned with MOTHERS OF INVENTION.

Herman Diaz was in the second picture. He was on his back, staring at a ceiling he could not see. The blood had pooled around his head, fanning from his face like red petals.

The third picture showed their twelve-year-old son, Richard. He was partially hidden under the kitchen table, but a thin smear of red trailed across the floor as if left by a mop. Her brother had been trying to escape.

I felt light-headed, and realized I had stopped breathing. I looked up and breathed deeply.

I flipped past pictures of splatter patterns and smudgy footprints. Sheriffs Department criminalists had isolated a partial thumbprint on the kitchen door and three print fragments on the baseball bat, but had been unable to establish an identity. They also found partial impressions on the kitchen floor consistent with a cleated, size-twelve work boot, suggesting an adult male assailant of average size and weight.

Most of the remaining reports, statements, and interviews were entered into the murder book during the three weeks following the crime. Tolbert entered the lab reports as they arrived, but their results – like the interviews and the rest of the investigation – offered nothing useful. No suspects had been identified, and after a time the investigation turned cold.

Tolbert's last report was dated sixteen weeks after the murders. Maria's sister, Teresa Evans, had gone through her sister's possessions, and reported that a heart-shaped necklace was missing. The necklace was described as a simple silver heart that had originally belonged to their grandmother. She told Tolbert that Maria wore it as her everyday necklace, but it was not among the items returned to the family by the coroner, and had not been found in the house. Teresa had sent Tolbert a picture of Maria Diaz wearing the necklace. Tolbert had entered the picture into the murder book. Maria Diaz was wearing a bright spring dress. Her shoulders were tanned and pretty, and she was standing on someone's patio at twilight. She could have been Kelly Diaz's sister. The necklace stood out plainly. Kelly Diaz had been wearing the necklace when I went to see her at Central Station, and on the morning I stood with her over George Reinnike's body.

I closed the murder book, then went to the kitchen. I turned on the tap, and cupped my hand under the cool stream to drink. When I finished, I wiped my hand on my pants, then returned to the dining room.

Alvarez and Tolbert hadn't tied the Reinnikes to the murders because their disappearance was never reported; they had simply paid their rent and vanished. Their landlord had no reason to suspect a crime, and was happy to be rid of them. Six years later when the police busted his then-current tenant for mail fraud, the murders were forgotten news. Nothing in the murder book identified the Reinnikes as suspects, but Kelly Diaz had ended up in an alley with George Reinnike. And clippings about me.

Diaz probably hadn't found Reinnike; George had probably found her. He paid them to pray. After a lifetime of guilt, George had probably sought out Diaz to beg her forgiveness, and brought her mother's necklace as proof that he was involved in the killings. Even his alias spoke to his guilt: Keller . . . Kelly. He had taken her name as he had desecrated his flesh – to suffer a daily reminder of his sin. Reinnike probably hadn't known of me, and had never heard of me; he had come to Los Angeles looking for Kelly Diaz.

The more I thought about it, the more convinced I became that Diaz planted the clippings about me. She planted the key card in the alley and more clippings in Reinnike's motel room to hook me into tracing Reinnike, and it had worked. Maybe Reinnike confessed everything to Diaz except for David's whereabouts, so she needed a way to find him that wouldn't put herself at the forefront of the search. Me. The World's Greatest Detective would find David, then she could kill him just as she had killed his father.

I dialed her cell again, but her message still answered. I called Pardy.

CHAPTER 45

Starkey

Starkey walked from Musso back to her office, feeling sullen and antsy. The morning sun beat hard through the broken sky, making her sweat on the short walk back to Hollywood Station. Her collar itched, and so did her scars. She wanted to peel off her blazer, but the blazer hid her pistol, so she slogged on. Starkey wished it was still raining. She wanted to walk in the rain with limp dangling hair and smoke soggy cigarettes and show everyone she was perfectly purely pathetic.

She loved Cole more than ever.

She realized – the two of them sitting in Musso's with Starkey trying to keep her feelings in check like some kind of crash-test dummy – that Cole kept himself buried; he hid behind flashy shirts and funny banter not unlike how his friend Pike hid behind dark glasses and a stone face. But hidden is hidden; for a moment just now in Musso's, Cole had let Starkey see the hidden and hurting part of himself, and now she loved him even more deeply. For letting her see. For trusting her.

God*damn* it sucked being her.

Starkey stripped off the jacket as soon as she reached her desk. She forced Cole out of her head by organizing the reports on her desk. She had just closed a teenaged prostitution case. All that was left was correcting her report. She had just gotten her head into it when Metcalf strolled by with a fresh cup of coffee.

'How's it going, Starkey? Did Cole come across for the little favor you did?'

When she glanced up, Metcalf leered, and pushed out his cheek with his tongue. He laughed as he went to his desk.

Starkey stared at the report, but now the feelings for Cole filled her again, and – just like that – she made up her mind.

Starkey decided to lay it on the line. She would tell Cole exactly how she felt about him; no more biting her tongue, no more hoping the goofy doof would wake up to realize Starkey was the real deal and Lady Puffin-stuff Southern Belle was yesterday's news. Some guys, you had to put it straight up their noses, and Cole – clearly – was one of them. If he freaked, then he freaked; if he chose Lady Macbeth, then –

Starkey pushed away that thought.

She ate two antacids, slugged down some water, then ate two more.

She squared the report again, then eyeballed Metcalf, muttering into his phone at his desk. He was either taking notes or talking to one of his girlfriends. His coffee was still steaming in its cup. He needed one of those cups with a slogan on the side: World's Biggest Asshole.

Starkey got up, slipped on her blazer, then walked over to Metcalf on her way out.

'Hey, Ronnie.'

Metcalf looked up.

Starkey pushed her tongue into her cheek like she was giving a blow job, then tipped his steaming coffee into his lap. Metcalf shrieked as he stumbled out of his chair. He was still hopping and cursing when Starkey left.

She headed for Cole's house.

CHAPTER 46

'It's Diaz. Diaz killed George Reinnike.'

Pardy said, 'I'm listening.'

'Her family was murdered when she was four years old. Father, mother, and brother – she was the only survivor. Did you know that?'

Pardy made a soft whistle in the phone.

'No. I had no idea. I figured her for the shooting, but I had no idea. Jesus.'

'The original murder book is here in her house. The Reinnikes disappeared eight days after the murders. They are not named in the investigation, but the silver heart she wears belonged to her mother. It was reported missing at the time of the crime. That's all in the book. The investigators believed the killer had taken it as a trophy. Now she's wearing it. I think Reinnike brought it to prove who he was.'

'She could say she had a copy made.'

'She can say anything she wants. I'm telling you she's good for it, and you know it, too – that's why you didn't care about Golden.'

Pardy hesitated, like he still had trouble admitting what we both knew.

'I had her for it, I just didn't know why. I have the gun.'

'The murder weapon?'

'One of my street people found it behind Union Station. A Browning .380. Your boy Chen just matched it to the bullet in Reinnike. It's not clean, but I can put the gun with her.'

'Your own private Walk-in Wednesday.'

'I couldn't have made the connection without that, Cole. This gun was used in a murder last year up at the top of Angels Flight. Wits saw the gun at the scene, but somehow that weapon wasn't recovered. Diaz worked that case, Cole. That gives her access.'

'Thin.'

'You're goddamned right it's thin, so I need the *i*'s dotted. I have two wits who saw Reinnike with a dark-haired woman the night he was killed. I gotta have time to put that together. This business about her family gives me enough to go to O'Loughlin. Here I am, my first lead, and I'm making a case where it looks like the shooter is a senior detective in my own station. I need this thing stitched before I bring it forward.'

'What are you going to do?'

'Leave everything like you found it and get out. I can put together a search warrant, and go to O'Loughlin. He's going to shit, but he'll do the right thing.'

I thought about Chen calling Pardy and Beckett.

'Did she get the ID information about Payne Keller?'

Pardy hesitated, so I knew that she had. She could have gotten Keller's address from O'Loughlin, or she might have called Chen herself.

'Pardy, she's on her way up there. If she has Reinnike's address, she's going for his son.'

'Just settle down, forchrissake. We don't even know David Reinnike is still alive, let alone whether he was with his old man. We need to get together our evidence, then bring her in nice and easy. This woman is an LAPD homicide detective.'

'If she finds him, she'll kill him. That will make it even worse.'

'And if she finds out we're onto her she'll take off or lawyer up, or maybe do something even more stupid. I've already spoken with the sheriff up there. Reinnike lived alone. As far as the sheriff knew, he didn't have any family, so there's probably nobody to find.'

'Then where is she, Pardy?'

'Let's take it easy. Let me talk to O'Loughlin, and then we'll head up to take a look – I don't want this to get out about Diaz until we have her in custody.'

'Take all the time you want, Pardy – I'm going.'

I hung up, and went out to my car.

CHAPTER 47

Frederick

Cole had a pretty nice place; it was small, with a tiny bedroom and bath on the ground floor and a loft bedroom and bath up above. The high pointy ceiling made it feel more like a cabin or a tree house than a real house. Frederick fantasized moving in after he killed Cole. He knew it was only a fantasy, but he liked the idea.

Frederick quickly checked the rooms, then returned to Cole's kitchen. He searched through the drawers, and selected a chopping knife with a heavy blade. He thought he might try to stab Cole instead of shooting him – less noise. Then he could go to work with the vise-grip pliers.

Frederick peeked out the curtained kitchen door into the empty carport, then went into the living room. He was getting used to being in the house, and feeling more relaxed. He saw the papers spread over Cole's table. The top page was a newspaper article about the disappearance of George and David Reinnike.

Coldness swept over Frederick, and the house swelled around him, growing huge and cavernous.

He pushed through the other papers, finding more newspaper accounts and what appeared to be official-looking police documents. A bill from the Home Away Suites was part of Cole's file. Then he saw Payne's name and address scrawled in the margin of one of the documents.

Frederick's eyes burned, and he trembled.

Cole had everything.

The voices whispered as Frederick searched the papers and documents for his own name. Cole had Payne's name and address, but not Frederick's. Cole was probably up at Payne's right now. Frederick wouldn't find him here at his house; he would find him at Payne's. Frederick saw Cole's path in an intuitive flash: Cole would search Payne's house, then go to the station. Elroy would tell Cole about Frederick, and Cole would go to his home. Frederick saw it unfolding with a pure bright clarity, and knew what to do. He would find Cole in Canyon Camino, and that's where he would kill him.

Frederick decided to go. He decided to let himself out through the kitchen door. He had left the table and was crossing the kitchen when a car pulled into the carport.

Cole!

Frederick's face split into a wide jagged grin, and he ran to the door, but when he peeked past the edge of the curtain he saw it was a woman.

CHAPTER 48

Starkey

Starkey frowned when she saw that Cole's car was gone. Just her goddamned luck, having to put off the big scene after she worked up her nut. She turned into his empty carport and shut off her car.

'Damnit.'

Starkey lit a cigarette. She fumed as she smoked, then decided to call him. She fished her cell phone from her purse, but when she tried to speed-dial his number, her phone couldn't lock on to a signal.

Starkey said, 'SonofaBITCH!'

She thought it might be her battery, so she plugged the phone into the power cord trailing from the cigarette lighter. She still couldn't get a signal.

Starkey thought, well, shit, she'd use Cole's phone. She got out of her car, and went to the spare key she once saw him use. He kept it on the side of his house. She retrieved the key, returned to the carport, and let herself into the kitchen.

She crossed to the cordless phone cradled on the

counter between the kitchen and dining room, and pressed in the number for Cole's cell. She stood with her back to the living room, impatiently listening to the ring.

CHAPTER 49

Frederick

Frederick watched the woman getting out of her car, and realized she was the police officer who was guarding Cole's house. His pulse sped with horrific images of his capture and torture. He was caught in a panicked indecision between killing her or hiding, and he didn't know which to do. Secret cameras might be letting them watch his every move RIGHT NOW! More police might be surrounding Cole's house RIGHT NOW!

Yet, she wasn't hurrying. Her gun wasn't out. He didn't hear the sound of approaching sirens.

Frederick backed out of the kitchen, ran across the living room, and ducked into the entry closet. He clutched the shotgun across his chest, and gripped the knife tight. He heard her enter the house just as he pulled the door closed.

CHAPTER 50

Starkey

Starkey was about to hang up when Cole answered.

'Hello?'

Mr. Witty. She wanted to make a wisecrack, but didn't. Cole wasn't smarting off the way he usually did because he was hurting.

'Hey, it's me, Starkey. I'm standing in your house.'

She was about to launch into it when Cole cut her off.

'Starkey, it's Diaz. Diaz killed him.'

He went off into this blur of a story about the Reinnikes and Diaz, and Pardy building the case, and Diaz probably being on her way to Canyon Camino to find and kill David Reinnike. When Cole said he was going to stop her, Starkey flashed on her dream.

. . . his inevitable death.

'Cole, don't. Wait for Pardy.'

She felt it so deep a taste like cold nickels coated her tongue – the medicinal taste of his death.

He said, 'It'll be fine.'

It was the last thing he said, and then the signal was gone.

'Cole?'

Dead air.

'Goddamnit, Cole.'

Starkey punched the redial on his phone, but this time his voice mail picked up right away. No signal.

'SHIT!'

Carol Starkey had been dead, and then risen; she had been drunk, then sober; she had been a cop for thirteen years and had seen every imaginable human depravity; she did not believe in God; she did not believe in premonitions, telepathy, channeling, ESP, clairvoyance, remote viewing, fortune-telling, astrology, or the afterlife. She believed that Cole would be killed.

'SHIT!! *SHITSHITSHIT*!'

She punched in the number and waited out the ring. His personal number. The one he gave her.

'Yes.'

'Pike. Pike, it's me.'

Starkey told him where to meet her, and told him why.

CHAPTER 51

Frederick

Frederick heard the door slam when she left. He listened to her engine roar, and the rubber shriek as she shredded away. Then he opened the door.

There in Cole's closet, he made peace with his own death, which was preordained and certain. They were too many against him, Cole and all these others. They were tightening their net, they would find him, and they would kill him. It was the punishment Payne had predicted. It had finally come to pass, and in a swell of emotion that filled his eyes with tears, Frederick realized now the truth of why Payne had gone to Los Angeles without telling him – Payne had gone to protect him. Payne had sacrificed himself in the final demonstration of his love.

Frederick could do no less.

Cole was going to Payne's, and that's where Frederick would find him. Frederick went back to his car, and drove hard toward Payne's home.

CHAPTER 52

The I-5 curved across the eastern edge of the San Fernando Valley and through the Newhall Pass. Hundreds of thousands of commuters followed that route every day, traveling to and from the bedroom communities that sprout from the freeways like budding flowers. Most everyone turns east when they reach Newhall, where the rolling hills and desert flats are covered with housing developments. The land wasn't flat to the west. The mountains grew steep overlooking Magic Mountain, and the little towns tucked in the pine-filled ridges felt isolated even though they were only twenty minutes from the city. Canyon Camino was a good place to hide.

The Sheriffs Substation was a small brown building located between a convenience store and a video store. I parked at the video store, and walked to the Sheriffs.

A slender deputy in a khaki uniform was leaning back with his feet up, talking on the phone when I walked in. He dropped his feet when he saw me, and hung up.

'Can I help you?'

His name tag read *Biggins*. I identified myself, showed him my license, then put Pardy's card on the counter.

'I'm here about a local named Payne Keller. Detective Pardy at LAPD spoke with someone.'

'I was here. What a bunch of crap, getting killed like that. The sheriff's out now, letting people know. He had to secure Payne's house. What a bunch of crap.'

'When is the sheriff getting back?'

'All I can tell you is he'll get back when he gets back. We been real busy this morning.'

'It's going to get even busier. Pardy is coming up, and a couple of other homicide cops are going to meet us here. Has Detective Diaz checked in?'

'You're the first.'

'Maybe she called.'

'A woman?'

'Yeah.'

'Someone from Sheriffs Homicide called – Mullen, I think she said. Then there was Pardy and someone named Beckett –'

Diaz had probably posed as Mullen.

'Okay. I need directions to Keller's house, and I'm also interested in talking to his friends. Maybe you could give me a few names.'

Biggins was looking nervous.

'Tell me again – what's your involvement in this?'

'I'm working for the family.'

I tapped Pardy's card.

'Call Pardy. He knows I'm working the case, and he's good with it. Give him a call.'

Biggins frowned at the card, then pushed it aside.

'I didn't know Payne that well, just to trade a cup of

coffee when I rolled by his station. I lived in Riverside before we moved up here.'

'He had a gas station?'

'Yeah, a little bit out of town – Payne's Car Care.'

'Did he have a family?'

'Listen, why don't you talk to one of those guys at the station. He has two guys out there.'

Biggins gave me directions to Keller's home, and said I would pass Keller's gas station on the way. He told me that Keller's employees were Elroy Lewis and Frederick Conrad, and that either one of them might be able to answer my questions. Biggins was helpful. After I copied the directions, I wrote out my cell number, tore off the page, and put it beside Pardy's card.

'If I miss the sheriff and he gets back, tell him I need to talk to him. It's important.'

Biggins glanced at the number.

'Cell phones don't work up here. You can't get a signal with the mountains.'

'I live in the middle of Los Angeles, and I can't get a signal.'

Biggins laughed.

'It was like that in Riverside, too.'

I turned to leave, then stopped.

'If Diaz or Mullen check in, tell them I'm here. Tell Diaz I asked after her parents, and she should talk to me before she does anything.'

'Okay. Sure.'

'There's something else you and the sheriff should know. Pardy didn't know this earlier, or he would have told you. Payne Keller and his son are suspects in a multiple homicide. If Keller's son is up here, he will be dangerous.'

Biggins stared at me without comprehension.
I nodded toward the transceiver.
'You should tell the sheriff.'

CHAPTER 53

Frederick

Payne's cabin was as lonely as yesterday, but that was good. The air still carried the smoky scent of the fires he had used. It wasn't so bad. It smelled like a cold fireplace.

Frederick unlocked the front door, then stepped into Payne's living room. He was trying to decide where best to wait for Cole when a car pulled up the drive. Frederick jumped at the sound, and hurried to the window, thinking –

'You bastard! This is what you're going to get for Payne, you bastard!'

But when he looked, it wasn't Cole; it was the Canyon Camino sheriff, Guy Rossi.

Frederick stood back from the window, watching as Rossi parked alongside his truck. The sheriff eyed Frederick's truck, probably wondering who it belonged to. The sheriff walked along the length of the truck, and that's when Frederick saw the shovel. Here he had been driving all over Los Angeles, here he had worked so hard at cleaning up Payne's place to get rid of the evidence, and the shovel he used to dig up the stuff was still in his truck. The shovel, with evidence on its blade.

Sonofamotherfuckingbitch.

He had forgotten to clean the shovel.

The sheriff started toward the house.

Frederick set the shotgun behind Payne's couch, then put on the face and stepped out. Maybe Cole had already spoken with the sheriff. No, not likely – a murderer wouldn't talk to the cops.

Frederick said, 'Boy, this sure is a sad day.'

Rossi stared when Frederick appeared on the porch. In that moment, out of context, it was obvious the sheriff didn't recognize him.

Frederick said, 'It's me, Frederick Conrad. I work for Payne.'

The sheriff finally placed him.

'I didn't expect anyone to be here. You heard the bad news?'

'Oh, yeah. I've been feeding Payne's cats. Payne has three cats around here somewhere. I don't know what's going to happen to them now.'

Frederick ambled over as he gave the sheriff the business about the cats, and stood so the sheriff had to face away from the shovel. Frederick shook his head sadly.

'I guess we can put up a sign at the station, try to find them a home. I could take one, maybe, but three –'

Frederick sighed heavily, as if the unfairness of what was about to happen to Payne's cats was crushing.

The sheriff seemed to consider Payne's house, then put his hands on his gun belt like he wasn't sure what to do next.

'Did Payne ask you to take care of'm before he went away?'

'Not before, no, sir. My understanding is it was some kinda family emergency. He called later and asked me to come out.'

The sheriff grunted like he wasn't really thinking about the cats.

'He tell you what happened?'

Frederick assumed the sheriff had already spoken with Elroy, so he fed out the same line.

'His sister was hurt in some kinda car wreck. They didn't think she was gonna make it.'

'He call you from Los Angeles?'

'He was in Sacramento.'

The sheriff grunted, and Frederick was suddenly worried the L.A. police had told the sheriff a lot more than he was letting on.

'He leave a number up there?'

'No, sir, he just said he would call back when he knew what he was going to do. That was the last time I heard from him.'

The sheriff drifted in a slow arc around Frederick toward the house. Rossi studied Payne's roof like he expected something to be up there. Then he studied the trees, then Payne's garage. Frederick didn't like the slow way the sheriff was moving and the way he studied everything. Frederick's palms grew clammy and a pulse started in his ears. *What did the sheriff know*?

Frederick said, 'You want me to leave the door open, or should I lock it?'

'You have a key?'

'Payne keeps one under the pot there.'

'Better give it to me. I'm gonna take a look around

344

before the L.A. people get here.'

Frederick gave him the key, wanting to move away from the truck but scared to do anything out of the ordinary.

The sheriff dropped the key into his pocket. He studied Frederick.

'I've been up at the Catholic church all morning. I understand Payne spent a lot of time up there.'

'Payne was a devout man. Me, I don't go so much, but Payne was very religious. You'll see when you go inside. Jesus is everywhere.'

'Was Payne close with the priest, Father Willie?'

'I really don't know. I guess he must've been.'

Sweat crawled down Frederick's sides like bugs. He was certain that Cole would drive up at any second, and he didn't like the way the sheriff was looking at him. Now the sheriff was wondering how Payne and Father Willie were connected. Maybe Payne had confessed to Father Willie, and Father Willie had told someone else. The sheriff just kept *staring* at him, and Frederick's breath came faster and faster.

'Let me ask you something.'

'What's that, Sheriff?'

The sheriff walked to the truck. He glanced into the truck's bed, studied the shovel, then draped his arm over the side panel. Frederick's heart thundered.

'How long have you known Payne?'

'I dunno,' Frederick mumbled. 'Must be ten, twelve years.'

The sheriff seemed to study him even more closely.

'You know he once went by another name?'

'I didn't know that.'

'He never mentioned another name to you?'

'No, sir.'

'George Reinnike?'

'No.'

'He tell you about his son?'

Frederick's vision blurred, and his lungs couldn't get enough air. He barely managed to speak.

'He didn't tell me anything.'

Frederick was certain the sheriff was watching him. The sheriff's head floated up and down in a slow-motion nod. His head tilted ponderously as he considered the shovel again. He studied the shovel forever before his eyes returned to Frederick. They rested on Frederick. They crushed him.

The sheriff smiled. Not a happy smile, but wise. Knowing. As if he could see the connections between Frederick and Payne.

'Looks like Payne had a few secrets.'

The sheriff moved past Frederick toward the house.

'Looks like they're about to come out.'

Frederick said, 'Sheriff?'

As the sheriff was turning, Frederick picked up the shovel. The blade bit deep, and then it was done.

CHAPTER 54

Biggins's directions led me to a small independent service station with a single pump island and a tow truck parked at the rear. Large yellow signs at the edge of the turnoff announced WE HAVE PROPANE and DIESEL. A thin man in a blue windbreaker came around the side of the building as I pulled up. A yellow lab gimped along behind him, then flopped to the ground by the station's front door. When the man saw me, he waved like he was waving good-bye. He was too young to be David Reinnike.

'Sorry, partner, I just turned off the pumps. We're closed.'

'Are you Lewis or Conrad? I just left the Sheriffs Substation. The deputy said I would find Lewis or Conrad here. I'm from Los Angeles, about Payne Keller.'

'I'm Lewis. This is the goddamnedest thing, isn't it? The goddamnedest thing. I'm supposed to take the wife up to Cambria tomorrow, and now this. I gotta get this place closed.'

Lewis was looking around the station, with his lips

silently moving as if he was making a list of everything he needed to do. I pointed up the road.

'Mr. Lewis, is this the right way to Payne's house?'

'Yeah, right up there. It's not much farther. The sheriff's up there.'

'Okay, good.'

I felt a little better thinking the sheriff was at Keller's house. Diaz would probably avoid him.

'Have any other officers come by?'

He stared at me like he was having a hard time concentrating.

'Yeah, another one from Los Angeles. She might be up there with the sheriff. She asked about it.'

'Was that before or after the sheriff?'

'After. Listen, I gotta get this place closed. We got a gas truck coming up here, and I gotta get that gas canceled. Payne's dead, and we got a whole damn truck of gas on its way.'

His eyes suddenly filled, and he hurried past me into the service bays. I helped him pull down the overhead doors, and talked to him as he shut the power to the hydraulic lifts.

'I know this is a bad time, Mr. Lewis. I'm sorry.'

'I know. I understand. They said Payne was using a fake name. What in hell is that all about? I never knew Payne had another name.'

'George Reinnike.'

'I didn't know. I been here for eight years; all I knew was Payne.'

'Payne had a son. Did you know about his son?'

'Jesus Christ, no. That's what the sheriff said. I didn't know anything about a son.'

'His name was David.'

348

'Jesus, next you're gonna tell me Payne was Elvis-fucking-Presley.'

We moved into the office. If Lewis had worked with Reinnike for eight years, he could probably name Reinnike's closest friends. I asked him. Lewis hesitated, and I could see he was bothered by how little he knew about the man with whom he had worked so closely.

'Payne didn't have friends. He kinda stayed to himself.'

'Everybody has someone.'

'Maybe up at the church. Payne was big on the Bible. He was up at the church a lot.'

'Anyone else?'

'Just me and Frederick, that's all I know. We helped him here at the station, then up at the house when he needed it. Frederick's been here longer than me.'

'How long has Frederick been here?'

'I don't know – ten, twelve years, something like that. You want his number?'

'What does Frederick look like?'

'Little younger than you, maybe. About your height, but heavy. I dunno. Why you asking about Frederick? What does that have to do with Payne?'

'Did Payne tell you why he was going to Los Angeles?'

'I thought he was in Sacramento.'

'He told you he was going to Sacramento?'

'He called Frederick. His sister got T-boned in a bad wreck, he said. I thought he was in Sacramento taking care of her, not down in L.A. getting himself shot.'

'He called Frederick.'

'Yeah. Frederick talked to him.'

'Payne didn't have a sister.'

Elroy Lewis muttered under his breath, and we were

both wondering why Frederick had gotten all the calls and not Elroy Lewis. Lewis turned off the last lights, then locked the door behind us.

He said, 'If you see the sheriff up there, you tell him I went home. He said he was gonna call.'

'I'll tell him you went home.'

'You going up to Payne's right now?'

'That's right.'

'Look for the big dead sycamore right by the drive, otherwise you'll miss it.'

'All right. Thanks, Mr. Lewis.'

The dog lifted its head when he saw us approaching, and struggled to its feet. It wobbled sideways before it steadied itself. Lewis stared at the dog as if it were homeless.

'I don't know what in hell we're gonna do now.'

He stared at me, then started blinking again.

'Payne read the Bible all the time. He would read it sitting here in the station. He had these statues of Jesus. He went to Mass, I dunno, three times a week, and now he gets shot to death down in L.A. I'm not a religious man, but it doesn't seem right.'

Lewis walked away, and the dog gimped along after him. I climbed back into my car, but I didn't leave right away. I thought about Frederick Conrad. Payne Keller's house was close, and the sheriff was supposed to be there. I had Conrad's address, and could have gone to his home, but I decided to see the sheriff first. Like failing to return to my office, it was exactly the wrong decision.

CHAPTER 55

Lewis warned me to look for a dying sycamore, and that's where I found it – an overgrown private lane little more than a break between the trees without even a mailbox to draw passing attention. It looked more like a trail than a road, with nasty potholes and cuts that would discourage the idly curious with a broken axle. It was a good place to be an invisible man and live an invisible life.

I worked my way over the potholes and through the trees. Reinnike's house was a rustic cabin built of clapboard and river stones, with a covered porch in front. I had expected to see the sheriff's vehicle, but Kelly Diaz's Passat was parked alongside the porch. No other vehicles were present. I pulled up behind her, and shut off my car. The front door was open.

Diaz would have heard me drive up, but she did not come to the door. I got out, and went to the porch.

'Diaz?'

I crossed the porch, and stepped inside.

'Diaz, it's Cole.'

Furniture was upended, magazines were scattered

over the floor, and books had been swept clean from a bookcase that was twisted away from the wall. Statues and portraits of Jesus were everywhere; watching from the walls and the television and the tables. More little statues were strewn over the floor.

'Diaz, you in here?'

Reinnike's house had been searched, but not by Diaz. Cops know you can't find something by throwing things in the air. Someone with a disordered mind had searched this house. An image of a collie with a garden stake through its chest flickered in my head. I was frightened of what I would find.

'David?'

I moved to the kitchen. Drawers had been emptied; the cupboards were open, and Tupperware raked to the floor. I didn't want to go into the back of the house. I wondered if Diaz had been here when David Reinnike came to call.

I backed out of the kitchen, and turned toward the living room. Kelly Diaz was waiting in the mouth of the hall, holding her pistol loose down along her leg. She could have killed me; she could have shot me down from behind, but she didn't. Her face was strained as if she had caught up in time with her mother, and carried her mother's lost years, but she gave me a wicked bright smile.

'Damn, Cole, you really are the World's Greatest Detective. You found the sonofabitch – Payne-fucking-Keller.'

'I found a suspect in his murder, too.'

Her shirt was taut over the swell of a bullet-resistant vest. Detectives never wore vests, but Diaz had come up here to do business. She waggled her gun at the room.

'He's here, Cole. The sick freak is shitting his pants. We can get him.'

'Pardy knows. He's talking it over with O'Loughlin right now. They're going to issue a warrant.'

'Pardy doesn't know his ass.'

'He found the gun and put it with one of your cases. You had access. He has a witness who saw a woman matching your description with Reinnike the night of the murder. I found the murder book in your house –'

She waggled the gun again, but a sheen of sweat slicked her face and her eyes were bright.

'We'll see with the jury.'

'Your footprints are all over this, Kelly. You're wearing your mother's necklace, forchrissake.'

The tough smile wavered, but strengthened with anger.

'Well, so fucking *what*? I made my choice, and I'm good with it. This bastard murdered my family. I am officially mentally ill. I snapped under the strain of being confronted by the man who murdered my family. I feared for my life, and reacted accordingly. I then proceeded with an investigation in preparation to come forward. We'll see what the jury does with it.'

She must have told herself those things a thousand times, convincing herself it would work.

'There were better ways, Diaz. You could have made the case. You could have arrested him.'

Her gun came up.

'Oh, fuck that, Cole – *please*. You don't *know*. You weren't *there*. Man, it was *intense*.'

'Look, I understand –'

'You can't –'

'You don't know me well enough to know what I

can know – all you know is what you read in the papers.'

I was shouting, too, and maybe that's what made her smile, the two of us in that house, shouting.

'The papers got a lot right, buddy. You stayed with it. You found him. Here we are in his house.'

'You led me. You planted the clippings and the key card. You baited me to the Medical Examiner's so I would see him again and you could set the hook even deeper. You didn't need me for any of this, Diaz – you could have found him without me.'

Her eyes glistened like black buttons, and she lowered her gun. She tipped back her head against the wall, and spoke without seeing me.

'But then everyone would have known I was in on the kill. I wanted them to think it was just you, you see?'

She laid it out and confirmed my guesses. She had me trace Reinnike to find David. She needed me to do the legwork to set me up for the murders, both George's and David's.

I said, 'But it didn't work out that way.'

She tipped forward again, and the sad smile returned.

'It was so intense, Cole; everything happened so fast, and I was making it up as it happened.'

'Did you find George or did he find you?'

Now she drew herself up, and straightened.

'When I finished the Academy and came on the job, the *Daily News* ran a little piece about what happened to my family. He saw it, and kept it. Man, that was years ago – *years*. I guess it took him all these years to work up his nut. He called last week. Out of the blue, he just called. He said he had information about the death of my family.'

She touched the necklace, and I knew my guess about it was right, too – he had brought it as proof. She was still in that awful moment when he called. *I have information about the death of your family.*

'What did he tell you?'

Her fingers caressed the silver, and her eyes were lost. I moved slowly, and took her gun. She did not resist.

'Did he tell you what happened, Kelly? Was it just David or was George part of it?'

Her fingers fell away from the necklace as if their weight was too great. Her eyes filled, and she clenched them shut. Her chin quivered. She fought hard to stop it.

She said, 'Shit.'

I put my arms around her. She shuddered, and cried for a while, and I cried along with her, for everything she had lost and for all the things I never had. And when we wore ourselves out with it, she told me how her family had come to die: Her father and brother were driving, and saw David Reinnike hitchhiking. David Reinnike would have been three or four years older than her brother, but the two kids got along, so her father probably brought the hitchhiker home to play or have a little dinner or whatever. Diaz only knew what she had been told by George Reinnike, and George only knew what he had been told by David. David hadn't been at their home for more than fifteen or twenty minutes when something set him off. Her brother showed his baseball bat to David. David probably tested it out with a few warm-up swings, but her brother probably wanted it back. Then David started swinging for real. He hadn't been in their home long

355

enough to know a little girl was playing in her closet. Between what George provided and the information available in the murder book, David Reinnike beat them to death, and then he just walked away and hitchhiked home, and not one goddamned person saw him. Not one person in a neighborhood filled with people saw or heard the murders, or David leave the scene. When he reached home, covered in blood – he had to be covered in blood, wouldn't you think? – George cleaned him up, took him away, and never told a soul. His son had problems, he said. His son needed care.

I said, 'He contacted you because he had to get it off his chest, but he wouldn't tell anything about David.'

'The sonofabitch wouldn't tell me where David was or even if he was alive, but I know he's up here. George would have to keep him close to control him. That sonofabitch cried like a baby, saying it was eating him alive. Well, fuck him.'

I nodded.

'So you killed him.'

Diaz cleared her throat, then pulled herself together and stepped away from me. She seemed angry again, and ready for hell.

'That's right, Cole. So what are you going to do? You going to slap the cuffs on me and wait here for Pardy and my lawyer, and let this bastard get away? Look at this place – he knows we're coming. Daddy's been keeping him out of jail all these years, and now Daddy's gone. You think he's going to wait?'

'I'm not going to let you kill him. If you kill him, you're just killing yourself.'

'Then what?'

'We're going to identify David, and you're going to take him into custody. You're going to arrest him, and bring him in to show you did the right thing. You're going to show them you didn't let what happened destroy you.'

Diaz sighed deep, pushing out air like she was trying to get rid of something that was trapped inside her. She tipped back her head again and stared at the ceiling.

'What a goddamned mess.'

'Pardy's coming. We don't have all day.'

She squared herself, and nodded.

'My gun.'

I gave her the gun. She put it into her holster.

'Do you know who it is?'

'Probably the other guy who worked at the station. That's what it sounds like from talking with Lewis. I can't be sure, but that's what it sounds like. Lewis told me how to get to his house.'

Diaz stepped past me and went to the door.

CHAPTER 56

Starkey

Starkey picked up Pike where the 405 crossed Mulholland. If Pike wondered why she was frantic, he didn't ask, and he didn't quibble over which car they would take. Her car had the lights and a radio. They would make better time.

Starkey flipped on her grille lights, and blasted out of the parking lot. When they were rolling north on the freeway, she keyed her radio, surprised that the damn thing worked.

'Six-whiskey-twelve.'

'Six-whiskey-twelve, go.'

The 'six' identified her as being from Hollywood. 'Whiskey' told them she was a detective. The 'twelve' was her car number.

'Ah, I need a patch to the Sheriffs Department Sub-station in Canyon Camino.'

'Stand by, six-whiskey-twelve.'

While Starkey was busy with the radio, Pike called Cole's cell number. Pike phoned it three times, but never once got through. By the time Starkey had the patch, they were passing Van Nuys Airport, twenty-six minutes away from George Reinnike's home.

CHAPTER 57

Frederick

The sheriff changed everything. He could have radioed that Frederick's truck was at Payne's, or told Biggins he was stopping at the house, or called in more police. Frederick's mind raced with the changing plans. He felt certain that Cole wouldn't approach with a patrol car out front, and Frederick wanted to get away quickly. Also, if the police found Rossi's vehicle, they might roadblock the area and stop Frederick's escape. He fought the urge to run. He loaded Rossi's body into the back seat, then drove the patrol car behind Payne's cabin and into the trees. He drove as far as he could, then huffed back to the house. He piled into his truck.

Frederick wept as he drove. He missed Payne, and he wanted to punish Cole, but now he realized he had to leave and vengeance would never be his. Maybe if he got away. Maybe in a few years. He knew where Cole lived. He knew where he worked. Maybe in a few years.

Frederick heard a voice as he entered his trailer, but it was Elroy, leaving a message.

'– call me back, goddamnit. The L.A. police are coming up to talk to us, and I don't know what in hell's –'

Frederick scooped up the phone.

'Elroy, it's me. Why do they want to talk to us?'

'Goddamnit, why haven't you called me back? I got –'

'I been so upset about Payne I didn't know what to say.'

Elroy calmed down. Even Elroy could understand grief.

He said, 'Payne ever say anything to you about going to Los Angeles?'

'Not to me.'

'Well, that's what they're asking about. The sheriff was here. He said some police are coming up from Los Angeles, and they want to know why he went down there. He said Payne's name wasn't really Payne. Did he get over there to talk to you?'

'He called. I just got off the phone.'

'I'm closing this damned station. I don't know what else to do.'

'Okay.'

'That private detective get over there yet?'

'Good-bye, Elroy.'

Frederick put the phone softly in its cradle. His eyes felt like they were swelling. They filled with a tremendous pressure and felt like they would explode. Cole knew who he was. Cole was coming right here to his house. Frederick felt trapped. They were being punished just like Payne always said. Frederick sobbed, then remembered Juanita. He wasn't done yet. He might be able to get the jump on Cole, and still get away.

Frederick got together the cash he had taken from the station, then locked his trailer and took the shotgun from his truck. He hurried across the courtyard to Juanita's double-wide. It was midafternoon, so Frederick knew she was taking her nap. Juanita woke at three or four every morning with the night terrors, then nodded out again after lunch. That's the way it was with old people. Sad.

The two little girls were playing on the far side of the motor court. He called out to them, and waved. They ran as soon as they saw him, which is exactly what he wanted.

Frederick went to Juanita's door, but didn't knock – he twisted her door handle and shoved through the cheap aluminum frame. Juanita woke with a start, but Frederick shut the door fast, and smiled.

Juanita, still foggy with sleep, said, 'Frederick?'

Frederick took care of her, then settled into the shadows just as two cars turned in from the road.

CHAPTER 58

High Mountain Communities was an older mobile home park with single- and double-wide mobile homes set among the trees. It had probably been a nice place to live at one time, but now it had the feel of an outdated summer camp with declining enrollment. Some of the mobile homes were well maintained, but others were grimy with stains. Frederick Conrad lived in Number 14, at the rear of the park.

Diaz followed me in her Passat. We crunched past the central motor court, watching the numbers until I found #14. Conrad's mobile home was clean, nicely maintained, and quiet. The entire mobile-home park was quiet.

I parked beside an F-150 pickup truck, and Diaz pulled up beside me. We got out of our cars at the same time, glancing over the surroundings. Her eyes were dark, like two polished black stones.

She said, 'His son's going to be up here. If he isn't here now, he was. He was never far from his son.'

'Let's take it easy. We don't know this guy is him.'

Two little girls appeared across the motor court. They

bubbled out of a pale green mobile home, the smaller of the two trying to keep up with her older sister. The older girl said something I could not understand, and the younger one loudly told her to wait. The older girl ran around the far end of their home, laughing. Her younger sister laughed as she followed. Diaz stared after them.

I said, 'Diaz?'

She turned back, and touched the locket that swung in the hollow of her neck.

'I'm good. Let's see what he has to say.'

We approached Frederick Conrad's door. Diaz walked with her hand on her gun under her jacket.

I knocked on the door, then knocked harder, and called out.

'Mr. Conrad?'

No one answered.

Diaz slammed her palm on the trailer.

'Fucking prick.'

'Take it easy.'

The truck was parked like it belonged with his trailer. I went over to the truck. The engine ticked, but the ticking was slow, as if it had been parked for a while. The two little girls had disappeared. Everything was so quiet it left me feeling creepy.

Diaz said, 'Let's talk to his neighbors.'

An older Dodge sedan was parked in front of the mobile home closest to Conrad's, suggesting the mobile home might be occupied. The mobile home's door was closed and drapes covered the windows, but all the other mobile homes were closed the same way. I followed Diaz across the gravel, wondering if these people were vampires.

All you can do is knock.

Frederick

Juanita liked it dark. She kept the lights off and the drapes pulled so prowlers and rapists couldn't spy on her. Frederick always told her, oh, Juanita, that's silly, there aren't any prowlers around here, but Juanita would wave her hand like he was foolish, telling him she saw it on the news every night – murderers were *everywhere*!

Now Frederick thought, thank you, Juanita.

Frederick stood in the broad daylight darkness within her mobile home, watching Cole and the woman pound on his trailer. This wasn't the same woman who had come to Cole's house, but she carried herself like a cop. She *strutted*.

They knew. It was clear to Frederick that they had identified him. He watched them stand on either side of his door as they knocked, and knew they intended to kill him.

If Cole had come alone, Frederick would have thrown open the door and cut loose with the shotgun. At this range, it would have been easy. But now Frederick hesitated. Taking two of them would be more difficult. He could get one for sure, but two . . .

As much as Frederick wanted to kill Cole, he hoped they would get into their cars and leave. If they left, he might still get away in Juanita's old Dodge, just get in that baby and ease down the hill, and head up to Bakersfield. Live to fight another day. Live to hunt down Cole on a better day.

Frederick heard Payne said, 'That's my boy.'

Payne had been a good father.

Cole and the woman turned away from Frederick's

mobile home, and Frederick thought he was home free, but then they started toward Juanita's. Frederick held the shotgun so tightly that his forearms cramped.

Cole stepped around Juanita's Dodge and came toward the broken door.

Cole

The Dodge sedan was silted with a thin layer of undisturbed dust. It probably hadn't been driven in at least a week, but for all I knew it hadn't been driven in years. If Conrad's neighbors used a second vehicle, they probably weren't even home.

I went up to the door and knocked.

'Hello?'

Diaz stood well to the side.

I knocked again, then turned to see if anyone had come out of the other trailers. I turned back to the door, and knocked again.

Diaz said, 'I'll check the next trailer.'

She moved away, and I knocked again at the door.

'I'm giving away money.'

Humor.

Diaz said, 'Hey, Cole.'

I glanced over. She pursed her lips, then wet them, and I thought she was sad.

'I'm sorry.'

I nodded.

The door's handle was bent and wilted. The entire mobile home looked wilted.

'Last chance.'

I knocked for the last time.

Frederick

A thin edge of light lay across Frederick's face like a scar as he held his breath. He stood to the side of the door, watching Cole and the woman through a break in the drapes. He heard Cole say her name. Diaz?

Her name rang a bell, but Frederick didn't have time to think about it; she told Cole she was going to check the next trailer, and then she turned away. They were separating, and now he could kill Cole!

Frederick flicked off the shotgun's safety, then eased forward, reaching for the handle.

She was walking away as Cole hammered at the door.

Thank you, Juanita.

Frederick touched the bent and broken handle with his fingertips, then heard the approaching sirens –

Cole

Diaz and I heard the sirens at the same time. I turned away from the mobile home and took eight steps toward my car so that I could better see the street. Exactly eight; then I stopped.

Diaz said, 'Goddamnit – that must be Pardy.'

'I told you he was taking it to O'Loughlin.'

Her face was creased with disgust when she turned back toward me, and I saw the moment when her eyes focused on something behind and beyond me.

I wish I could have been everything the articles made me out to be, and leaped into action to save us, but true crime and true cops are never that good. I didn't hear anything. I didn't see it coming. The blast kicked me down as if I had been broadsided by a car. I went down, and looked up, and saw Diaz with a perfect clarity as if my eyesight had grown inhumanly sharp. Her hand was under her jacket, reaching for her gun when she suddenly snapped backward against the old Dodge. A cluster of black grapes appeared below her breasts. Diaz staggered, but the vest had saved her and the Dodge held her up. She was still on her feet.

A man I did not know ran forward from the open door of the trailer. He was heavily built, but he moved quickly. He ran past me with a short black shotgun to his shoulder. Diaz brought up her gun, but the shotgun went off as she fired, and Diaz was knocked away.

The heavy man staggered sideways, looked down at himself, then looked at me. A red heart grew on his chest. He lifted the shotgun again, but now he wasn't moving so fast.

He screamed, 'You killer!'

I was flat on my back, but I had my gun by then. I squeezed the trigger, and kept squeezing, pointing the gun up at him. He staggered in a circle as I shot him. I shot him until he fell, and kept shooting into the air up where he had been because I was too scared to do anything else, and never gave a thought where the bullets would hit or whom they might hurt. I kept shooting even after he fell.

'Diaz?'

I could see her feet, but she didn't answer me. She had fallen behind the Dodge.

'Diaz, answer me.'

I tried to get up, but couldn't. I tried to roll over, but my body flared with an outrageous heat that made me scream. I touched myself, and my hand came away gloved in bright red.

I heard a little girl screaming, and thought it must be Kelly Diaz.

I said, 'It's okay. I'm not your daddy.'

Blood pulsed out over my fingers, and the trailer park dimmed. The last thing I saw was David Reinnike climb to his feet. He raised up from the dead, climbed to his feet, and picked up the shotgun. I tried to raise my gun again, but it was too heavy. I pulled the trigger anyway, but it only made clicking sounds. David Reinnike stood over me, weaving unsteadily from side to side. His red shirt glistened brightly in the pure California sun. He lifted the shotgun, and pointed it at my head. He was crying.

He said, 'You took my father.'

All the world fell, and then I was gone.

CHAPTER 59

Starkey

Starkey knew her nightmare was real when she got Biggins on the patch, midway between Van Nuys and Newhall. Biggins had checked out a tag number registered to one Frederick Conrad, a former employee of Payne Keller's, after the substation sheriff reported the vehicle at Keller's home. When the sheriff did not respond to Biggins's return call, Biggins had gone to Keller's home and discovered the body.

Starkey got directions to Conrad's mobile-home park on the fly, and called in the State Sheriffs herself. She didn't trust Biggins to do it. He seemed too upset.

Pike said, 'Faster.'

'Shut up.'

'Push.'

They came around the curve and screamed into the turnoff, and reached the trailer park first through clouds of dust and spraying gravel that rimed her soul with ice. Starkey had died in a trailer park. She had lost Sugar Boudreaux in a place exactly like this, and the echoes from that explosion now rippled through her, and she thought, Oh God, not again.

When she saw Cole, she knew he was dead. Dead people have that look. She didn't know what Pike saw. She wasn't thinking about Pike.

Diaz was down near the front end of an old car. Cole was down, too, halfway between the car and a trailer. A thick squat man was standing over Cole with a shotgun, and looked up at her as if he was peering through the wall of an aquarium. All of them were red. All of them glistened in the brilliant hot sun, and Starkey knew Cole was dead.

Pike made a sound, a kind of sharp grunt, and after that Starkey wasn't sure what happened. The steering wheel snapped out of her hands; Pike's foot crushed hers into the accelerator; the car surged forward, crushing over low shrubs and rocks and a wrought-iron bench. The squat man raised the shotgun. The windshield burst into lace, and then Pike stomped the brake pedal as he yanked the hand brake, and they were sideways. Pike was out of the car before they stopped sliding, and she heard the booms, two fast booms so close she thought they were one – BOOMBOOM – and the shotgun went up, twirling into the sky as David Reinnike windmilled backwards and fell.

Pike reached Cole as Starkey fell out of her car.

'Nine-one-one. Clear the perp and check Diaz.'

Pike never even gave the others a thought, but that seemed right to Starkey, so very very right. Her eyes filled and snot blew from her nose as she radioed emergency services. She stumbled forward to Cole and threw up as Pike worked. The side of Cole's chest was red pulp. It bubbled as Pike pushed on his chest.

'You gotta plug him. We gotta –'

Starkey, crying and shaking, pulled off her shirt and bundled it and pressed it into Cole's wound. She pressed and held hard.

Pike was shaking. She would never mention it to him, but she felt him shaking. Pike tipped back Cole's head, then blew hard and deep into Cole's mouth, once, twice, again.

Starkey said, 'Hang on. Hang on.'

She pressed harder on his wound, trying to hold the blood inside.

'Don't you die.'

Pike blew. He blew deep and hard into Cole's mouth, and kept blowing, and did not look up even as the sirens arrived.

CHAPTER 60

Elvis Cole's Dream

Death brought me home. Cool air came through the windows, carrying faraway calliope music and the scent of grilled hot dogs. The hour could not have been more pleasant in that perfect little house.

My mother called from downstairs.

'Wake up, you! Don't stay up there all day!'

My father's mellow voice followed.

'C'mon, son. We're waiting.'

Our house was small and white, with a tiny front porch and velvety lawns. Lavender hedges snuggled beneath our windows, and a wall of towering cypress, each identical in height and width, trimmed the drive. The cypress stood like immaculate soldiers; protecting us from a light that was bright, but never harsh.

I rolled out of bed and pulled on some clothes. My room was upstairs, with windows looking out to the street. It was a terrific room, really just the best, but it was a mess – Spider-Man comics, toys, and clothes were scattered all over the floor; my shoulder holster hung from the bedpost, and my pistol was on the dresser. The bullets had fallen out, but I didn't take time to find them. I wouldn't need the gun for breakfast.

The shirt I wore yesterday was patchy with blood. I didn't want my mother to find it, so I balled it up, shoved it under the bed, and hit the stairs at a sprint. Man, I don't know how my folks stood it; I sounded like a herd of stampeding buffalo – BOOM! BOOM! BOOM! They were saints, those two; really just the best.

'Elvis!'

'COMING!'

We had this family tradition. Every Saturday, my Mom, my Dad, and I had a late breakfast together before starting our day. It was the best. We would share the good things that happened the past week and pick a movie we could see together on Sunday. After that, we would sit around, just being a family and enjoying each other.

Now, you have to understand, we had never done this before, but that day was the day. Before I died, my room was in a cheap apartment or a mobile home or at my grandpa's, conversations with my mother were always disturbing, and I had never met my father.

But that day was the day. I was finally going to meet the man, my mother would come to her senses, and we were going to be a real live All-American nuclear family, normal in every way. So, me, all anxious as hell, Mr. Anticipation, I crashed down the stairs, through the house, and skidded into the kitchen.

Mom was at the sink and Dad had his head in the refrigerator.

374

Dad, not looking up, said, 'Milk or Schlitz, partner?'

'Milk.'

'Good choice.'

Mom, her back to me, said, 'Did you wash off the blood?'

'Clean as a whistle.'

'It looks so bad at the table.'

'I know.'

Me, rolling my eyes because that's what normal mid-American kids in normal mid-American towns always do; television said so, and television doesn't lie.

Neither of them turned.

My mother stayed at the sink, and my father stayed in the fridge. The kitchen drapes swayed, but their slight movement made the house feel still.

'Hey, I'm hungry. I thought we were going to eat.'

Water burbled in the sink. Eggs fried in bacon grease on the stove. Outside, boys and girls chased the ice-cream man, and fathers and mothers laughed. Outside, the day was so beautiful you could hear sunlight and taste its joy.

My perfect house felt hollow.

'Dad? Daddy, look at me. You have to look at me. I'm supposed to know you! Hey, that's why we're here. That's why I made this place. I took it in the chest to know you!'

The man in the fridge grew milky and pale, and faded as he stood.

'Daddy!'

He stood, but it was too late. I told myself he tried. I told myself he wanted to know me, and would have if he could.

'Mama, don't let him go!'

He thinned until he vanished, and then she faded, too. The refrigerator swung open. The door bounced once, and was still. Cool air came through the windows, carrying faraway voices. The hour could not have been more pleasant in that perfect little house.

It isn't so bad, not knowing who you are. You get to make up whatever you want.

I walked back through the house. The hall was long. My footsteps echoed. The living room was smaller than you might think, but comfortable with Early American furniture, framed pictures on the mantel, and a grandfather clock. It ticked like a dying heart.

The voices I heard earlier grew louder, riding in on the breeze. They sounded familiar. I ran back to the kitchen.

'Mom?'

The voices came even louder, a man and a woman, all jumbled and mixed, and I got the crazy notion she was bringing him back. I didn't see anyone out the kitchen window, so I ran back to the living room.

'Is that you? Where are you?'

Footsteps came from the ceiling; someone was moving. I ran to the stairs, and took the steps three at a time. We could still do it. I could still find them.

'Where are you?'

I ran upstairs, following the voices.

CHAPTER 61

The Intensive Care people weren't big on chairs, though they said visitors were good so long as they didn't stay too long. Because lengthy visits were discouraged, they provided only the one chair. Pike had been at Cole's side since the beginning, and had not left the hospital. He slept in the chair when the others had gone, or stood in the room or the hall. He washed in the lavatory, and Starkey or the guys from his gun shop brought fresh clothes and food. Pike was particular about what he ate. He was a vegetarian.

Visitors came and went throughout the days and evenings, and Pike felt them move around him with barely a word or nod exchanged. Lou Poitras and his family came by almost every evening. Starkey visited twice a day, usually once for a few minutes during the day shift, then again in the evening. The first time, she stood quietly in the corner, arms tightly crossed, bunched together, eyes red, mumbling, *I knew this was going to happen, goddamnit, I knew it.* The second time, she came in blowing gin, and sat in the chair with her face in her hands.

Pike gently pulled her to her feet. He removed his dark glasses, then held her. He smoothed her hair, and made his voice soft.

'Don't do this. Be stronger than this.'

Starkey told him to fuck himself, but the next time she came she didn't smell of gin. She left every five minutes to cheat a cigarette in the bathroom, and often smelled of Binaca.

Detective Jeff Pardy showed up on the third night. He eyed Pike like he was embarrassed by the scene he had made in Cole's home, and then he apologized. Pike respected him for the apology, and told him so.

Pardy said, 'Well, listen, I'm going to go. We're having a service for Diaz.'

Pike nodded.

'If Cole wakes up, tell him we found Reinnike's Accord in a long-term parking lot at LAX. We found Diaz's prints on the seat. It looks like she put it there, but we can't be sure.'

'I'll tell him.'

'We wouldn't have found it if you guys hadn't gotten the tag. That was good work.'

'I'll let him know.'

One of their former clients, a film director named Peter Alan Nelsen, came by late one evening. He came alone, wearing a fishing cap and a high-collared shirt, hoping he wouldn't be recognized. Pike and Nelsen stood in the hall outside Cole's ICU bed for a long time, talking about what happened. Nelsen sat by Cole's side for a while, praying, and didn't leave until much later. The next day, one thousand roses were delivered, so many roses that the floor staff put roses in every room on the floor, and spread them throughout the hospital.

The following day, another former client arrived, but he did not come alone. Frank Garcia had once been a White Fence gangbanger, but he built a billion-dollar food empire that included salsas, chips, Mexican food products, and his legendary Monsterito tortillas. When Frank's daughter was murdered, Pike and Cole found the killer. Now, Frank arrived with his attorney, Abbot Montoya, a city councilman named Henry Maldenado, and an army of hospital directors in tow. Frank Garcia had built the hospital's children's wing.

Frank wasn't as strong as he used to be, and latched on to Joe's arm for support.

'How is he?'

Pike glanced at the bed.

Frank made the sign of the cross, then waved angrily toward Montoya.

'The best. Put him in the same room they put the fucking president. Is this the best these bastards can do? This man avenged Karen. He carries my heart!'

Pike said, 'Frank.'

'The best doctors, the best nurses – take care of it, Abbot. *Para siempre.*'

Frank stood clutching Pike's arm, weeping like a child as he stared at the bed.

On the fifth day, Pike was standing beside Cole's bed at one-sixteen that afternoon. Starkey had just left. Earlier, Ellen Lang and Jodi Taylor had dropped by, but at one-sixteen, Pike was the only one.

Cole appeared to be dreaming. His eyes, though closed, fluttered in REM sleep.

Pike took his hand.

Cole's eyes opened, just little slits, squinting at the light.

379

Pike said, 'Welcome home.'

Cole wet his lips and tried to speak.

Pike said, 'Don't talk.'

Cole went back to sleep. Pike held his friend's hand, and never once moved as he held on, and held, waiting.

That evening, Pike stood at the foot of Cole's bed, and it was Starkey who held Cole's hand.

'Hey, buddy. Cole, can you hear me?'

Throughout the afternoon, his eyes opened a little more each time. The nurses told Pike that talking to Cole was good, and would help him come back.

When Pike told Starkey that Cole was waking, her strained miserable expression blossomed into a sunburst smile, and she stormed straight to Cole's bed.

'That's great, man! That's fantastic! Hey, buddy, you with us? You hear me?'

They took turns talking to Cole, and holding his hand, and Pike was pleased to see Starkey in such good spirits. She seemed like her old self again, saying funny outrageous things, and bouncing around the room.

– 'Cole, check this out – I'm flashing my boobies.'

– 'Guess what, Cole? I moved into your house. You're not using it, so I figured what the hell. I shot your cat.'

– 'You know, Cole, this is a really stupid way to avoid buying me dinner.'

At seven-thirty that night, Pike left Starkey with Cole, and stepped into the hall. He stretched deeply, bending far forward to ease the stiffness in his back. When he stood, Lucy Chenier was rushing toward him. She slowed to a fast walk. Her face was gray with fatigue and strain, and sagging with worry.

She said, 'Where is he?'

Pike nodded toward the door.

Lucy blew past him into the room. Pike watched Starkey as Lucy went to the bed. The edgy light in Starkey's face dulled, and her energy, it seemed to Pike, faded. Starkey stepped away from the bed to make room for Lucy, and Pike resumed his place at the foot of the bed.

Lucy took Cole's hand in hers. Her eyes filled, and the tears showered onto the sheets.

She said, 'You better not die on me. You better not. Do you hear me, Elvis Cole? You –'

Lucy heaved with a terrible sob, and she gasped as she cried.

Cole's eyes fluttered. His left eye opened more than his right.

'Luce?'

Lucy cried harder, but now her face broke into a smile.

Cole's rolling eyes focused.

'Luce –'

'Yes, baby. I'm here. I'm here. You come back to me now. You come back.'

Starkey backed away. Pike saw her watch Lucy, then turn her eyes to the floor. After a while, Starkey left to stand in the hall. Pike considered the meaning, but would not leave Cole's side. He patted Cole's leg.

'Elvis.'

Cole looked at him.

Pike said, 'I'm the one who's supposed to get shot.'

Cole managed a smile, then slipped back into sleep. Pike stayed. Every day, visitors came and left, but

Pike remained at the hospital. He stayed at the hospital nonstop for twelve days before taking a break, and, then, he left only because they were sure his friend was past the worst of it; Elvis Cole was with them, again; he would live.

Part Five
THE FORGIVEN MAN

CHAPTER 62

I said, 'Here is good.'

Pike eased the rental car to the side of the gravel road under the lush canopy of a beautiful willow tree.

'You know where it is?'

'Over there somewhere. I can find it.'

Pike had flown with me back to the place she lies buried. I still had trouble walking, and didn't trust myself to drive. I would rather have come alone, but having Pike's company was good.

Pike said, 'You want me to come with you?'

'No, you wait. I won't be long.'

I had to use a cane, and my side stitched with sharp pains when I moved. The therapists warned me the pain would linger for months, and might never completely leave, so I had made peace with it.

My grandparents and my mother were buried near each other at the rear of the grounds. My aunt had died in an auto accident fifteen years earlier, and was buried outside Chicago where she had lived with her husband. I had two cousins, but I never saw them. I had not been to my mother's grave since the day she was buried.

I found the little black rectangle and stared down at her name. The stone was dirty and weathered, but green grass softened its edges and made it look better than it was. No one was left to put flowers. Probably no one had put flowers since my aunt moved away. It hurt to bend, but I bent anyway, and placed the roses on her name.

I said, 'Hi, Mama.'

My eyes filled, and I cried for a while. I felt bad that I never came to see her, and bad that I had blamed her for so much over the years, because now it all seemed selfish and cruel. Her sickness was a sad thing, and beyond anyone's measure. Her only true crime was giving me a dream, and I had resented her for it. My true crimes were greater. Like the pain in my side, some things simply need to be accepted, and overcome.

I limped back to the car, and tried to make myself comfortable. It wasn't easy.

'Okay. I'm done.'

'You good?'

'Yeah. We had a nice talk.'

Pike and I drove back to the airport, and returned to Los Angeles the same day.

It was good to be home.

If you have enjoyed

THE FORGOTTEN MAN

Don't miss the thrilling
novel from Robert Crais

THE SENTRY

Available from Orion

New Orleans
2005

MONDAY, 4:28 A.M., the narrow French Quarter room was smoky with cheap candles that smelled of honey. Daniel stared through broken shutters and shivering glass up the length of the alley, catching a thin slice of Jackson Square through curtains of gale-force rain that swirled through New Orleans like mad bats riding the storm. Daniel had never seen rain fall up before.

Daniel loved these damned hurricanes. He folded back the shutters, then opened the window. Rain hit him good. It tasted of salt and smelled of dead fish and weeds. The cat-five wind clawed through New Orleans at better than a hundred miles an hour, but back here in the alley—in a cheap one-room apartment over a po'boy shop—the wind was no stronger than an arrogant breeze.

The power in this part of the Quarter had gone out almost an hour ago; hence, the candles Daniel found in the manager's office. Emergency lighting fed by battery packs lit a few nearby buildings, giving a creepy blue glow to the shimmering walls. Most everyone in the surrounding buildings had gone. Not everyone, but most. The stubborn, the helpless, and the stupid had stayed.

Like Daniel's friend, Tolley.

Tolley had stayed.

Stupid.

And now here they were in an empty building surrounded by empty buildings in an outrageous storm
that had forced more than a million people out of the
city, but Daniel kinda dug it. All this noise and all this
emptiness, no one to hear Tolley scream.

Daniel turned from the window, arching his eyebrows.

"You smell that? That's what zombies smell like,
brought up from the dead with an unnatural life. You
get to see a zombie?"

Tolley was between answers right now, being tied
to the bed with thirty feet of nylon cord. His head just
kinda hung there, all swollen and broken, though he
was still breathing. Every once in a while he would
lurch and shiver. Daniel didn't let Tolley's lack of
responsiveness stop him.

Daniel sauntered over to the bed. Cleo and Tobey
shuffled out of the way, letting him pass.

Daniel had a syringe pack in his bag, along with
some poppers, meth, and other choice pharmaceuticals.
He took out the kit, shot up Tolley with some crystal,
then waited for it to take effect. Outside, something
exploded with a muffled *whump* that wasn't quite lost
in the wind. Power transformer, probably, giving up the
ghost, or maybe a wall falling over.

Tolley's eyes flickered amid a sudden fury of blinks,
then dialed into focus. He tried to pull away when he
saw Daniel, but, really, where could he go?

Daniel said, all serious, "I asked you, you seen a zombie? They got'm here in this place, I know for a fact."

Tolley shook his head, which kinda pissed Daniel
off. On his way to New Orleans six days earlier, having been sent to find Tolley based upon an absolutely

4

spot-on lead, Daniel decided this was his one pure and good chance to see a zombie. Daniel could not abide a zombie, and found their existence offensive. The dead should stay dead, and not rise to walk again, all shamblin' and vile and slack. He didn't care for vampires, either, but zombies just rubbed him the wrong way. Daniel had it on good authority that New Orleans held quite a few zombies, and maybe a vampire or two.

"Don't be like that, Tolliver. New Orleans is supposed to have zombies, don't it, what with all this hoodoo and shit you got here, them zombies from Haiti? You musta seen something?"

Tolley's eyes were bright with meth, the one eye, the left, a glossy red ball what with the burst veins.

Daniel wiped the rain from his face, and felt all tired.

"Where is she?"

"I swear I doan know."

"You kill her? That what you been tryin' to say?"

"No!"

"She tell you where they goin'?"

"I don't know nuthin' about—"

Daniel hammered his fist straight down on Tolley's chest, and scooped up the Asp. The Asp was a collapsible steel rod almost two feet long. Daniel brought it down hard, lashing Tolley's chest, belly, thighs, and shins with a furious beating. Tolley screamed and jerked at his binds, but no one was left to hear. Daniel let him have it for a long time, then tossed aside the Asp and returned to the window. Tobey and Cleo scrambled out of his way.

"I wanna see a goddamned zombie. A zombie, vampire, *something* to make this fuckin' trip worthwhile."

The rain blew in hard, hot and salty as blood. Daniel didn't care. Here he was, come all this way, and not a zombie to be found. Anything was good, Daniel missed out. A life of miserable disappointments.

He looked at Tobey and Cleo. They were difficult to see in the flickery light, all blurry and smudged, but he could make them out well enough.

"Bet I could kill me a zombie, one on one, straight up, and I'd like to try. You think I could kill me a zombie?"

Neither Tobey nor Cleo answered.

"I ain't shittin', I could take me a zombie. Take me a vampire, too, only here we are and I gotta waste my time with this lame shit. I'd rather be huntin' zombies."

He pointed at Tolley.

"Hey, boy."

Daniel returned to the bed and shook Tolley awake.

"You think I could take me a zombie, head up, one on one?"

The red eye rolled, and blood leaked from the shattered mouth. A mushy hiss escaped, so Daniel leaned closer. Sounded like the fucker was finally openin' up.

"Say what?"

Tolley's mouth worked as he tried to speak.

Daniel smiled encouragingly.

"You hear that wind? I was a bat, I'd spread my wings and ride that sumbitch for all she was worth. Where'd they go, boy? I know she tol' ya. You tell me where they went so I can get outta here. Just say it. You're almost there. Give me a hand, and I'm out your hair."

Tolley's lips worked, and Daniel knew he was about to give it, but then what little air he had left hissed out.

"You say west? They was headed west? Over to Texas?"

Tolley was dead.

Daniel stared at the body for a moment, then drew his gun and put five bullets into Tolliver James's chest. Nasty explosions that anyone staying behind would have heard even with the lion wind. Daniel didn't give a damn. If someone came running, Daniel

6

figured to shoot them, too, but nobody came—no police, no neighbors, no nobody. Everyone with two squirts of brain juice was hunkered down tight, trying to survive.

Daniel reloaded, tucked away his gun, then took out the satellite phone. The cell stations were out all over the city, but the sat phone worked great. He checked the time, hit the speed dial, then waited for a link. It always took a few seconds.

In that time, he stood taller, straightened himself, and resumed his normal manner.

When the connection was made, Daniel reported.

"Tolliver James is dead. He didn't provide anything useful."

Daniel listened for a moment before responding.

"No, sir, they're gone. That much is confirmed. James was a good bet, but I don't believe she told him anything."

He listened again, this time for quite a while.

"No, sir, that is not altogether true. There are three or four people here I'd still like to talk to, but the storm has turned this place to shit. They've almost certainly evacuated. I just don't know. It will take me a while to locate them."

More chatter from the other side, but then they were finished.

"Yes, sir, I understand. You get yours, I get mine. I won't let you down."

A last word from the master.

"Yes, sir. Thank you. I'll keep you informed."

Daniel shut the phone and put it away.

"Asshole."

He returned to the window, and let the rain lash him. Everything was wet now: shirt, pants, shoes, hair, all the way down to his bones. He leaned out, better to see the Square. A fifty-five-gallon oil drum tumbled past the alley's mouth, end over end, followed by a bicycle, swept along on its side, and then a shattered sheet of plywood flipping and soaring like a playing card tossed out like trash.

Daniel shouted into the wind as loud as he could.

"C'mon and get me, you fuckin' zombies! Show your true and unnatural colors."

Daniel threw back his head and howled. He barked like a dog, then howled again before turning back to the room to pack up his gear. Tobey and Cleo were gone.

Tolliver had hidden eight thousand dollars under the mattress, still vacu-packed in plastic, which Daniel found when he first searched the room. Probably a gift from the girl. Daniel stashed the money in his bag, checked to make sure Tolliver had no pulse, then went to the little bathroom where he'd left Tolliver's lady friend after he strangled her, nice and neat in the tub. A little black stream of ants had already found her, not even a day.

Cleo said, "Gotta get going, Daniel. Stop fuckin' around."

Tobey said, "Go where, a storm like this? Makes sense to stay."

Daniel decided Tobey was right. Tobey was the smart one, and usually right, even if Daniel couldn't always see him.

"Okay, I guess I should wait till the worst is over."

Tobey said, "Wait."

Cleo said, "Wait, wait."

Like echoes fading away.

Daniel returned to the window. He leaned out into the rain again, watching the mouth of the alley in case a zombie rattled past.

"C'mon, goddamnit, lemme see one. One freaky-ass zombie is all I ask."

If a zombie appeared, Daniel planned to jump out

the window after it and rip its putrid, unnatural flesh to pieces with his teeth. He was, after all, a werewolf, which was why he was such a good hunter and killer. Werewolves feared nothing.

Daniel tipped back his head and howled to match the wind, then doused the candles and sat with the bodies, waiting for the storm to pass.

When it ended, Daniel would find their trail, and track them, and he would not quit until they were his. No matter how long it took or how far they ran. This was why the men down south used him for these jobs and paid him so well.

Werewolves caught their prey.

Los Angeles
Now

THE WIND DID NOT WAKE HIM. It was the dream. He heard the buffeting wind before he opened his eyes, but the dream was what woke him on that dark early morning. A cat was his witness. Hunkered at the end of the bed, ears down, a low growl in its chest, a ragged black cat was staring at him when Elvis Cole opened his eyes. Its warrior face was angry, and, in that moment, Cole knew they had shared the nightmare.

Cole woke on the bed in his loft bathed in soft moonlight, feeling his A-frame shudder as the wind tried to push it from its perch high in the Hollywood Hills. A freak weather system in the Midwest was pulling fifty- to seventy-knot winds from the sea that had hammered Los Angeles for days.

Cole sat up, awake now and wanting to shake off the dream—an ugly nightmare that left him feeling unsettled and depressed. The cat's ears stayed down. Cole held out his hand, but the cat poured off the bed like a pool of black ink.

Cole said, "Me, too."

He checked the time. Habit. Three-twelve in the A.M. He reached toward the nightstand to check his gun—habit—but stopped himself when he realized what he was doing.

"C'mon, what's the point?"

The gun was there because it was always there, sometimes needed but most times not. Living alone with only an angry cat for company, there seemed no reason to move it. Now, at three-twelve in the middle of a wind-torched night, it was a reminder of what he had lost.

Cole realized he was trembling, and pushed out of bed. The dream scared him. Muzzle flash so bright it sparkled his eyes; the charcoal smell of smokeless powder; a glittery red mist that dappled his skin; shattered sunglasses that arced through the air—images so vivid they shocked him awake.

Now he shook as his body burned off the fear.

The back of Cole's house was an A-shaped glass steeple, giving him a view of the canyon behind his house and a diamond-dust glimpse of the city beyond. Now, the canyon was blue with bright moonlight. The sleeping houses below were surrounded by blue-and-gray trees that shivered and danced in the St. Vitus wind. Cole wondered if someone down there had awakened like him. He wondered if they had suffered a similar nightmare— seeing their best friend shot to death in the dark.

Violence was part of him.

Elvis Cole did not want it, seek it, or enjoy it, but maybe these were only things he told himself in cold moments like now. The nature of his life had cost him the woman he loved and the little boy he had grown to love, and left him alone in this house with nothing but an angry cat for company and a pistol that did not need to be put away.

Now here was this dream that left his skin crawling—so real it felt like a premonition. He looked at the phone and told himself no—no, that's silly, it's stupid, it's three in the morning.

Cole made the call.

One ring, and his call was answered. At three in the morning.

"Pike."

"Hey, man."

Cole didn't know what to say after that, feeling so stupid.

"You good?"

Pike said, "Good. You?"

"Yeah. Sorry, man, it's late."

"You okay?"

"Yeah. Just a bad feeling is all."

They lapsed into a silence Cole found embarrassing, but it was Pike who spoke first.

"You need me, I'm there."

"It's the wind. This wind is crazy."

"Uh-huh."

"Watch yourself."

He told Pike he would call again soon, then put down the phone.

Cole felt no relief after the call. He told himself he should, but he didn't. The dream should have faded, but it did not. Talking to Pike now made it feel even more real.

You need me, I'm there.

How many times had Joe Pike placed himself in harm's way to save him?

They had fought the good fight together, and won, and sometimes lost. They had shot people who had harmed or were doing harm, and been shot, and Joe Pike had saved Cole's life more than a few times like an archangel from Heaven.

Yet here was the dream and the dream did not fade—

Muzzle flashes in a dingy room. A woman's shadow cast on the wall. Dark glasses spinning into space. Joe Pike falling through a terrible red mist.

Cole crept downstairs through the dark house and stepped out onto his deck. Leaves and debris stung his face like sand on a windswept beach. Lights from the houses below glittered like fallen stars.

In low moments on nights like this when Elvis Cole thought of the woman and the boy, he told himself the violence in his life had cost him everything, but he knew that was not true. As lonely as he sometimes felt, he still had more to lose.

He could lose his best friend.

Or himself.